About Tania

Published in 2015 with Momentum Books (Pan Macmillan), Tania Joyce is an Australian author of erotic, contemporary and new adult romance novels. Her stories thread romance, drama and passion into beautiful locations ranging from the dazzling lights of Sydney Harbour or the glitter of New York, to the rural countryside of the Hunter Valley or Darling Downs.

She's widely traveled, has a diverse background in the corporate world and has a love for shopping, shoes and shiraz. She's rarely seen without glitter, sparkle and stilettos.

Tania draws on her real-life experiences and combines them with her *very* vivid imagination to form the foundation of her novels. She likes to write about strong-minded, career-oriented heroes and heroines that go through drama-filled hell, have steamy encounters and risk everything as they endeavor to find their happy-ever-after.

Tania shuffles the hours in her day between part-time work, family life and writing. One day she hopes to find balance!

Visit: www.taniajoyce.com

Distractions

by
Tania Joyce

Distractions

EPUB format: ISBN: 978-0-9945774-3-6

Mobi format: ISBN: 978-0-9945774-4-3

Paperback: ISBN: 978-0-9945774-5-0

Cover design by Gatwick Enterprises

Edited by Belinda Holmes

To report a typographical error, please visit http://taniajoyce.com/contact-form

Visit http://taniajoyce.com/ to read more about her books and to buy books online. You will also find features, author interviews and event news.

To finding true love.

Chapter 1

Somehow I'd survived the summer holiday from hell. A cheating boyfriend, a broken heart, and the drunken embarrassment of New Year's Eve are thankfully all behind me. I tilted my head back and enjoyed the fresh mountain-range air and sunshine on my face as I sat with my friends outside on the grassed area in between the rows of low-set accommodation blocks. Fellow students raced around the grounds unloading their belongings from their cars into their dorm rooms. Shrieks pierced the air as friends reunited after the holiday break and our gathering outside grew. Parents' faces looked daunted as college life sprang into action. Yep, so far the first day back living at Steele Rudd Residential College to start my last year at the University of Southern Queensland (USQ) was normal.

Phizst...

"Here you go, Wiley." Kelly Harp cracked open and passed me another ice-cold can of rum and cola from her small Esky.

"You're an angel sent from heaven. You know that, right?" What would a girl do without her best friend?

She threw her arm around my shoulders and squeezed me tight. "Here's to a great year ahead." Kel raised her drink, clinked her can against mine before sculling down its contents.

Yep, everything was normal.

My eyes glazed over as the thought of all the study in front of me made my stomach knot. I already felt the pressure. Pressure to maintain my GPA for my scholarship. Pressure to be considered for an internship at Huntersville Accounting. Pressure from my parents to do well. Pressure from my own expectations. I closed my eyes and rubbed at my forehead to erase the onslaught of a headache. With no boyfriend, my trust in guys shattered and a massive workload ahead, my purpose for the year was clear. My study was my priority; there would be no other distractions.

A gust of wind made me turn my head to avoid getting dust in my eyes. As it passed, movement in the end room of D-block caught my attention. With the sun reflecting off the glass it was difficult to see clearly, but I could make out the shape of a guy standing with his back to me. Transfixed, I watched him stand up straight and draw his broad shoulders back sharply. Subconsciously I splayed a hand across my chest, my breath hitched and a warmth rippled across my skin. Now that ... was not normal.

Who is that?

I squinted, trying to get a better look, but a glass-shattering screech burst from my lungs as I was showered with the spray from a shaken up soda. I gasped as the cold, sticky liquid saturated my skin and trickled down my face.

"Good one, you idiot." Jumping to my feet I swore at Aaron who laughed and flicked his thick, sun-bleached blond curls out of his eyes. "What was that for?" I snarled, wiping the mess off my face. I didn't know whether to laugh or cry as I stood there with dripping wet hair, a soaked singlet top and drenched shorts.

"Wilhelmina Cayton, you need to lighten up," he smirked. "Come on, you have to admit that was funny."

Glaring at him, I shook my head. Not only did I hate being the center of attention, but I hated being called by my full name. No one called me *Wilhelmina*. I was simply known as *Wiley* to everyone. *Wiley—like Kylie!*

You'd think that after two years he'd know not to call me that. No one could spell it, read it or even say it properly.

I glanced over my mismatched bunch of friends. Half were stunned. Half tried not to laugh. Dave and Megan quickly returned to making eyes at each other and cute PDAs; Lachlan, Justin and Rick applauded Aaron while continuing to drink vast quantities of beer. Kel readied herself to go into battle with me. Yep, she was back to her bouncy, bubbly self now that she was out of home, away from her very strict parents. Ashleigh, however, laughed hysterically at her boyfriend's actions, yep she'd had too much alcohol already.

"Funny, ha?" Planting my hands on my hips, I jutted my chin towards Aaron. The heat from the sunshine combined with the sugary syrup made all the hairs on my arms stick together. With every move I made I wanted to itch and rub at my flesh. Flies buzzed around me like manic rock-star fans.

"Totally," Aaron chuckled. "Come on, Wiley, you need to stop being so serious. Maybe that's why your relationship ended with Michael. You're too uptight and study too much. This is our last year, you need to get out more with us and paaarrrttttyyy." He opened another bottle of beer and drank half of it in one big gulp.

I sniggered at him. I didn't really care what Aaron thought of me, although his words still packed a punch to my guts. Yes, I studied hard. I had to. I didn't go out much. I wasn't a big drinker. Okay, New Year's had been an exception. But with my future at stake, nothing was going to change my ways. "Well, party's over for me now, isn't it? I'm off to have a shower. It's getting late anyway, so I'll see you all at dinner."

After finishing my drink, my gaze drifted toward the end room in D-Block hoping to catch a glimpse of the mystery guy again, but he was nowhere to be seen. *Oh, well.* I threw my can into the bin and headed for my block. I wasn't going to let Aaron's soda spraying antics or some unknown guy dampen my mood. There was an electric vibe in the air and it brought a spring to my step. Was it the hype of being back at residential college for the start of university tomorrow, or was there something more to it?

***

It looked like nothing had changed in the dining hall over the summer break. Round tables, covered in unattractive heavy orange or deep maroon vinyl tablecloths, were placed randomly about the room while the food-serving area was hidden behind a glass-bricked wall at the far end. The smell of greasy, overcooked food filled the air as I walked in with my friends. We claimed our table by placing our room keys on it, and joined the queue.

Crumbed chicken, watery vegetables and fruit salad was our delightful first meal. In the overall scheme of residential college food, it was pretty good. I loaded my heavy white dinner plate as I shuffled past the steaming hot trays of food before heading back to our table.

My girlfriends and I were all in varying stages of inebriation and feeling the effects from drinking in the sun. With rosy cheeks, we swayed in our seats and shoveled food into our mouths. Making an excessive amount of noise, we laughed and joked with Dave and the guys at the table next to ours. The main glass doors at the top of the hall swooshed open with a loud rush of air, as fast as a snap of one's fingers, my head turned in its direction.

And in he walked.

Silence flooded the room.

Everything seemed to move in slow motion as my eyes fell upon the breathtaking sight of him. *Wow!* As I absorbed every inch of his tall, athletic physique, my skin tingled all over like I was being wrapped up in a cloak of luxurious silk. His short, rusty, dark brown hair was tousled. Scruffy facial growth accentuated his chiseled jawline and his fair skin showed hints of a summer tan. The faded khaki singlet he wore clung firmly to his chest, and his knee-length beige cargo shorts hung low across his hips as he strolled in toward the front of the hall.

The exhilarating rush that ran through me was like nothing I had ever experienced before. I'd seen plenty of good-looking guys in my time, but this guy made me fluster.

In a trance, my gaze followed him as he strolled towards the serving area. I was unable to comprehend the sensations coursing over my body. Thankfully, the abrupt shattering of a china plate in the kitchen brought me out of my coma-like state.

Kel had been sitting with her back to the door and had missed the newcomer's grand entrance. With curiosity, she turned to see what I'd and many others had been staring at.

"Who's that?" Her eyes widened at the sight of the new student before he disappeared into the food area.

We all shook our heads. We'd met most of the new first year students during afternoon drinks and this guy hadn't been among the crowd. This had to be the mysterious guy I saw in D-Block.

The clatter of cutlery, clinking of glasses and alcohol-infused, excited conversations filled the room once more. Why was I so buzzed when this guy walked in the room? Had I drunk too much this afternoon? *I didn't think so.* Was it from months of not having had sex? *I doubt it.* Was it the heat of the day affecting me? *Hmm, could be.* Was it just the excitement of being back on campus? *Highly possible.*

Shrugging my shoulders, I put an end to my overactive thought process and continued with my meal. Remember — no distractions! But no matter how hard I tried, I couldn't ignore there was a change in the air around me. Shuffling about in my seat, I tried to ward off the warm rippling sensation on my skin, but my eyes were instantly drawn in his direction when he ventured out of the serving area. With his plate full of food, he jostled past several tables before taking a seat at Dave's table. I couldn't help but smile as I heard a flurry of disappointed sighs from all the females in the room.

The boys made audible grunting sounds in greeting and continued with their chitchat. Dave blew a puff of air into the fringe of his preppie-cut, strawberry-blond hair. Rick, Justin and Aaron stuffed food into their mouths while Lachlan led the pack in their conversation.

I sat diagonally across from the newcomer, trying not to ogle. For a split second our eyes met. My heart skipped a beat as he held my gaze for a brief moment too long. A smile tugged at the corner of his mouth and his eyes shimmered, highlighting their vivid, metallic-blue color.

Color flushed my cheeks. I quickly looked away, down toward my fumbling fingers that were resting on my lap. I blinked. I didn't understand what was going on. I begged for this strange sensation to disappear.

Ashleigh, who was rather tipsy after too many beers, leaned back on her chair in toward the boys table. "Hi, I'm Ashleigh. You are?"

"Cameron. Cameron Wilks." The sound of his velvety voice sent a ripple of warmth through my insides. Yep, had to avoid that from ever happening again.

"Nice to meet you," Ashleigh slurred. "Welcome to Steele Rudd. I see you've met the boys. God, they're a gentlemanly bunch, aren't they?" She winked at him playfully. "Well, Cameron, first things first. Tonight is Scholars Drinks. Are you coming?"

"Should I know what that is?" he questioned.

"Guys, what do you talk about? Nothing useful, obviously." She accused everyone sitting at the table. "Scholars is the student bar held here in the foyer of the dining hall. It's not as good as The Club over at the university, but it's cheap drinks to help raise money for our residential college."

Dave piped up. "It's a Mexican theme tonight. Tequila, Coronas, whatever! So are you in? It starts at seven-thirty."

"Better wear your drinking shoes and get ready for initiation," Ashleigh added jovially.

"Sounds interesting. But I don't think I've anything Mexican in my suitcase," He stabbed at his chicken with his fork and placed it in his mouth.

"Oh, shit no!" Ashleigh squawked. "You don't have to dress up — you just have to come along and drink! There's no harm in that, right?"

Chapter 2

Scholars Drinks was busy. Music boomed from the sound system, making my heart beat in time with the heavy bass. Students filled the room, bustling and bumping into each other like a mosh pit crowd at a rock concert. Nearly all one hundred and thirty residents were here, their voices raised trying to speak over the noise.

The temporary bar operated out of a small room on the left-hand side of the hall. The massive beer fridge was loaded with alcohol — beer, pre-mixes and cheap wine, while bottles of spirits were lined up in rows along the benchtops. I couldn't wait to quench my thirst. I wasn't a big drinker but was certainly looking forward to another cold one or two.

As I walked through the crowd with Kel, I found Cameron. Like a compass always finding north, I found myself homing in on his location. This strange pull toward him was starting to unsettle me.

Cameron stood not far from the bar, circled by a bunch of girls. His face displayed a broad array of playful expression as he talked to them. They all looked eager to attract his undivided attention. Surprise, surprise! Front and center was Louie. The pit of my stomach churned and constricted into a tight knot at the sight of her.

Louise Clark, alias *Louie*, was now a second-year business student. She towered over the crowd, tousled her long blonde hair when she laughed and had a smile that demanded attention. She was stunning, model material. And extremely well-off. Her father was a successful investment banker. I didn't care she had money, but I loathed how she flaunted it around and thought everything was rightfully hers. With her looks, her fancy car and dollars to splash around, she was very popular with the guys — in and out of the bedroom.

Zigzagging through the sea of people, Kel and I made our way over to the bar and met up with Ashleigh and Megan buying drinks. Lachlan was working up a sweat serving behind the bar.

"Slammers!" he yelled out, lining up ten shot glasses in a row and filling them all with tequila. Along with the saltshakers borrowed from the dining room and a huge bowl of lemon slices, slammers were ready to down.

"Boys," Lachlan called out, coaxing my friends to gather around. "And come on, Cameron, we told you this was an initiation."

Cameron looked over at us when he heard his name called out and made his way to the bar.

"Thanks, I needed to get away from over there." Cameron rubbed the back of his neck, glancing back over his shoulder to the now sulking group of girls.

"Ready to lick, sip, suck?" Kel hollered as we all grabbed hold of a shot glass. "Go!"

In unison we gulped the cool, sticky concoction down our throats — licking salt off our hand, slamming the tequila and finishing off with sucking on a lemon slice. Our faces screwed up at the sour taste of the fruit and the horrid aftertaste of the liquid.

"Another round!" Lachlan demanded, and down the glasses went in a line for a refill and the ritual once more.

Lachlan did the introductions. "Cameron, if you don't remember everyone from the dinner table — this is Dave, Justin, Rick and Aaron; and the girls — Ashleigh, Kel, Wiley and Megan.

We all waved and nodded our hellos with rinds of fruit still wedged between our teeth.

"So where did you come from?" Ashleigh sucked on her lemon skin. "What are you studying? Come on, give us the rundown."

"I'm from Sydney. " Cameron replied. "I'm in my final year of studying Commerce Biz Law."

I choked on my piece of rind. *OhMyGod! He's in my course!*

My initial reaction was panic. He'd be in my lectures, maybe some of my tutorials, and always hanging around. But then I furrowed my eyebrows. Why should I care what course he was in? It shouldn't matter what he did. I wasn't interested in him in any way or form. My sole focus was on my study, nothing else.

"So why move on to campus now?" I asked out of curiosity, dropping the remains of my lemon slice into a rubbish bowl on the bar.

"I've been studying externally from back home and was slacking off. My parents thought this might be good for me. Plus, I have a gran who lives up here in a retirement village, this will give me a chance to see her. It's all a bit boring really." Cameron replied. But I watched his eyes closely as the air around me grew heavy. Something about him didn't add up. His mysterious dark look didn't match his playful tone. There was something more intriguing lurking behind this façade.

"Goddamn!" Ashleigh shrieked at Cameron, breaking my inner thoughts like shattered glass. "You're fucking good looking, aren't you?"

Cameron smiled and swigged on his beer.

During the course of a third round of shots, my group of friends and I interrogated Cameron. No girlfriend. Not gay. He was twenty-one. And yes, it was him that resided in the room in D-Block, directly across from me in F-Block.

As Lachlan prepared another round of slammers, I gracefully bowed out to the sounds of boos and moans from my friends. I rubbed my grumbling tummy, unable to face another tequila shot. Leaving them to drink, I shuffled off into the crowd to chat with some other students.

Music blared and the hours passed. As I stood talking to some new first year students, I noticed Louie flitting in and around Cameron. She was being blatant with her intentions. There was the hair flicking, the loud giggles and the seductive look in her eyes. I did like the fact Cameron didn't look interested. I hoped he stayed like that and did not fall for her advances. If he was going to sleep with someone, anyone here would be better than Louie.

Midnight came quickly and Lachlan started to shut up the bar. The stragglers and I sat around, leaning against the walls, engaged in useless conversation.

Cameron staggered as he sat down next to me on the floor. With only a foot of distance between us, my body reacted. Heat swirled underneath the surface of my skin and the magnetic draw toward him kicked in. My body ached, like it wanted and needed to be closer to his. As if that was going to happen. Ever! I resisted the urge and shuffled an inch or two away.

"You look smashed." I noted his sway and bloodshot eyes.

"Yep — feeling it too," he blurted through intoxicated breath.

"And you stink." Leaning away from him, I screwed up my nose at the sickly stench of tequila and beer.

"I'm glad I've made a memorable first impression," he chuckled. "God, I'm never going to make class tomorrow." He rubbed his hand across his face.

"Possibly not." I agreed.

Cameron looked toward me with his long-lashed blue eyes that made my heart beat with a strange irregularity. Stupid heart.

"So you're a Sydney boy. Whereabouts do you live?

Cameron half smiled but didn't reply.

"Is that a touchy question? Or is it too hard for you to compute?" I crumpled my empty aluminum Coke can between my hands.

He blinked a few times, grinned, and then took a large swig of his drink before responding. "I live in Vaucluse."

"Oh ... that's in the Eastern suburbs, right? Your folks loaded or something?" Why was I being so snide? This was not like me.

"My old man's in mining."

"What's he do?"

"Runs a company."

"Which one?"

"Do you ask this many questions all the time?" He raised an eyebrow and a hint of a smile touched his lips.

My stomach did that flutter somersault thing.

"I'm sorry. I was just trying to make conversation." I shrugged and drew my eyes away from his.

Cameron sighed heavily. "If you must know, my father owns Wilks Resources."

"Wilks Resources." My mind repeated the name over and over, trying to remember where I knew it from. I'd heard of it. I'd read about it. Where? Where? Why did I know that name? It finally clicked. "Holy shit! You mean *the* Wilks Resources? As in one of the biggest mining companies in Australia? We studied them in Environmental Law last year." Then it dawned on me. "Is your dad Robert Wilks?"

"Yep. The one and only." He sounded far from impressed.

"OhMyGod! Robert Wilks is one of the richest mining magnates in the country, if not the richest."

"So," he mumbled, peeling at the label on his beer bottle.

Dumbfounded, I sat there reveling in the information that had come to light. Cameron Wilks was the son of one of the richest people in Australia. It was hard to comprehend someone like Cameron would be here in the rural city of Toowoomba. Just what we needed — another rich, arrogant student flitting around campus thinking they owned the place.

Rick walked over and squatted down before us, alcohol heavy on his breath. "Wiley, you coming?"

Rick Thornton was a final year engineering student. With his messy dark brown hair, short stocky build and squinty eyes, he reminded me of a furry mole struggling to see in the bright light of day. Over the past nine months, he'd changed so much and had become more and more reliant on drugs for his highs. Totally not my scene. I stayed well clear of him, as much as one could do on residential college anyway.

"What for?" I snapped, still bewildered from my conversation with Cameron.

"We're going for a bit of a hit. You wanna come?"

"Rick, that's not even funny. You know I don't do that shit."

Rick laughed as he struggled to maintain his balance. "No harm in asking. I'll get you one day." He diverted his attention to Cameron. "You?"

"No, thank you. Definitely not." Cameron shook his head. "You shouldn't either, you've been drinking too much." The frosty vibe emanating from Cameron made my skin prickle.

"Already on the jet, man." Rick's hazy eyes clearly showed he was already under the influence of something illegal. "Come on, have some fun on your first day. It's all part of your initiation."

"No chance." Cameron's jaw strained.

"Some other time, maybe?" Rick winked, stood and left.

Cameron stared up at the ceiling and I heard him take several deep breaths.

I was about to ask what the matter was, but my head started to ache after all the drinks I'd had, interrupting my train of thought. My stomach swirled with tequila, rum and cola. Not a good combination. I needed to get off this emotional roller coaster I'd been riding on since I'd first seen him. A good night's sleep sounded like a cure to rid myself of the unexplainable feelings I got when he was around. Keeping my distance from him would surely resolve the issue.

The room felt claustrophobic as I felt the color drain from my face.

"Excuse me, but I'm going to call it a night. I'll see you around," I said, staggering to my feet.

"Shall I walk you to your room?" he offered graciously.

"No thanks. I'm good."

"So that's it? You are just going to leave me here?" he smirked.

"Yep." I looked over at Louie, who noticed me about to leave. "I'll leave you to be entertained by the remaining few." I had to get out of there and get some fresh air.

Too much tequila.

Too much Cameron.

Chapter 3

By the middle of the first week, timetables were sorted out and lectures were in full swing. Regardless of how much I tried to shuffle around my classes, Wednesday ended up being a full day of lectures and tutorials. By midafternoon, I fought off my weariness and hauled myself to the last two-hour lecture.

I entered the decrepit old lecture theatre. Musty, oatmeal-colored carpet covered the floor underneath the rows of hard and extremely uncomfortable tiered lecture chairs. The overhead projector in this hall made a constant dull hum and flickered every now and then — just annoying and often enough to prevent you from falling asleep.

I looked up among the swarm of students for a familiar face. Where was Dave? He was in this class, but not here yet. Traipsing up the stairs, I found a few vacant seats halfway up the theatre and readied myself to take notes.

Seconds later, in strolled Dave. Loping in tow was Cameron. Without warning, my heart started to dance like a kite in the air when I saw him approach.

Why did that happen?

"Hey!" Shuffling back on my chair, I made way for Dave to pass in front to take a seat on one side of me while Cameron remained on the other.

"What time do you have the tutorial for this?" Dave asked as he settled into his chair.

"Friday at two o'clock," I replied.

"Damn," Dave said. "I have Monday at three o'clock." He leaned forward and spoke to Cameron. "When's your tute?"

Cameron opened his timetable on his iPad. "Um, Friday at two o'clock."

"That's the same time as me." I gently nudged my arm against his. I jolted back in surprise as a hot, thrilling, tingling sensation ran up my arm when my bare skin brushed against his. He stared at me and looked just as startled. Did he feel that sensation too? How does that happen from touching someone? My cheeks flushed with color and I quickly looked away.

"Well, it'll be nice to know someone in my class," he managed to murmur after roughly clearing his throat.

Carefully avoiding any body contact, I grabbed Cameron's iPad and glanced over his timetable. "You're in nearly all my classes." My worst suspicions were confirmed as I read through his schedule.

As I handed back his iPad, his fingers crossed over mine. I gasped as a shock shot through me gain when our skin connected. Our eyes met. I nearly dropped his tablet as I slowly pulled my hand away.

What was wrong with me? I'd never experienced anything like it before. It was nothing like an electric shock; this was exhilarating and exciting. It snaked through my veins like tendrils of fire. I was mystified and intrigued...and beyond baffled.

Having missed the introduction, the lecturer brought us

to attention. I blinked my eyes to adjust to the dimming of the theatre lights.

As the room darkened, I had an urge to test this extraordinarily strange body contact experience and to see if it happened again. Yes, conduct my own little science experiment. How was I going to do this subtly? Dave was going to be my control specimen. I leaned over toward him and rested my arm against his. Skin on skin.

I waited a split second or two. Daring not to breath.

But...nothing happened.

It was just Dave.

I straightened back into my chair and smiled to myself. I then casually leaned over in Cameron's direction to see what he was typing on his iPad. My arm rested against his. He inhaled deeply and at the same time my blood started to swirl like the ocean in a wild storm and my heart pounded like a runaway racehorse. The hairs on my arm stood on end. He stared at me, his penetrating metallic-blue eyes shimmering in the dim lighting. My mouth gaped open. I couldn't move and simply forgot how to breathe.

He closed his eyes. "Are you okay? Did you want something?"

I stuttered, but finally managed to form some words. "Um, no, I'm all good."

Yes, I'd finally come up for air. I flopped back in my chair and could feel his eyes linger on me as I tried to understand what had just happened. This was not normal. Exhilarating, intense, but not normal. I was being stupid or out of my mind. Was I having an allergic reaction to the lotion or soap he used? Surely there had to be a logical and realistic explanation?

Whatever it was, I wanted and needed it to stop. It was way too much of a distraction.

Shaking my head and coming back to reality, I refocused

on the lecture at hand. With iPad, pen and paper ready, I listened to the drab talk on accounting and the course outline for the semester ahead.

Chapter 4

By second week, the holiday cobwebs in my head had fully disappeared and I had submerged myself into studying. Mid-Thursday morning, I was sitting at my desk reading up on Consumer Law in preparation for tomorrow's tutorial, when the inviting weather outside and the constant dribble of pedestrians passing my window got the better of me. I couldn't concentrate anymore. I needed coffee. Grabbing my wallet and travel mug, I headed over to the university café for a caffeine fix.

The coffee shop was located in the main building, nestled between the library and the main university refectory. When I arrived, it was bustling with patrons eager for their takeaway coffees, sandwiches, milkshakes, or a slice of decadent chocolate mud cake that was hard to resist.

Like a lion with its eyes on its prey, I headed with determination, straight past the crowded tables to the takeaway counter. Coffee — I *needed* coffee. The sweet smell of freshly ground beans and baked cakes filled the air. The first sip of the hot beverage warmed my belly, coursed through my veins and cleared my head. *That's what I needed.* With my mug in hand, I was about to head off when I heard my name.

"Wiley," Dave called from one the tables. "I thought that was you."

"What are you guys up to?" I walked over to the table where Dave sat with Cameron. Both wore sunglasses inside, baseballs caps drawn down low on their heads. The telltale sign of a good hangover.

"Big night?"

"Definitely was," Cameron rubbed his brow.

"And I had to return a book to the library and needed caffeine, lots of it, if I'm going to survive today." Dave looked like he was about to barf.

"I know that feeling." I pipped my mug toward them. "Dave, you were in the library? I didn't even know you knew where it was!" I teased.

"Ha! Funny." Dave swayed when he stood up. "I did have to ask for directions. Anyway, I gotta go and try to make it through my lecture without throwing up. What are you up to, Cameron?"

"I have an hour to kill before class … if I decide to go."

"Wiley will join you. Won't you?" Dave shuffled around the table, offering me his seat. "Catch you guys later."

Rolling my eyes, annoyed that I couldn't think of an excuse to get away, I unwillingly plunked myself down on the chair. Within seconds of sitting across from Cameron, I felt my heart pound that little bit faster. The weird chemical imbalance flooded through me, bubbling and boiling away like a beaker on a Bunsen Burner. Why did I feel this way when I didn't want to? I was a smart, intelligent girl. What forces of nature were playing havoc with my mind and my body?

Cameron slouched in his chair. Even hungover he was handsome, dressed in a gray t-shirt, black shorts, ever-present sunglasses and baseball cap. Of all the people living at my residential college, Cameron had fallen into hanging out with my group of friends, and with him being in most of my classes, I was finding it near impossible to avoid him. Maybe if I got to know him better, it would put an end to all these crazy feelings happening to me when he was near. "How are you settling in to life on campus?" I asked.

He grinned while fumbling around with his coffee mug. "It's okay. I'm still finding my way around the place. Actually going to classes is different. I think I prefer studying online." He took a sip of his drink and licked the moisture from his lips. *Oh wow!* They were so pink, so perfect, so ... *What?* I blinked my thoughts away when he spoke again. "More importantly, what can one do in this town for fun?"

I narrowed my eyes, wondering if he was the type to laze his way through university, party the nights away and waste his time and his daddy's money?

"Do you know where you are? This is Toowoomba! The rural gateway to the agricultural west and the Darling Downs." My sarcasm was swift. I winced at the sound of the tone in my voice and wanted to pinch myself to stop my sharp tongue. "It's not a city renowned for its fun factor. I'm not the one to ask, if all you're out for is a good time."

"So I've heard. I gathered you're the studious type since I haven't seen you out at night anywhere. Is there nothing fun to do in this city? What's a good distraction to get away from studying?" He folded his arms and leaned on the table.

I turned my gaze down and stared at my hands. Brushing against his skin, the way he looked on the first day when he'd walked in the hall, the way he sat here now in front of me. Cameron's very presence was a distraction, but I would never let him know that. I inhaled deeply to suppress the annoying butterflies fluttering in my stomach and wished they'd go away. "There's not much to do. There's some pubs and nightclubs down town if that's what you're after."

"What do you do for downtime?" He asked while taking off his sunglasses. His eyes were bloodshot, bit too bad. Still metallic blue.

"Not much. I go to The Club here on campus on Friday nights, that's it. I work on Saturdays down at the local tavern and the rest of the time I study. I maybe on a scholarship, but I don't take it for granted and have to work hard to maintain my grades. Not all of us have the luxury of your circumstances."

"Whoa! What do you mean by my circumstances?" Cameron's eyebrows furrowed deeply. "Do you think I get everything handed to me on a silver platter because of who my father is? Do you think I'm floating through uni just to get a piece of paper?" His tone, all rough and defensive, vibrated though me. "Do you think I'm wasting my time because I can go and work for my father at any time?"

Recalling I hadn't seen him in many classes yet and he did go out a lot with the boys, I couldn't help but wonder. "No. Not at all." I lied, who wouldn't? "Most of us would kill to land a job in a company like your dad's though. If you don't want to work for your him, what *do* you want to do?"

He inhaled deeply, then sighed heavily. "Sorry, I didn't mean to bite. It's a touchy subject at the moment. The thing is, I have no idea what I want to do after uni."

I was fortunate to not be in that position. I always knew I wanted a professional career and have my own independence. I dreamed about going to work in a tailored suit, high-heel shoes and carry a designer handbag into one of the big city skyscrapers in Brisbane; somewhere like KPMG or PWC and now Huntersville. My degree had me on track to make my dreams come true.

"Maybe you could be a model." I subtly pointed in the direction of a group of girls eyeing him off as they walked past.

"You certainly aren't lacking in the ability to attract attention."

"I wasn't doing anything, just sitting here having coffee." His plea for innocence made me laugh. "On that note," he jumped up, "I need another. Are you okay or would you like one more?"

"Sure. Why not. White with one please." I handed him my coffee mug.

"It's the only way to have it," Cameron replied and walked over to the counter to order another round of drinks.

OhMyGod! What was I doing? I could have kicked myself. I didn't want to spend more time with Cameron. I had the perfect opportunity to escape and I missed it. Muttering to myself, I slumped back down in my chair.

As he returned to his seat, curiosity niggled at my insides. If I had to spend time with him and have another coffee, I best find more out about him.

"If you don't want to talk about your family, what do you like doing outside of uni?" I asked while stirring my coffee.

"I don't mind talking about my family. It's just most people, when they find out who I am, want to know which celebrities I know, if I can get them tickets to various sports events or concerts and what it's like to be rich." Cameron stared blankly at his cup. "But in the short time I've known you, you haven't, which is a pleasant change."

"That stuff doesn't interest me." I peered at him over the rim of my mug.

"It's nice to have a conversation with someone who isn't trying to sponge off me to go somewhere or have them throwing themselves at me trying to get me into bed," he grinned cockily.

"Maybe I'm approaching the matter the wrong way." Flippantly, I responded without thinking. My eyes widened and my cheeks flushed. I was flirting like a floozy trying to pick up for the night. Where did that come from? I laughed my comment off, ignoring the rush of blood to my head at the thought of him in bed all naked, hot and sweaty. I struggled to swallow and shook the images away. Thoughts like that were totally off limits. "You've probably slept with way too many girls for my liking."

His eyes sparkled. "I think you'd be pleasantly surprised."

"Your sex life doesn't concern me. But I'm sure you'll find plenty of that type of entertainment while living on campus if it's what you're after. It's full of sex, drugs and alcohol."

"Alcohol yes — I do like to drink. It helps to numb the…" A flicker of pain shot through his eyes, but he continued in a lighter tone. "Sex is definitely good, although it's been a while, and I'm adamantly not into drugs."

"Me either. I hate seeing how they affect people, it freaks me out. I've never even tried them. What about you? Have you had any bad benders?"

Cameron's playful mood disappeared. His jaw tightened and eyes dropped to stare at nothing in particular on the table. I watched the muscle in his cheeks flex and when the color drained away from his face a shiver ran down my spine. When he looked back up at me, his eyes had turned a dark grey.

"Wiley." His tone changed, edged with pain, so different from when we'd been engaged in our playful banter. He drew in a deep breath and exhaled slowly. "I've tried pot when I was sixteen, but never again. I won't touch anything since … my ex-girlfriend overdosed on heroin," his voice was barely audible above a whisper, "and she died."

I gasped. "What?"

Cameron grabbed and twisted a napkin around in his hands. "Her name was Gillian. We were together for two years and not once did I suspect anything. I never knew she was on drugs. According to her friends she was a regular user. She O.D'd one afternoon after we had a fight and I was the one who found her in her apartment." He paused, lost in thought for a moment. "I blame myself for being naïve and not noticing she had a problem."

A chill ran through my veins as he spoke. His eyes glassed over, haunted with so much pain. "As a result, I've no tolerance for drugs. None."

"Should you be telling me this stuff?" I shivered as his words sunk in and touched my soul. "Are you still drunk from last night?

He shook his head. "I didn't mean to make you uncomfortable? I'm sorry. I do go to a shrink back home, but he's useless. I only go to one because my parents think it will help. I thought talking to a friend would be better. That's what I'd like to think you are. I don't know what it is about you, Wiley, but something tells me I can trust you." He sat up straighter in his seat, like a weight had been lifted from his shoulders.

I sat there drowning in mixed emotions. I was horrified by what had happened to him and confused as to why he trusted me with something so personal. Me, of all people, who had issues trusting anyone — especially guys, considering what my ex-boyfriend did to me.

"Seriously," I shook my head. "I don't think I'm the one you should be talking to about this stuff. The uni has counselor's if you need more help."

"I don't need another counselor. I'm opting for peer therapy. You don't seem to be the gossipy type to go blurting my fucked-up problems around to everyone. Am I wrong in my assumption?"

"No. No. Of course not." *Jesus, who did Cameron think I was?* I could listen, but I had no idea on how to handle trauma. I placed my mug down on the table, unsure of what to say. "How long ago did Gillian die?"

"July last year. That's why I came up here. I needed to get out of home. My parents became suffocating and I needed to start somewhere to get my life back on track. I'm truly damaged goods, aren't I?" He rubbed his fingers across his forehead.

"We're all damaged in some way," I sympathized. But Cameron was a complete train wreck, while I was only a decoupled caboose in comparison. "You'd best avoid Rick then. He's the only druggie I know. He never used to be like that and now hangs around with some weirdos who live off-campus."

"I worked out Rick already," he nodded. "And thanks for listening."

His eyes locked on to mine, making my chest tightened and my head spin. I couldn't move. I couldn't think. I couldn't speak. This broken man in front of me lost his girlfriend and blamed himself for it. While I felt flattered and humbled Cameron had confided in me, I couldn't begin to fathom why. There was so much more to him than I could have ever imagined. He was a basket case full of problems and I had enough of my own. While I'd never tell anyone what he told me, it was clear in my mind — it was best to stay well away from him.

"You okay?" he asked.

I managed to move my head and nod.

He gathered his bag and stood up. "You're seriously the first person I've managed to talk to about this stuff. I don't know why that is, but thanks."

"Yeah sure. No worries." I snapped out of my trance. "Don't worry, I won't tell anyone."

He smiled. "Cool. I have to get to class."

"Thanks for the coffee." As I stood up, I hit my leg hard against the table, "Ow!"

"What did you do?" He caught me by the arm and a rush shot through my body where his hand clasped around my skin. It was just like the one the other day. The one I'd been trying to avoid. I gasped as heat swirled beneath his touch.

Stunned, I looked at him to see if he felt the same thing,

but he only stood there and laughed at my clumsiness.

"I hit my leg. I'm fine." My head felt woozy but I quickly freed myself from his clutch, collected my mug off the table and hobbled out of the shop.

But Cameron stopped me when he glanced down at my leg and I noticed I had a small cut bleeding and bruising rapidly. "Do you want me to get you some ice for that?"

"Are you checking out my legs?" I grabbed a napkin off the nearest table to stop the blood from trickling down my knee.

"When they look that good, well, yes."

"Ha, ha." I playfully punched him in the arm and left, hobbling back to my room.

Chapter 5

"Come on. It's Saturday night. Please come out with me." Kel pleaded with her hands clasped together. "It's only a hall party in B-Block. You don't have to stay long."

"I can't go. I have two assignments due soon, I've worked all day and I'm tired," I said as I ate the last of my cold fish and chips dinner in the dining hall.

"Just for a few hours. You can study all day tomorrow. I've some beer in the fridge ready to go. Please. Please. Please."

Other than to The Club on Friday night and work, I hadn't been out anywhere since the start of university three weeks ago. Kel's pleas were relentless and I knew she wouldn't let up. "All right, just for a little while."

After dinner we returned to F-Block; all ten girls who lived under its single-storied roof, readied themselves for the B-Block hall party. Music pumped out of the stereo in Kel's room and vibrated off the brick walls. After showering, I shimmied into my old bootcut jeans and a black t-shirt, perfect for sitting around on the horrid dirty carpet in the boys' block. I ripped my brush through my long hair, and applied a coat of baby pink gloss to my lips. Glancing at my reflection in the mirror, I thought I scrubbed up okay.

Kel knocked on my door and entered without waiting for my answer. She bound over to me and gave me a massive hug as we examined each other's attire in the mirror. She looked fabulous wearing my skinny Levi's. Her curly chocolate-brown hair fell loose around her shoulders and her cherry-red, lip-glossed smile was contagious. Together, we were like fraternal twins — different in looks, but identical in average height and the same slender build. Our similar taste in clothes made our wardrobes wonderful as we were constantly mixing and matching outfits.

"Ready?" She released me from her hold and grabbed my hand.

"Let's go."

It was nearly eight o'clock when Kel and I entered the upper level of the old double-storied B-Block. The air was hazy from cigarette smoke and it stank like a brewery. Along the narrow hallway, students sat along the floor, squished in the narrow passage like a can of sardines. Everyone present was consuming excessive amounts of booze. Music blared from Rick's room in the middle of the hall as Kel and I parked ourselves among our usual crowd of friends. Ashleigh sat opposite Aaron who was sneering at everyone who walked past. Dave sat across from Megan, and Kel and I took a seat next to her.

Where's Cameron? He should be here. I glanced up and down the corridor to see if I had missed him. A stupid ache thudded in my chest when I wasn't able to locate him. It was enough to give myself a mental slap in the face. Why was I concerned about where he was? I'd had enough of this silliness over Cameron. It had to stop. No boys — no more distractions.

"What's up?" Kel looked concerned as she handed me a beer.

"Nothing." I opened the bottle and took a drink of the cold amber ale.

By ten o'clock the party was rolling, the music was louder, a new slab of beer was opened up and the shotgun races of sculling cans commenced. No one could outdo Rick, he was the champion.

As two first year students took on the challenge, up the steps bounded Cameron. My eyes instantly drawn toward him. There he stood, in his dark denim jeans and a pale-blue button-up shirt, glancing up and down the hall. He paused when he caught sight of me and smiled. I waved hello without realizing. *Well, at least now I didn't have to dwell on where was.*

"Hey Cameron!" everybody cheered as he entered the hall.

Rick grabbed a can of beer and threw it at him. "Shotgun!" he yelled.

"Serious?" Cameron laughed as he was drawn into the crowded hall party and into the drinking games. He placed his six-pack of beer down and prepared himself for the race. Cameron towered in height over short little Rick. On the count of three, both guys speared their cans open and downed them at breakneck speed. Cheers erupted as Cameron and Rick crushed the beer cans on their heads to see who won first.

"Oh — so close," yelled Aaron. "But I declare no winner. Do it again."

Roars of laughter and encouragement filled the hallway as another two beers found their way to the willing participants.

"Ready, set, go!" Everyone shrieked with excitement.

The second shotgun disappeared in record time, but Rick was the clear winner.

Shaking Cameron's hand, Rick slurred. "Good go, my man, good go. But I'm the champ!" He boasted to the hallway of people as he flexed his arms up in the champion stance.

Cameron coughed and spluttered beer everywhere, bowing out gracefully. Picking up his six-pack, he headed down the corridor and took a seat on the floor across from me, in between Dave and Justin.

"Where've you been?" Over the noise, Kel raised her voice toward Cameron.

"I was sorting out my flights for going home for Easter holidays." He replied, opening up a beer in the process.

Kel opened her mouth to speak again but was interrupted when Rick yelled out, "Pizzas are here!"

Brown cardboard boxes and garlic bread were passed down the line to be shared by everyone. We dived in to the food like crazed, starving beasts. The stench of meat, grease and garlic briefly overruled the sickly sweet smell of alcohol and cigarettes.

Ashleigh leaned forward around Dave and directed her probing question and lust for gossip at Cameron. "So, what was with you and Louie last night at the Club?"

I froze with a piece of pizza halfway to my mouth.

What? Not Louie. Oh God! Please no!

My heart hung heavy in my chest and my gaze bore into Cameron, searching his face for answers. I felt sick to the stomach at the thought of him with Louie.

"She was trying to get all over you last night. So spill the beans because if you don't, she certainly will." Ashleigh warned him.

"Nothing — we just danced." His eyes caught mine, a flicker of concern crossed his face, but I quickly looked away. I shouldn't be surprised, Cameron would be a prime target for Louie. They were both attractive people. Maybe they were perfect for each other.

"Where were you last night?" Cameron jutted his chin in

my direction.

"I had to work today. I left The Club early, at about eleven o'clock."

"You left with Justin?" His eyes chiseled into mine and a muscle in his jawline twitched as he waited for my answer.

Why should he care if I went home with someone or not?

"What did I do now?" Justin innocently joined our conversation.

"Yeah, I did go home with Justin," I admitted honestly. "He walked me home to make sure I got back safely."

"Oh." Cameron raised a questioning eyebrow at me.

"Yeah, I'm Mister Chaperone." Justin twinkled his fingers up in front of his face.

"You're just a big softy," I threw my pizza crust at Justin who promptly caught it and stuffed it in his mouth.

Kel jumped in. "We all know Wiley isn't with anyone. She's still hung up on Michael." She gently shoved me in the side.

I shook my head firmly. "No, I'm not. Definitely not." I was, without a doubt, not hung up on a scumbag like Michael. Kel should know me better than that.

"Good." Cameron whispered.

What was that?

I saw a smile touch the corner of his lips before he swigged on his bottle of beer.

Timing!

I rolled my eyes when Louie bound down the hallway and wriggled herself in between Justin and Cameron. Why did she have to be here? Her presence made me nauseous. My muscles tensed and a burning hatred built inside of my gut. Did she revel in making my life an uncomfortable hell?

The corner of my mouth twitched as she leaned against Cameron.

Yeah right, nothing happened last night!

"Hi Cammie." Wearing skinny, tight jeans and a t-shirt top falling off one shoulder, revealing her black bra strap, she nudged closer to Cameron. With her flawless makeup, Louie looked like she'd stepped off the catwalk. How could anyone compete with her? She had stunning looks, an outgoing personality and all the guys were waiting in line to be with her. I drew my legs up close to my chest, trying to pull myself as far away from her as possible.

But as she sat there cuddling into Cameron and rubbing against his well-toned, bicep muscles, I couldn't help but feel a little... No, definitely not. I was not jealous. Not in any way, shape or form. Cameron was not mine, I had no claim on him. Reaching for another beer, I snapped it open and took a long drink to stop the crazy thoughts in my head.

Louie giggled and touched Cameron on his leg. She glanced across at me, her smile sinister. She flicked her hair and pathetically fell in toward him again. *Ergh!* She made me sick.

"Louie. Enough." Cameron boomed, everyone around could hear. He grabbed her hand off his leg and pushed it firmly away. "I'm not interested, so stop it, please."

All eyes stared at Louie.

"Oh, come on, Cam," she flirted.

With jaw ticking and eyes fuming he turned to face Louie. "Fuck off!"

The sound of his stern voice was music to my ears.

Everyone laughed at her. "Oo! Burned, Louie."

I would have been so humiliated, but she didn't seem fazed. She smiled, flashed her perfect white teeth and turned to talk to Justin on the other side.

That was my cue. If she was staying, I was leaving.

"Where're you going?" Cameron asked as I stood up.

"It's got way too crowded in here for my liking."

With a quick wave goodbye I headed off back to my room.

Chapter 6

Friday came quickly and it was time for my Consumer Law tutorial with Cameron. A smile tugged at my lips when he greeted me at my window with a soft single tap on the glass. I quickly gathered my things and we walked over to the university together.

Our classroom lay on the second floor of the Business School building. The room was small and cramped with white desks and hard black chairs. Mr Barnes, our tutor, started to outline the course assignment and writing details on the whiteboard the moment we took a seat.

I glanced out of the corner of my eye at Cameron. His unruly hair fell in all directions, his eyes were focused on the front of the class. Occasionally when he'd look down to write, one long strand of hair fell across his eyes and made my fingers twitch; I desperately wanted to move it away. His stubble-free jawline moved subtly every time he swallowed. I couldn't decide if he looked better cleanly shaven or with his normal three-day growth appearance.

I still had no explanation for the weird tingles I got on my skin when we accidently touched, or the way my heart fluttered whenever he was near. Constant thoughts of him rattled around in my head. I wondered what it'd be like to give him...? *Oh dear!*

I bit my lip and tried not to giggle at my outrageous thoughts.

So much for no distractions. Cameron was my constant distraction and I was struggling with the emotions I was beginning to feel. But I had to lock them away, like a prisoner in the dungeons of a castle where the guards had thrown away the key. I had to keep my distance to avoid being hurt again. And my priorities were my studies.

"Wiley?" Cameron interrupted my overactive train of thought.

"Yeah."

"So do you want to do it together?"

I dropped my pen and moved awkwardly in my chair. "What do you mean? Do it?" Where my thoughts had been, I wanted to do many things to Cameron Wilks.

"This assignment. We have to do it in pairs. Do you want to do it with me?" His eyes darted across my face. "Where were you? You were totally zoned out."

"Sorry," I blushed. "You want to do the assignment with me? Why?"

"Because you're smart and I'll need all the help I can get."

That bit may be true, but spending more time with Cameron was not part of my plan. But how could I refuse. "Sure. That would be great."

After the tutorial, I made my way across the overly crowded hallway and waited by the wall for Cameron. The narrow walkway was full of students and staff exiting classes and moving on to the next.

But he must have followed right behind me because when

I turned around I stared into the hard plane of his chest. With him in my personal space, my head spun.

The crowd thickened as people shuffled their way past. The deafening shrill of conversations and muffled footsteps echoed loudly in the concrete passageway. Cameron was bumped toward me and he braced himself against the wall with his hand to prevent me from being squashed up against the bricks.

I was trapped by his arm hovering beside my head.

Mm...

He smelt divine. Dior Homme. I'd seen the bottle in his room. His heady scent filled my senses, his face only inches away from mine.

"I was thinking about our assignment and wondering if you'd like to start on it this weekend," he said. "Since you have to work tomorrow, how about on Sunday?"

"Yeah, we can do that." Wow, I was impressed that he was keen to start on it straight away.

"Other than the library, where in this thriving metropolis can we go?" His hand hadn't moved and his eyes remained locked with mine, making me curl my toes inside my shoes.

"Geez, Toowoomba has so many options available, I don't know where to begin," I said sarcastically, knowing all too well that this rural city didn't have too much to offer. "We could go to a coffee shop downtown, or to one of the parks like Queen or Picnic Point?"

"Let's do Picnic Point. That's the park at the top of the range, right?"

I nodded, unable to draw my gaze away from his lips. Watched him lick them and move his tongue around behind his perfect teeth. My mouth ran dry when he inched closer toward me. His breath danced across my face. I closed my eyes and stood deathly still. "It's a date." I whispered.

"It's not a date," he chuckled.

Damn, his lips were close. Just one more inch and I could taste them. I gripped into the handle of my bag hanging over my shoulder, tugging on it so hard I was going to break the buckle.

"Ah-ha!" Ashleigh's voice blasted in my ears. I turned to see her walk toward us from the direction of the other tutorial rooms. Aaron and Dave were in tow. Ashleigh's eyes narrowed and she waved her finger at us. "Okay, what the hell is going on with you two?"

My throat seized.

Cameron dropped his hand away and took a step back. Dave and Aaron's gazes ping-ponging between the two of us. Their eyes popping out of their heads like Pop-Tarts from a toaster.

"These two?" questioned Dave.

"What do you mean?" I leaned back against the wall, the coolness in the bricks aided in lowering my escalated body temperature. "Nothing is going on!" Unfortunately, that was the truth.

"Bullshit, look at you two." Ashleigh jammed her hands onto her hips.

"Look at what?" Cameron rubbed his forearm.

"This!" Ashleigh wiggled one of her fingers at us again. "I know there is something fishy between you two. It's not quite sex, because I goddamn know what that is, but something is going on."

"There's nothing going on!" I repeated. "We were discussing our assignment."

"Is that what you call it? Why don't you two go and have sex? Get it over and done with," she laughed.

I was so embarrassed I was unable to move. Was my body language and the way I reacted when Cameron was near becoming obvious to everyone? I didn't think so. I wanted to slink away, back to my room and hide so no one could ever see me again.

"Sorry Ashleigh." Cameron snapped his fingers and pointed at her. "I can't do that right now, because I'm off to The Club for lunch with Justin. Would you all like to join me?"

"Hell yeah," they nodded.

Cameron glanced over at me and smiled. It was as if nothing happened. Maybe it had only been my imagination thinking he tried to kiss me. "Want to come Wiley?"

The tug-of-war between my two frames of mind was unrelenting. I could go to The Club, eat lunch and be further harassed by my friends, or I could go home to my room and study.

Warning sirens and flashing report cards with big red F's on them danced through my mind. I stepped away from the wall, shaking my head. "No thanks. I have work to do." I'd had enough embarrassment for one day.

Chapter 7

On waking, I drew back my curtains and was greeted by a glorious Sunday morning with rays of sunshine warming the earth and a playful breeze wafting through the trees.

By midmorning, Kel and I were lazing about on her bed, reading magazines and listening to music. Well, Kel was reading, I flicked through the pages, not even taking notice of the pictures and glanced at her clock every few minutes.

"What's with you, Wiley? You've been jittery all morning."

I snapped the magazine shut.

"I'm going to start my law assignment with Cameron today. I don't want to be late." I jumped up off the bed and knocked all the magazines beside me onto the floor. With shaky hands I picked them up and placed them back on the bed.

"Cameron, hey? Nice!" Her eyes lit with excitement.

"Kel. It's study. Nothing else." She of all people knew I was not interested in a boyfriend this year. What would I have done if Cameron had kissed me outside class the other day? Nothing good would have come from it anyway. It was time to put my silly crush behind me and get this assignment done. I waved goodbye to Kel and returned to my room.

I busied myself while I waited for Cameron. I sent my parents an email, folded my washing, straightened up my cupboard and changed my shirt several times, trying to decide what to wear. Finally I settled on jeans and a long-sleeved cream t-shirt.

I hated waiting.

A fraction past midday, the highly anticipated single knock came on my door. I bit my lip to contain my smile and counted to five before I opened the door.

Cameron stood in the hall, leaning against the wall, looking breathtaking as always. His faded blue jeans hung low on his hips while his rugby jersey fit snuggly around his toned torso. And his smile was absolutely dazzling.

"I'm sorry I'm late," he said, stepping into my room. "I was at Gran's. Once you get her talking she's hard to shut up. She was still rambling on about something when I walked out the door."

"So, you ready then?" I grabbed my heavy backpack full of books and slung it over my shoulder.

"Yep, my stuff's already in the car. Let's go." He pointed to my bag. "Here, let me carry that for you." I let it slip off into his hand, impressed by his thoughtfulness. "I hope you don't mind," he continued, "but I've already bought lunch. You like chicken wraps, right?"

I nodded, walked out the door and followed him to his car.

I sank into the soft leather seats of his black Toyota Hilux as he started the engine. He grinned and revved on the accelerator before he slipped the car into gear, reversed out of the car park and headed on down the street.

Picnic Point was about a ten-minute drive from campus.

Cameron drove up the steep drive, past the iconic funnel-shaped water tower that took prime position at the top of the mountain range, and pulled into the car park down past the kiosk. The park was beautiful, as always. The grounds so green, the hedges freshly trimmed and the tall, straight gum trees rustled in the light breeze above.

"Stay there," Cameron said, hopping out the car and ran around to open my door for me.

"Thank you." I said and exited the car.

Cameron grabbed his backpack and a small cooler bag off the backseat along with the standard, college-issued, beige woolen blanket from the bed in his room for us to sit on.

The fresh mountain air filled my lungs and a subtle scent of burning wood from the barbecues up at the main picnic area drifted in the breeze. We walked over to the crest of the mountain to a clearing overlooking the range. In the distance, patches of farmland stretched for miles toward the eastern horizon. We lay the blanket under a group of gum trees, took a seat and I leaned back against one of the pillar-like tree trunks.

"Let's eat," Cameron opened the cooler bag, took out the wraps and offered me a beer. "This is good to get off campus for a while. I'm not used to living with one hundred-odd other people, I think I was starting to feel claustrophobic."

"Yeah, it gets like that sometimes. And this is only the start of week five. There's no such thing as privacy living on residential college. My escape's the library." I said, then took a huge bite out of my chicken wrap.

He laughed, as if that didn't sound like an option for him.

Cameron certainly was a tough one to work out. He came across as a party-hard type of guy around my friends and often went out with them during the week, but when he was alone with me, I always saw such a different side. What was with that? Cameron had trusted me with his past and it touched me in a way I didn't think possible. Like most people, he hid so much of himself and his problems deep inside. Well, so did I. But his made mine seem insignificant.

I wondered if it was his family that made him so guarded. I was intrigued to find out more about the real him. "Can I ask you something about your family?" I questioned him while brushing crumbs off my legs.

"I suppose." He grunted.

"How did your dad become successful?"

"That's what you want to know?" He looked at me with raised eyebrows. "You're one of the first people to ever ask me that."

I shrugged, unfazed.

"You certainly are different, aren't you?" He shook his head while trying to rip the label off his bottle of beer. "Okay. Well you probably know the basics, right? Dad made his money through property developments and mining. When he was younger, one of his first ventures was his own drilling and exploration company. It paid off when large deposits were found on the land and tenements he bought. The Pilbara, Hunter and Central Queensland have been his most successful developments and are now all being mined. The rest is history, I suppose. More mines, mergers and acquisitions, and now he's expanding into Africa and Mongolia. Plus he still has a bit of property development on the side. That's the summary in very short detail. I could bore you with more detailed facts, if you like?"

"Short stories are good for now." I sat gazing at him, mesmerized by his voice rather than at the information he provided. "Why don't you want to work for your dad after uni?"

He rubbed at his forehead and sighed heavily. "Everyone at home expect me to be like Dad. Taking on Wilks Resources is so much responsibility and I don't want to let anyone down. I'm not sure I can do it."

Cameron struggled with his thoughts. This obviously bothered him a great deal; the stress evident on his face. Like most of us, his life was far from perfect.

"Dad always says, '*When Cameron comes on board at the company...*' and things along those lines. It's like I have no choice. It's even harder now that my sister Lisa, who's a lawyer, works for him as well."

"So what are you going to do?"

"I'm not sure yet. I like what I'm studying and there's no way in hell my dad would let me be a bum and live off his money. He has worked hard for every cent he has made. You may not think it — hell, I certainly haven't given you much to go on, but that trait is instilled in me. I do want a career."

"That's good to know." I sheepishly smiled at him.

"My parents, although suffocating, have been really good over the past few months since Gilly died. Losing her screwed me up, and they're giving me some space. Coming up here to go to uni has certainly helped."

My head spun like a roulette wheel. The real Cameron, this Cameron, continually blew my mind.

He shaded his eyes as the sun broke through the tree canopies. "Do you think I might get a chance to ask you some things?"

I looked down at the blanket and picked at the pilling balls of fluff. "I'm not very interesting. There's nothing to tell."

"I tell you everything, yet I hardly know anything about you."

"I like it that way," I mumbled. "Aren't we supposed to be doing our assignment?"

"Soon."

I edged back against the tree, the bark scratching into my skin. Avoiding getting close to him, or anyone for that matter, meant I couldn't get hurt again.

"Let's start with something easy. What do your parents do? Do you have any siblings?"

I sighed. At least that question was harmless to answer. "Dad's an endodontist. He owns his own practice and has three other endos working for him. Mum works in reception and does the books. Their life revolves around socializing at golf, tennis and rugby. I've a brother, Chris. He's two years older than me and works for a tech company in Brisbane."

"Do you get along with your parents?"

"Most of the time. Dad's a gem, but my mother can have her moments." No, wait. That was an understatement. She drove me up the wall. Drama queen was her specialty. Center of attention her number one priority. Since moving away to university and experiencing so many new things, my eyes were finally opening up to the world. I was no longer as naïve as I had been when I was living at home under the protective shield of my parents. I knew what I wanted to do with my life and was determined to make it happen. I loved my parents dearly, but now when I went home for holidays our differences were becoming more notable. "All I seem to be now is slave labor. When I'm home, they always go away on holidays and I get to work in the reception at Dad's practice."

"Your parents sound like mine." He chuckled. "They just want you to learn, work in and run their business. See, we have so much in common!"

Yeah — I was trying to avoid that.

"And we've both had screwed-up relationships!" I winced after the words had left my mouth. How heartless of me. *Me and my stupid quick tongue.*

"Well, mine certainly was." He licked his fingers after the last bite of his wrap. "But what happened with yours? What was his name?"

A shudder ran through me and my throat constricted. Dare I go down this path? Kel was the only one who knew what had happened and I made her swear black and blue not to tell a soul. But Cameron rattled me. He trusted me and had made my hardened heart thaw a little. Wiping my clammy palms off on my jeans, I inhaled deeply and dared to tell him the truth. "His name was Michael. I caught him cheating...and it was with Louie."

Once I started, I couldn't stop blurting out all the details of my horrific encounter of walking in on Louie and Michael going for it in his house. To this day, I don't know how they met, where they met — I don't ever want to know those facts.

"Well, that explains a lot!" Cameron nodded slowly. "No wonder you get your back up around her."

"All the guys are desperately trying to get in her pants. Aren't you?" I scoffed, feeling a bitter taste rise in my mouth.

"Nope. She's attractive, but not my type."

Opening up and letting my guard down even a fraction, however, terrified me. If this information got out around college, I would be so humiliated.

As he looked at me, a strange warmth settled around my heart. With no expectations other than friendship, something magical passed between us. Was it our brutal honesty with each other, or the sharing of our past wounds, or a kindred connection that joined us together? Who knows, but the vibe between us was nothing short of intense.

The afternoon lingered on as we lay down on the blanket next to each other. His arm rested up behind his head, while I used his backpack for a headrest. We stared up at the clouds and played stupid games of trying to make out shapes in them. We slowly coaxed more information out of each other as we talked about our family, our private school days, career aspirations and all that our worlds centered around at that point in time.

We even loved the same band — Cold Play. I don't think I had ever been this candid and truthful with anyone before in my life, not even Kel.

Maybe this was a sign of starting to grow up.

Cameron lay next to me, his hair shone with golden streaks in the sunlight. Sometimes his eyes were closed; sometimes he was staring off up into the skies above. He had the most beautiful long eyelashes I had ever seen. It took all my strength not to reach over and touch him. I longed to experience that sensation when our skin touched, but I didn't want to make a fool of myself and didn't want to ruin the perfect afternoon.

A strong gust of wind brought us to the realization the day was drawing to an end and we had to return home for dinner.

"I can't believe we've talked all afternoon." I noted the late hour on my watch. "You prattle on too much!"

"I think we both suffer from that. But this was great. Talking and having a few beers was nice."

We cleaned up the rubbish and jumped in his car to head back to campus.

"Bugger!" I gasped. "We didn't start the assignment. Seriously, we better get into it tomorrow."

Cameron sighed and nodded in agreement before speeding all the way back home. When we arrived, he walked me to my block.

"Thanks for today, I owe you a lunch," I said, turning toward him. "I hate to ask, but promise me you won't say anything to anyone about Louie?" Nausea swirled in the pit of my stomach.

Then I met his eyes. The depth of their blueness made me lose every doubt. Cameron reached up and hooked a piece of flyaway hair in behind my ear, his finger brushed along the side of my cheek as he did so. I shivered and leaned into his gentle stroke wanting more. His eyes widened and he quickly pulled his hand away.

Could he not see or sense the effect he was starting to have on me?

"You've got to stop doing that," I whispered, hoping he didn't hear me.

"What was that?"

"Nothing!" Blushing, I stared at the ground.

"Okay then." He smiled. "Dinner! I'll see you there." And off he walked over to his block.

I dashed inside to my room and flopped down on to my bed.

What the hell was that?

Thoughts spun around in my head at a million miles an hour as I replayed our amazing afternoon. We laughed. We liked the same things and had the same crazy ideas for the future. It wasn't what I expected at all. Cameron was nothing like I first thought. The way he smiled left me breathless. The way he looked at me was mesmerizing. The way I felt when I was in his presence was nothing short of incredible. What a turmoil I had landed myself in. In the span of an afternoon he had somehow weaved his way in and started to open my heart. In the space of a few hours he had found out more about me than most of my friends did. How did I let this happen? Why did this happen? The obvious finally dawned on me. I was, without a doubt, head over heels for Cameron Wilks.

Chapter 8

It had been a rough week. Attending classes, working with Cameron on our assignment, and trying not to think about him during every waking hour was proving to be more and more difficult as each day passed. I needed to take the edge off somehow.

On Friday afternoon, after my tutorial finished at four o'clock, I ventured via The Club knowing some of my friends would be there having drinks. Cameron had not been at class and I wondered if he would be with them.

I walked in through the main entrance of the beer garden and headed toward the bar. Music blared from the speakers and the tables and chairs were filled with patrons, students and teachers, all glad to see the end of another week.

It was a Bundaberg Rum promotions day. The Bundy Girls, wearing very little clothing, had nearly every male within a ten-mile radius hovering around the bar trying to score photos with the girls, win free drinks and Bundy Bear merchandise.

I found Dave, Justin, Ashleigh and Kel sitting on old

wooden bar stools with rum drinks in hand. But no Cameron.

"Hey, Wiley!" they cheered as I walked in.

"Oh darn," said Justin. "That means we have to have another drink before we go to dinner."

"Yippee!" Ashleigh waved her hands up in the air.

I ordered a drink, took a seat and savored a few quick sips. The alcohol hit me straight away, helping me to relax for the first time all week. The rum went down easily and before I blinked, two had disappeared down my throat.

But it was enough. I picked up my bag to leave, when Kel insisted on buying me another drink. She was hard to say no to when she looked at me with her puppy dog brown eyes. As I reclaimed my seat, guess who walked through the door? Cameron. I looked at the floor and shook my head. I should not drink around him. I'd had enough already and I needed to go and read a case study or do something, anything before dinner to avoid being around him. My willpower and self-control were starting to falter around him. I didn't want to be one of those girls he had mentioned he didn't like, the ones who threw themselves at him. I was getting close to being at that point. I had to find my inner calm. One more drink and I'd be out of there.

"Hey, Cameron!" Dave shouted. Cameron pulled up a bar stool, sat right behind me facing the boys to my left. I was trapped.

Cameron rested his arm on the back of my chair and leaned toward the boys, shouting over the music. "Bundy promotion, any deals?"

"Not really, it's just five dollar drinks," Justin bellowed.

I glanced over my shoulder to say hello to Cameron and was instantly captured by his metallic blue eyes shining in the soft lighting. I was caught, hook, line and sinker. *Hmm, not good!*

"Hey girls," he said, still holding me captive and under his spell. "Glad you're here for a drink."

"Always up for a drink." Kel beamed, holding up her glass.

I forced myself to turn away and sipped on my rum. I could feel Cameron staring at me but resisted the temptation to turn around again. Closing my eyes, I took a deep breath and tried to settle my heart from thudding too loudly in my chest.

Cameron leaned on to the back of my chair while talking to Justin. I froze when goose bumps shot down my neck, arms and legs, making me shiver in my seat. I'm sure I did not imagine it, Cameron had blown softly against my skin. What was he doing?

I was about to turn around and face him when Ashleigh caught my attention. "What are you girls going to wear out tonight?" she asked.

I rubbed the back of my neck, trying to keep my breath at an even pace. "The usual jeans and shirt." I muttered, my mind clearly elsewhere.

"I'm wearing Wiley's slimfit jeans and my gold sequin top," Kel said before taking a sip of her drink.

"I brought a new top today when I went shopping with Aaron. He picked it out for me, I can't wait to show you." Ashleigh was in her usual high spirits after a few drinks and struggled to sit straight in her chair. "You're going to love it."

"Really? Aaron picked it out?" Kel and I exchanged glances.

"Yep, he's got great taste. He loves shopping!" Ashleigh laughed, oblivious to our concerns.

"Gotta find me one of them," I said, swirling the ice around in my drink with the straw.

"He could be right behind you." Ashleigh gulped down her rum and pointed directly at Cameron.

I turned, Cameron looked at us and smiled his gorgeous smile.

"What?" he straightened up in his chair, trying to look

innocent.

"Nothing." Ashleigh, Kel and I giggled together.

I took the last sip out of my rum eager to make my exit when Cameron's hand rubbed across the back of my shoulders; his face brushed up against my ear and whispered. "Do you want another drink?"

My eyes closed at hearing his voice rumble in my ear, his warm breath cascading down over my skin. I pictured his lips as he spoke. The need to taste them rose within me and my mouth began to water. Why was he being so cruel to me? Did he seriously not know he was having this effect on me? It was starting to cause me physical pain being around him. I couldn't contain my feeling for him any longer. With the alcohol coursing through me and giving me the boost of confidence I needed, I turned to face him.

Oh for the love of God! I threw my hands up in front of me. *You've got to be kidding!*

There stood the Bundy promotional girls, dressed in their little black hot pants and crop tops, vying for Cameron's attention. They offered him a free hat and drinks card "Buy 4, Get 1 Free". I dug my fingernails into the palms of my hands to try and calm down. My sanity was at breaking point. I'd had enough, I had to escape. Once the crowd cleared from around us, I was out of there.

The minutes seemed endless until finally the Bundy girls moved on after all the boys had their photos taken with them.

Cameron hollered, "My shout."

"No. Thanks. I gotta go," I slid off my stool to leave. A sobering Consumer Law case study awaited me and looming assignment due dates flickered through my mind.

"Please stay." He held up his drink card. "You have to have one of these." He stood to block my exit, called over the bartender and ordered a round of drinks for everyone.

"Are you trying to get me drunk?" I forced smile.

"Me? Never."

How could I resist? Study would have to wait.

The four rum drinks I had were enough to put me into a party mood for tonight. We all quickly finished off our drinks and headed back over to the dining hall. The aim was to bolt down some food, have a shower, and be back over here at The Club for happy hour at eight o'clock and dance the night away.

Chapter 9

After drinks at The Club and eating dinner, my friends and I, full of raucous laughter dispersed in all directions, back to our blocks to shower, dress, drink more and get ready to go out.

I managed to score a shower straight after dinner, ahead of the queue for a change. Two showers between ten girls usually resulted in a long waiting game. I proceeded with my Friday night ritual of washing my hair and shaving my legs. After soaping, sudsing, shaving and scrubbing, I was back in my room deciding what to wear. The first week of April saw the nights grow cooler and had me delving into the depths of my wardrobe to find warmer clothing.

I settled on my favorite dark blue hipster Levi's and red button-up checked shirt. All I had to do was blow-dry my hair and put on my lip gloss. I was not one for dolling myself with heaps of make-up. Just the basics, so it never took me long to get ready.

Kel burst through my door. "Sorry, Darl, I was chatting to Jessica next door. I'll go and jump in the shower, is that okay?"

Her cheeks were flushed from drinking and she stumbled around my room while trying to pull off one of her boots.

"Yeah sure, no rush. Come and get me when you're done. I need to do my hair anyway." I shooed her off back out the door and closed it behind her.

"I won't be long, I promise." Kel called out as she walked down the short hallway to her room. A smile charged across my face. Kel was notorious for taking really long showers; I don't know what she did in there for so long. But when she said she would rush, I knew I had a good twenty to thirty minutes up my sleeve.

I returned to the mirror hanging on the inside of my wardrobe door and started to dry my hair when I heard another loud knock.

"What did you forget, Kel?" I switched off the dryer, threw it on my shelf and turned to face the door. I stopped in my tracks. Cameron stood there, all freshly showered, cleanly shaven, dressed in Levi jeans and a black t-shirt and of course, he had a beer in hand.

Damn it! I should have recognized his knock.

"Hi!" My heart fluttered, like a baby bird testing its wings. Was I imagining things again or had he made an effort to look even more handsome tonight? Not that he had to do much at all. "Are you ready to go to The Club?" I reached for my brush and pulled it through my hair.

"I came over to see if you were ready to go." His eyes darted around my room while leaning against the end of my built-in wardrobe.

"Sure am. I'm waiting on Kel, though. She's just jumped in the shower." I furrowed my eyebrows, looking him up and down, thinking he was acting all weird.

"What's wrong?" I asked while continuing to brush my hair.

"Nothing." He took a step toward my bed, flopped down on the mattress and watched me. "You look good tonight, as always."

"Yeah, right!" I grunted. Was he complimenting me or being sarcastic? I wasn't used to receiving compliments; they made me feel awkward and embarrassed.

As I put my old overused hairbrush away on my shelf, he stood up quickly from the bed. He threw his empty beer bottle in my bin and then, there he was, standing right in front of me, only inches away. The smell of his cologne hit me. Dior Homme was my new favorite smell in the entire world. I closed my eyes and inhaled the woody scent. When I opened them, his Adam's apple lurched in his throat when he swallowed. My heartbeat started to race with him standing so close to me.

"Wiley," his brow burrowed. "I can't take this anymore." His deep voice rippled through me, curling its way across every inch of my skin. "I'm gonna go out on a limb here, but need you to know ..." I held my breath, wondering what was going on as he jittered on the spot. "I'm crazy about you."

"Oh wow...really?" A wave of ecstasy swept through my body, from my head down to my toes. Every nerve ending in my body tingled. Did I hear him correctly? Cameron was crazy about me or was I daydreaming again?

He stepped closer, took my hand and gazed at me with his blazing metallic blue eyes. "I want to know if this...is something. I need to know if you feel the same way about me."

The air around me grew thick, I struggled to draw oxygen into the depths of my lungs. I could no longer hear the music playing from my iPod; I could hardly make out my surrounds. There was only Cameron standing here before me.

Somehow I managed to nod. My ability to speak was rendered useless as words tumbled around in my head like they'd been thrown into a clothes dryer. "I thought you..." I couldn't finish my sentence, my voice faltered in the depths of my throat. It was all I could do to stand upright, let alone speak.

His hand slowly crept around my neck and nestled underneath my long hair, his other hand slipped around my waist. I trembled. My skin blazed beneath the touch of his fingers. I held my breath when he leaned in and kissed me. Nothing forceful, nothing fast; just a gentle, cautious kiss. His soft lips, laced with the sweet taste of beer, pressed against mine. I shut my eyes and soaked up every second. I wanted his lips to stay on mine forever and never wanted this moment to end.

I wanted this distraction.

He stopped and rested his forehead against mine. "Are you good?" he asked, wanting assurance that he had not crossed a line.

Trying to catch my breath, I wasn't sure if my feet were touching the ground. I was still savoring the taste of him and the feel of his lips. "Most definitely," I was still trying to comprehend Cameron had finally kissed me.

Nervous giggles escaped us and our mouths rushed to taste each other again. As I wrapped my arms around his broad shoulders and entangled my fingers into his thick hair, I drew him closer to me and pressed my body against his.

"I've been trying to ignore you, but can't do it anymore either," I confided over his kisses. "This afternoon at The Club was my limit. If it wasn't for those damn Bundy Girls, you would've been in trouble."

"Someone always seems to interrupt us at the most inopportune times, don't they? I don't know what it is about you, but I've wanted you since the moment we met. I didn't want to rush. I needed to make sure. And I get this insane buzz all over when I touch you," he confessed as he stroked his hands through my hair.

"Do you get that too? I thought it was just me. How weird is that? Is that normal?"

"It's intense to say the least. Freaky, but in a good way."

Gliding my hands down across his chest, the smooth cotton of his shirt was cool against my fingertip. Then when I snaked my arms around his waist, fire ignited in my veins.

His lips found mine again, more sure of himself this time. "This is better than I imagined."

"You've thought about doing this to me?" I did like that notion. I could never have anticipated being the object of someone's fantasies. It was doing wonders for my self-esteem that had been way below par over the past several months.

"Constantly," he whispered.

Cameron's hands were everywhere - on my ass, on my back, in my hair. His kisses intensified. The flick and taste of his tongue along with his hot breath on my face caused heat to swell in my core. I was bordering on delirious when he coaxed me toward the bed.

"Wait a sec," I gasped, "I think we should shut the door." I didn't want to let him go — not yet. I didn't need Kel or anyone else barging in to my room unannounced.

"Mm," was the only sound I heard rumbling deep within his throat.

I ducked around him to shut and lock the door and was caught off guard when he stepped in behind me. Shivers ran down my arm when he reached up beside me and flicked the bedroom light off. Then, took my hand and drew me on to the bed.

Even with the block-out curtains closed my room wasn't very dark thanks to the pathway and building lights outside. I shuffled up on to my pillows and melted into the mattress as he lay down on top of me. His long jean-clad legs fell in between mine.

Tilting my head to the side, he trailed ticklish kisses down the side of my neck. "Are you sure about this? About me, I mean?" I asked, rubbing my hands across his back. *Oh wow!* He was all rock, solid muscle.

"Do you really want to talk about the laws of attraction right now? I'll stop if you want me to."

"No, no! It's all good." There was no way in hell I wanted this to stop. In my wildest dreams I would never have thought Cameron would be attracted to, or would want a girl like me. I gently stroked his cheek. I had to touch him to make sure this was real. "I think you could be insane, though." I giggled, questioning his state of mind.

"My shrink says I'm not." He captured my hand in his, entwined our fingers together and pinned them down onto the pillow beside my head. "You're exactly what I need."

Propping himself up on one elbow, his other hand inched down my side, lingering on the arch of my breast before continuing over my hip and onto my leg. My body hummed and ached to feel more of him. I curled my leg around over his and slid my toes up and down the back of his calf. Placing my hand on his butt, I tugged him closer, feeling his hardness against me.

"Wiley," he groaned and pressed into me, arousing me more by the second.

I was trying to be controlled and not ravish him like some wild animal, but the rum I had earlier was not helping the situation. The more we kissed, the more difficult it was becoming to think logically.

The room temperature was rising and the heat cloaked itself around us. Cameron's eyes darkened and the low rumbles in his throat deepened.

A grin danced across my lips when his trembling fingers reached for the top button on my shirt. I'm glad he was as nervous as me. One by one, he popped each button undone and glided his fingertips down over my bare skin to the belt on my jeans. In one quick, swift maneuver, he unbuckled the clasp. "This seems to be in the way." He pulled the belt free from its loops with one almighty tug and threw it on the floor.

"So it seems." Running my hands down his back, I reached for the bottom edge of his shirt. "So is this." Grabbing handfuls of soft material I pulled it off over his head. He sat up to rid himself of the garment in full. Hungrily, I ran my eyes over the outline of his body. He was near perfection. Ripped stomach, broad shoulders, smooth chest and the feathering of hair that led below the rim of his jeans.

He cursed, struggling to undo the top button of my jeans and clumsily shimmied them down off my legs. As our clothing started to come off, I ached to explore every inch of him — preferably with my lips and tongue.

"How about we get under the bed covers." I suggested as he discarded my jeans on to the floor.

"You're reading my mind." He reached for my hand and dragged me up off the bed so I was able to pull back my quilt and sheet.

His hands drew around my waist and turned me into the hard plane of his bare chest. I lightly kissed his pecks as he peeled the shirt from my shoulders and threw it somewhere on the floor. Tingles shot through my veins and my fingers burned when I brushed them over his skin and headed for the top of his jeans. This was so surreal. My fingers were shaking and wouldn't cooperate as I attempted to undo the button.

Finally it came undone and I slowly drew his zipper down. Slipping my hand inside, I felt his erection straining inside his boxer briefs.

He nudged against my hold. "Wiley, here I was thinking you were a good girl." My head spun as we feebly removed the remainder of our clothes with a sense of urgency– bra gone,

Cameron's boots and jeans came off, panties and boxer briefs were discarded, all before we sank back into my bed underneath the crisp white sheets.

I gasped when Cameron's erection pressed hard up against me. His naked flesh seared against mine. I closed my eyes and imprinted this moment to memory; the way he looked, the way he felt, I had to savor every detail. Cameron was here, in my bed, with me.

"This is something I could definitely get used to," he said, kissing down my neck toward my breasts and licked one hardened nipple then the other. His warm, wet tongue made me quiver all over making me arch my back up to meet his pleasurable taunts. "Your boobs are fantastic," he claimed, cupping me in his hand and fondling my hardened bud.

I came to my senses, reached over into my bedside drawer, fished around and pulled out a condom. "I think we might need this." Only the other day, I was going to throw out the box, thinking I had no need for them at all.

He hesitated. "Are you sure about this."

I nodded. "Are you?"

His eyes twinkled and a cheeky grin spread across his face as he took the foil from me, tore it open with his teeth and rolled the latex onto his shaft.

"You're in trouble now." Flicking the sheet up high in the air, he rolled over on top of me and nestled between my legs. With his arms beside my head, holding his weight upon his elbows, his lips returned to mine. His pulsing erection throbbed against my opening, teasing me with gentle rubs. Arching into him, the want was getting unbearable. I needed him inside of me. I slid my hand down between us, stroked my hand up and down his length and guided him into place.

He probed me gently at first, pulling back ever so slightly before daring to go deeper. My breath caught in my throat and

I gasped.

He smiled when I wiggled my hips beneath him allowing my body to adjust to his size.

"Better?" He penetrated me slowly with the full length of his penis, sending shockwaves to my brain.

"I am now."

"You feel incredible. So wet. It makes me even harder for you. " He whispered into my ear.

With erratic breaths, I kissed his lips, his shoulders, nipped at his skin and tasted him with my tongue. I closed my eyes and bit my lip, trying not to think of fireworks going off in the night sky. Sweat started to lick our skin as our moves intensified. He was rubbing against me in all the right places as he thrust into me.

Then Cameron froze. Still buried inside of me. Every muscle of his body tensed.

Panting, I touched his cheek. "What's wrong?"

"Nothing." He grimaced. "I'm just trying not to come too quickly."

"Oh," I grinned. "So if I do this," I pulsed my hips up against his and wrapped my legs around his waist, "what happens?"

"Shit Wiley," he groaned.

And that's all it took to have him drive into me again and again.

My heartbeat pounded at a frightening pace. With his body against mine and his steel-like shaft inside me, my thighs shook, begging for release. I clasped on to his hips and my insides clenched around him. I wanted to cry out, but thin walls were such a bitch! When a guttural groan escaped from Cameron's throat, stars appeared before my eyes and everything exploded.

***

Only a few heated crazy minutes had passed until I lay embraced in his arms. I was hot, slicked with sweat and still trying to catch my breath. The smell of sex and Cameron filled the air. It had been all a bit intense, nervy and crazy, but *WOW*, that had come out of nowhere. I looked up at him.

"What?" he said through a sexy grin.

"What was that?" I smiled, pictures of what had happened still running through my head.

"That...was one hell of a bonus." He kissed me on the forehead. "Much more than I expected when I came to your room."

"What were you expecting?" I had to question.

"Everything from rejection to maybe a kiss and dance with you at The Club tonight."

"Oh!" I smiled, a little embarrassed at how far we went, but totally euphoric at the same time.

"Wiley?" We both jumped in our skin as a loud bash nearly knocked my door from its hinges. The window rattled above us from the force of the blow. "Come on, you ready?" Kel yelled out. "What are you doing? Why is your door locked? It's never locked. Are you there? Come on, it's time to go. Discount drinks are about to start."

I gasped. I'd forgotten all about Kel and The Club.

"Shit," I whispered to Cameron. "See, I told you about the door locking thing."

"Shh. She might go away." Cameron hugged my tightly and chuckled in to my ear.

"I can hear you, what are you doing?" Kel called out.

I tried not to laugh. "I think we're busted."

"I think so, too."

"Um...Kel, I'll meet you at The Club. I...I...I'm busy,"

"Busy? You? "What are you doing in there? Oh — who are you doing in there?" She demanded to know.

"Cameron," I flinched as the words left my mouth.

"What did you say?"

I knew she heard me clearly.

"Cameron." I repeated.

"Are you serious?" Her voice went up an octave. Shadows danced underneath my doorway, she would be jumping around all excited.

"Hi Kel," Cameron said.

"Holy shit!" She squealed. "You lucky bitch, Wiley! I mean, oh you know what I mean. You two have fun with whatever you're doing in there. I'll see you over at The Club later... maybe?"

"See you soon," I called out to Kel, then hesitated, before turning back to Cameron. "Are you ready for the news to spread like wild fire?"

"She won't tell anyone."

"Are you serious? Kel will be on the run at breakneck speed over to Ashleigh's room and then to The Club to tell everyone and anyone." I chewed on my thumbnail, I hadn't had the chance to get my head around what just happened. I had to keep pinching myself to ensure I was awake. Yep, Cameron was definitely here naked in bed with me. To be sure, I buried my face into his chest and cuddled deeper into his arms. His skin was so soft and warm beneath mine. I never wanted to him to leave. I didn't want to face reality.

"It'll be fine." Sounding assured of himself, he stroked my hair with his fingers.

"No, you don't understand. The whole of Steele Rudd College will know we were together by breakfast in the morning."

"I'm not worried." He propped one of his arms up behind his head.

"You have not been in the firing line of residential college rumor and gossip. The hounding we'll get tomorrow will be insane." I'd been through it before. The first time had been over Steven, the guy I lost my virginity to in my first year. He was a third year student and happily bragged to everyone. It was so humiliating. I never had anything to do with him again after that night. The second time was the night I met Michael. I was hoping I would avoid such circumstances again.

"It can't be that bad. I'm sure we'll be able to deal with it. At least there will be some truth in whatever story they come up with." He seemed so calm and in control, while my head was still wheeling in the aftermath.

"But —" I protested.

"Come on, let's go to The Club, have a drink, a dance and let's see what happens. And the best thing now is at least my balls won't be bursting every time I look at you; well, they might, so we might have to do this again."

"Again?"

"Most definitely."

Grinning, I lay in silence against his chest, listening to the sound of his rhythmic heartbeat. I didn't want to move. I didn't want this to end. I was afraid the minute he walked out the door it would be all over.

"Wiley, breathe. It will be okay."

He started to slowly run his fingers up and down my back. The sensual trails made me relax and nestle into him deeper. The gentle rise and fall of his chest started to deepen. Was he about to fall asleep?

"Do you want to go to The Club?" I asked. *Please say no, please say no* was going through my head.

"Not particularly," he whispered, rolled toward me, leaned in and kissed me. "I think there's a lot more here I would rather be doing than trying to control myself around you at The Club."

After making out again, we curled together, my head

resting against his chest. His breaths deepened and he drifted off to sleep. Listening to the gentle thud-thud-thud of his heart made my eyelids grow heavy and I gave up trying to keep them open.

***

Several hours later, I woke up busting for the toilet. My bedside digital clock showed it was half past one in the morning. Silently, I slipped out from under the covers without waking Cameron. The biggest smile spread across my face as I looked back at him lying in my bed. I rummaged around in the dark and cursed when I couldn't find any of my clothes. Where had they gone? I grabbed his t-shirt instead, slipped it on over my head and snuck out of the room to go to the bathroom.

My heart stopped when I returned and found my room empty. Cameron was gone.

Shit!

I sat down on the edge of my covers. Why did he leave? Was that it? It was all over. A quick roll in the sack and that was it? Was I that bad? OhMyGod — I just had a one-night stand. All these thoughts ran wild through my head. And tomorrow, I was going to have to deal with the consequences.

Light streamed into my room from the hallway as Cameron opened the door and snuck back into my room.

"Good timing," he whispered, closing the door behind him. "I needed the toilet as well. I just ducked into the boys bathroom next door in G-Block. I didn't want to wake you before because you looked so cute lying there snoring and snuffling away."

"I thought you'd gone." My eyes never left his as he walked around in front of me, his jeans hanging loosely around his hips.

"I'm not going anywhere." He leaned down to kiss me, ran his hands along my arms and pulled me up to stand. "Now this," he looked me up and down dressed in his shirt, "is hot." His voice, all soft and seductive, rang in my ears. He lifted me up, swung me around and placed me down on top of my desk, sending a pile of books crashing to the floor. His eyes sparkled, his warm breath tickled my face. His hands ran softly up across my thighs as he pressed his groin into mine. My fingers slid down across his bare chest to find the top of his jeans, and popped the buttons open slowly, one at a time. His lips found mine and it wasn't long before we were doing it again into the early hours of the morning.

Chapter 10

I awoke like clockwork at six-thirty the following morning; I had to go to work. The sun's rays broke through at the sides of my curtains, giving a hint to a fabulous day. I hated having to work when the weather was so nice.

"I'm going to have a quick shower before I have to leave," I whispered to Cameron, kissing him on the cheek then sliding out of bed.

"I forgot you had to work. Can you call in sick?" he mumbled, half asleep with his eyes closed and the hint of a smile upon his face. "Stay with me."

Cameron lay with the sheet drawn across his waist and his arm tucked under my pillow. His offer did sound mighty tempting. I didn't want to leave because once I walked out the door, the most amazing night ever would have to come to an end.

"Believe me, that sounds very enticing, but I need the money and my boss, Bruce, would hunt me down and kill me."

After a shower, I dressed for work in my unflattering long

black pants and white logoed tavern polo shirt, ready for the day ahead. I felt amazing, not only because of Cameron, but it was a rare occurrence for me to wake up on a Saturday morning not hung-over or sleep deprived.

Sitting beside Cameron on the bed, I leaned down closer to his ear and spoke softly. "Do you want to know what the funny side of this is?" Gently, I brushed his hair across his forehead. "You have to face everyone at breakfast and lunch without me today. I hope you're prepared. You haven't been privy to gossip yet. They will be brutal."

He smiled, "I'll be fine. You?"

"Absolutely!" I pressed my lips to his. "I gotta go, so lock the door when you leave. I'll see you tonight."

I heard a deep breath fill his lungs and assumed he'd fallen back to sleep so I quietly gathered my things and tiptoed out the door.

***

Every time I glanced at the clock, the hands had barely moved. The day dragged on and seemed like it would never end. I spent most of the day in my own little world, reminiscing about last night. But reality started to set in and I was terrified of the consequences. What had I done? Last night had been amazing, but Cameron was a party boy and was I just another notch on his belt? And more than anything, I didn't think I was ready for a relationship. In spite of all my crazy feelings for Cameron, could I risk getting hurt again? My priority had to be my grades. What would be the point of being together when the end of uni was not far off and we would no doubt venture off in separate directions? My emotions were playing havoc with me, flying up and down like a yo-yo.

From five o'clock on, I glanced at my watch every few

minutes. I didn't want to miss dinner. I was eager to get back, see Cameron and put an end to the butterflies swirling up a storm in my stomach.

"Bruce, I gotta get going. It's nearly six o'clock." I managed to corner my boss when there was a lull in serving.

"Sure, no worries. Thanks for staying back and helping."

It was nearly dark when I sped up the hill, back to campus. My hands sweated as I gripped and wrung them around the steering wheel as I drove along. I was not looking forward to the harassment from my friends about last night. There was no way to avoid it, so it was best to face it head on and get it over and done with. I parked my car, stepped out and sucked the cold night air into the depths of my lungs to calm my nerves before I entered the dining hall to face the onslaught of my friends — and Cameron.

Everyone sat around our usual table drinking coffee or finishing off their meals.

"Wiley!" Kel cheered as I walked in through the heavy glass doors. The others let out loud cheers and clapped. "Girl, we have some serious shit to discuss, get your ass into gear and get over here now."

Luckily, there were not too many people left in the hall, so I wasn't totally embarrassed by Kel's outburst.

Cameron looked at me with a sympathetic glance as he slouched over his coffee; his cheeks crimson red. The sight of him made me smile. It was a good thing he was not avoiding me. Right?

"I'll be there in a minute, I'll grab dinner first." I waved, walking directly to the kitchen.

Dinner of watery casserole looked unappetizing. I scooped some onto my plate along with a spoonful of soggy-looking vegetables before walking out to face my friends. I sat down in the empty seat next to Cameron and snuck a quick peek sideways. "Hi," I whispered.

"How are you doing?" He placed his hand on my leg underneath the table. I gasped, my skin tingling underneath at his touch. Sensing my overzealous reaction, he smiled and quickly drew his hand away.

Everyone's eyes were upon us. Waiting. Staring. Silent.

Ashleigh leaned forward, resting her elbows on the table. Kel's eyes beamed with excitement, her smile was as wide as the Darling Downs. The boys all nodded in unison and winked in Cameron's direction. Even Megan, who never cared for gossip, looked at me intrigued.

My stomach flipped and I swallowed hard. I was not looking forward to this at all. "What did everyone do today?" Trying to divert the subject was worth a shot.

"We want to know what you've been up too." Kel rubbed her hands together, eyes shining brightly.

I shrugged. "It was a boring day at work until the rugby finished and the crowd from Gold Park came in. That's why I'm late and tired."

"Tired! Too bloody right! You've been at it all night," Ashleigh blurted out. "I told you. I knew there was something going on between you and Cameron. God, I do love it when I'm right!" Ashleigh looked very pleased with herself as she crossed her arms.

"I don't know what you're talking about." I blinked, my tone was soft and full of innocence.

"Bullshit!" Justin coughed. "You sneaky little minx, Wiley."

"Come on, spill it. We've been harassing Cameron all day, it's your turn now." Kel wriggled around on her seat, busting to get the details out of me.

"What have you told them?" I lowered my voice, directing my question at Cameron.

"Not much, as little as possible."

"You look like you survived."

"Barely!" he sighed, scratching at the stubble on his chin.

"Come on, Wiley, you gotta give us something; Cameron won't tell us anything." Ashleigh dug for more information.

"It's enough that you know, you don't need details." I blushed, heat creeping up the side of my neck before I scooped casserole into my mouth.

"Yes we do! I need to know everything." Ashleigh pulled her chair in closer, keen for all the juicy gossip. She thrived on it, and until last night I hadn't given her any fuel to feed her fire in a long time, but now her eyes were drilling into me, burning with curiosity.

"Not going to tell," I shook my head. My friend's faces all filled with disappointment as they realized I wasn't going to give them any more satisfaction.

"You're boring!" Ashleigh huffed, sat back in her chair and pouted. "You have just slept with one of the hottest, if not the hottest guy on campus and you're going to tell us all about it?"

"Hey!" Aaron protested.

"Aaron, honey." Ashleigh glanced in his direction. "Sorry to say it, but Cameron is fucking hot!"

Aaron placed his hand across his heart and gasped. "No one is better than me."

"I still love you though." Ashleigh giggled, leaned over and gave Aaron a quick kiss on the cheek before turning her attention back to me and Cameron. "Now, Wiley, how did you two end up in bed last night?"

"Sorry, Ashleigh," I said. "You're not going to get anything out of me. That's it."

"So what's the deal with you two?" Kel strummed her fingertips on top of the table.

"Come on guys," Cameron rubbed at the muscles in his shoulder. "We haven't had a chance to talk about anything because she had to work today. Give us a break."

Ashleigh tisked and shook her head. Everybody knew everybody's business on residential college. "Oh Cameron, Cameron. Cameron. You will learn. We find out everything."

"I'm gathering that," he sounded drained as his shoulders slouched.

"I did warn you," I said to Cameron.

"You certainly did and you were right, I wasn't prepared for this extent of harassment."

I smiled at him and caught the pleading look in his eyes to get out of there. I finished my dinner in a few quick gulps, cleared my dishes away and went back to the table to grab my keys and bag. Cameron stood up, stretched and straightened out his jeans by running his hands down over his thighs. "Come on, I'll walk with you back to your room," he offered.

"Go, you two lovebirds," Kel grinned from ear to ear.

"Go get all crazy and sexed up," Ashleigh yelled as we walked toward the exit. "We'll talk more about this later, Wiley!"

I waved at her over my shoulder as I exited through the door.

Cameron and I walked back to my room and sat down on my bed. Facing him, I fidgeted with my pillow resting in my lap. I was anxious and nervous about being alone with him for the first time since last night and wondering what was the next step; if any.

"You were right about the gossip, it's insane." Cameron leaned his head back against the wall. "When I walked into breakfast, Kel sat there grinning, busting to know what happened."

"Wow. Kel was at breakfast?" That shocked me more than anything else. Kel rarely went to breakfast.

"I know! Right? I did acknowledge we were together last night. It was hard not to, especially when I ran into your neighbor,

Jennifer, out in the hallway when I was leaving this morning. But that's it." He sounded tired as he gave me a rundown of the day's events. "By lunchtime, it felt like everyone knew. It didn't help when Jennifer kept telling everyone we woke her up in the middle of the night making too much noise."

I bit my lower lip, remembering when books went crashing to my floor, "Gotta love the thin walls." He grinned, making my heart race. "So now what?"

He took my hand and entwined his fingers with mine. "I would like to see where us being together leads. Wouldn't you?"

I stared at my hand linked in his. Was I ready to take the plunge into another relationship? Cameron was ridiculously good looking and turned every female eye his way. How would I handle everyone vying for his attention? Was Cameron going to screw around on me like Michael did? Could I fit in time for him around my studies? I needed to be fair on Cameron because I wasn't the average type of girl.

"You do know I study heaps; my grades are my priority. I don't go out through the week and I work every Saturday. I thought you'd want some party-hard, adrenaline-junky type girl."

"You have me so wrong." Cameron shook his head. "You're exactly what I need. You're smart, beautiful, and funny — and you get me."

My head went dizzy, trying to grasp what he was saying. All the pros and cons of being together jumbled around inside my head, but my heart was overruling everything.

Cameron squeezed my hand. "You're the first sign of light I've seen since Gilly died and I want to see where it leads us. Will you please go out with me?"

As he looked at me with his shimmering eyes, it was hard to imagine doing anything else.

My hands trembled, my stomach was mastering

somersaults and my pulse throbbed in my ears. But something about him gave me a glimmer of hope that things may be all right. I was scared, terrified in fact. But I liked him, so why hesitate? I took a deep breath and jumped into the unknown. "Yeah, that would be nice."

He let out a huge sigh like he'd been holding his breath. "I was worried there for a moment you were going to treat me like a cheap one-night stand and kick me out."

I giggled. *Oh wow, I've just got myself a boyfriend!*

"Do you have plans tonight?" His brow furrowed with seriousness.

"Nope. I desperately need a shower. I smell of beer and I can't remember what this stain on my pants is from. It looks like gravy, I think."

"Would you like to catch a movie, or go out for a coffee?" he asked.

"Like a first date?" I smiled at him, his beautiful face gleaming back.

"Yeah, I suppose you could call it that." He looked so calm and cool, while my insides were bubbling like a bottle of champagne about to explode.

"I haven't been to the movies in months. Can we do that? Let me shower and get dressed. Do you want to come back and get me in about twenty minutes?"

"Done." We both stood up, he nervously kissed me on the cheek and departed. After he left, I closed the door behind him and leaned back against the smooth surface. Staring up at the ceiling, I closed my eyes and was convinced no one in this world would be able to wipe the smile off of my face. I couldn't believe I was going out with Cameron Wilks. On a date! As my heartbeat raced I said a silent prayer. I hoped I'd made the right decision.

***

Twenty minutes later, the soft one-tap knock came on my door. I did like his promptness.

"It's open," I called out as I finished applying my lip gloss.

Cameron swung open the door and stepped into my room. Freshly showered, he now wore dark navy blue jeans, white shirt and black dress jacket. I glanced up and down over his entire; handsome didn't cut it in describing how good he looked. My eyes widened and my mouth fell open when a single, long-stemmed yellow gerbera wrapped in clear cellophane appeared from behind his back.

"For you." He handed me the flower.

"You bought this for me?"

"Yeah. In anticipation of our first date."

"Wow." I nuzzled my nose into the petals, my feet feeling light upon the ground. I was amazed at how buzzed a simple flower could make me feel; or maybe it was just Cameron. But I had to play the devil's advocate. "What if I'd rejected you?"

"I would've thrown the flower in the bin and you'd be none the wiser." He grinned as his eyes surveyed me up and down. "I must say, you do look hot in that outfit," he said, admiring my low-rise bootcut Levi's and navy long-sleeved knit top. "And those high-heeled boots make you a little bit taller so I don't have to lean down so far to kiss you." He swept in and gave me a gentle kiss on my mouth. Having his soft, warm lips against mine again made my head dizzy. I closed my eyes to regain my balance. As I blinked them open he smiled at me.

"What?" I lowered my gaze to the ground, my long hair falling across my face. My equilibrium was out of whack; so much had happened in the past twenty-four hours I needed time to adjust. After trying to deny my attraction toward Cameron for the past six weeks, now I had to deal with the 180 degree turnaround. It was going to take some time to get used to. "Do I not affect you in the same way?"

He hooked his finger underneath my chin and tilted my head up so my eyes met with his. "More than you can imagine. But this is our first date and I aim to be a gentleman."

Heat rippled through me at the sound of his voice and my insides started to clench with want. Cameron was mine, and I wanted to take full advantage of the situation. I placed my hand on his chest, grabbed his shirt and draw him in closer for a kiss. His mouth drew into a smile beneath my lips as his hand grabbed mine. "Hmm. Come on, let's go or we'll miss the movie." I reluctantly let go of him, placed my flower on the desk, picked up my bag and followed him out the door.

***

The action movie, for a no-big-name movie, ended up being quite good. Well, what I saw of it. Cameron was much more entertaining to watch in the dark. His expressive responses, like seeing the vein protrude in the center of his forehead when he was stressed, his hooded eyes when he concentrated hard, or his wide open laugh and shining eyes when he was happy, were all imprinting into my memory.

After the movie, coffee and cake, we drove back to campus and my feet started to drag after the long day.

"Thanks for a great night, I had a really good time," he said when we arrived back at my room.

"Me too." My fingers shook as I placed the key in the lock. I swung the door open and turned to face him.

He grinned, noting my apprehension. "I said I was going to be a gentleman on our first date and I mean it. You've had a long day and need a good night's sleep. I'm not going to stay. I have to take Gran to Brisbane tomorrow for her birthday. My parents are flying up from Sydney and we're all going to a matinee show at the Lyric Theatre."

"Oh. Culture! I didn't think that would be your thing."

"Wiley, there's so much you don't know. But I, for one, am looking forward to spending more time with you and getting to know each other a whole lot better. Goodnight, beautiful. I'll catch up with you tomorrow evening."

He bent down and kissed me. The sweet taste of chocolate torte on his tongue as he flicked it against mine made my knees buckle. Flashes of last night burst in vivid technicolor behind my closed eyelids as I relived his body against mine.

"Are you sure you don't want to come in...and stay?" I rested my hands against his chest and could feel his heart race.

"Believe me, I want to." The muscle in his cheek ticked. If his want was anywhere near mine, I knew how hard it would be to part. "But it's our first date. Never sleep with anyone on the first date."

"A bit late for that."

"I'm lucky to know what's in store, so there'll have to be many more dates after this one. I've got to head off early in the morning, so I better get going." He chuckled as he removed my hands from his chest. "Night." He lowered his head and kissed me again before he backed out of the doorway, letting go of my hand and disappearing out through the common room door.

***

I spent the afternoon mulling over assignments. By three o'clock I'd had enough of studying. The hours seemed to crawl by ever so slowly as I anxiously awaited Cameron's return. Glancing up, I saw Dave and the boys walk past my window on their Sunday afternoon ritual of having drinks over at The Club. Cameron wasn't back yet and I needed a break as I could no longer concentrate.

"Hey!" I called out to them. "Can I come?"

"Really?" Dave faltered in his stride. "Are you okay? You never come out on a Sunday."

"My mind is elsewhere." I shrugged, turned to grab my wallet and rushed out to join them. Kel tagged along and we settled in with a few jugs of beer in the beer garden, listening to the afternoon music and entertainment. The cold ale went down well and I was pouring my second glass when my phone blipped with a text message.

Where are U?

My heart flipped when I saw it was from Cameron. I grinned and quickly replied.

Club

C U in 5.

Exactly five minutes later, Cameron strolled in from behind the latticed screens near the entryway. He walked over to our table and stood behind me and greeted everyone. He placed his hands on my shoulders and softly played with my long, loose hair, making me melt under his touch. When would I get used to his hands upon me?

"Grab a glass and join us," waved Justin, pointing to a spare chair.

"Maybe next time," he said before leaning down and whispering in my ear. "Do you want to get out of here?" His breath danced across my skin.

Raising my eyebrow, I turned to look at him. I didn't need much convincing.

"Sure do!" I sculled the remains of my drink and waved farewell to everyone. Cameron took my hand and led me out of the Club. I could still hear hoots and hollers from my friends as we departed.

I giggled, struggling to keep up with his pace as we walked

across the car park toward our residential college. I tried to find out how his day was, but he kept his responses short and insisted we walk faster. "What's going on?" I asked, amused at being whisked away.

"Just come with me."

He led me straight to his block, drew me into his room, closing and locking the door behind.

He spun me around and kissed me hard. His tongue delved into my mouth with hunger, making my head reel.

"What is this all about?" I asked over our kisses, threading my fingers through his hair and trying to catch my breath.

His blue eyes darkened with stormy desire. "The first date is over. I don't want to wait for a second or third. I've missed you all day. I want you. Now."

His hands clawed at my t-shirt and started pulling it off over my head.

"Oh. Well then." I grinned, raised my arms and happily obliged before we fell on to his bed.

Chapter 11

Shaking. Trembling. Scorching heat and sweat. I wrestled myself awake and stopped myself in time from falling out of Cameron's bed. *Damn single beds.* Startled, I sat upright and looked over at Cameron. His eyebrows were pinched tightly together and he mumbled incomprehensible words. His body was a lather of sweat as he tossed and turned his head upon the pillow. His hands were clenched into fists, pulling at the bedsheet as his body shuddered.

I rubbed my tired eyes and caught a glimpse of the green digits on his alarm clock, it was nearly two o'clock in the morning. "Cameron!" I whispered but he didn't respond. "Cameron." I spoke louder this time and nudged him on his shoulder. "Cameron!"

He bolted upright. "No. What? Wait." He gasped for air as his eyes shot open. His body glistened in the dim room light from the sweat slicked across his chest.

"Are you okay?" I looked at him with concern as he wiped his hand across his face.

Silence hung in the air as he tried to regain his composure. He rubbed his eyes and then the back of his neck. "It was just a bad dream. Sorry, I didn't mean to scare you." He took my hand in his, trying to offer me some reassurance. His skin was hot like a furnace as he wrapped his fingers around mine.

"What you were doing was freaky!" I had never seen anything like that before.

"Come here, beautiful. I didn't mean to frighten you." He lay down again, pulled me into his arms and held me tight like he never wanted to let go.

The terrors I had experienced were few and far between and were nothing like Cameron's. I was unsure how to deal with witnessing such physical nightmares and couldn't deny he had shaken my nerves. "How often do you have them? Do you want to talk about it?"

His chest rose and fell gently next to me, his skin was still hot to touch.

"I don't have them very often anymore. But it's the same dream over and over. It's usually Gilly's lifeless body on the floor and I can't save her. I can never get to her in time. But tonight the dream was different. This time it was you."

I shivered as an icy chill ran through me and I curled up closer next to him. "Well, let's hope that's not a premonition."

***

Just my luck to start dating someone one week before Easter holidays. I usually looked forward to the break, but now I faced fourteen days at home away from Cameron. The holidays started and my assignments offered little reprieve from constantly thinking about him. I dreaded the cost of my next phone bill, with all the calls and texts we were making.

Late one night, when I got home from dinner with my

parents, I decided to go to bed straight away. I had to work at Dad's practice tomorrow so an early night would be good. I checked my phone once more while I readied myself for bed. Cameron hadn't called like he said he would, and hadn't responded to my earlier messages. My mother was far from impressed at finding out I had a new boyfriend especially after I'd been adamant about not wanting one this year. Me getting top grades at uni was all she seemed to care about.

My relationship with my mum started deteriorating when I won the scholarship, moved on campus and discovered boys. My mum was a control freak and maybe she hated not being able to control me anymore. Needing to vent my frustrations about my mother's ever-increasing nagging, I settled with bitching about her on the phone to Kel. She was always good for that, but I ended up listening to her more than vice versa. My pettiness was nothing compared to her having to live with a verbally abusive, alcoholic father. It made me realize how lucky I was to have good parents...well...the majority of the time. And I did love them...most of the time.

Just as I turned off the light, my message tone beeped.

I reached over and grabbed it, and my eyes widened with excitement at seeing Cameron's name.

Hey Beautiful. How are you? Sorry it's late. You awake?

I grinned sheepishly as my worry dissipated into thin air.

Yep. Miss you. Where were you?

Late dinner with dad. All ready for bed. I'm in bed.

I wish I was in bed with you. I've got a hard-on just thinking about it.

Yeah, right.

Seriously — no joke!

I don't believe you.

Wait — I'll prove it.

Sitting up, resting back against my headboard, I wondered what he was doing. In the next instance my phone chimed again. A photo. What had he sent? Maybe a photo of him naked. I didn't need to see that! Well, maybe; on second thoughts. Giggling, I opened the attachment and before my eyes was a picture of him lying in his big bed on top of deep red sheets. He lay snuggled up among the pillows, his hair damp and messy from showering and his face a little scruffy with growth. His long-sleeved black t-shirt top was pulled firmly across his broad chest. But what really caught my attention was the rather large bulge protruding up from underneath the fabric of his black and red striped flannel pajama pants. I bit my lip, impressed by what I saw.

Nice!

I told you so, you drive me crazy.

Hope it stays that way.

Can you help me out with my predicament?

The ridiculous grin could not be wiped off my face as I speedily typed back.

You know what I would do with that!

Oh, the thought is making it harder.

Well then you won't need me! LOL. I am sure you can handle that all by yourself.

I think I'm going to have to — wish it was you.

Should not have gone back to Syd.

I'll get on the next plane.

Don't tease me.

Missing you heaps.

Same. Will sleep with your photo on my pillow next to me.

Cruel.

LOL. Night.

Chapter 12

The new term meant autumn was upon us. The air turned crisp and the mornings were chilly. I arrived back on campus on a drizzly Sunday afternoon, unpacked everything into my room and counted down the hours until Cameron returned in the evening. Common rooms were busy with students watching rugby league on television and reacquainting after the break. At five-thirty Kel and I headed over to the dining hall for dinner and half an hour later, Cameron walked in after flying back from Sydney. His eyes lit up when they met mine. The urge to run over and greet him burned within me; I literally had to hold on to my chair to keep from making a fool of myself.

Dinner passed with the excitement of holiday tales, and then Cameron and I made our excuses and headed for my room.

He swept me up in his embrace and kissed me feverishly. "Hmm, I've missed you so much. The only thing that got me through the holidays were those late night texts and calls." His warm breath brushed across my face as my hands dived for his belt. "It's so good to have you back where you belong."

My insides felt like melted chocolate as his hands slid my coat off and dropped it to the floor. Boots, jeans, shirts and underwear littered my floor as we dived under the covers. I had every intention of making up for time lost.

***

Four weeks into second term saw the days disappear and I to find balance in my relationship with Cameron and classes. Unfortunately, the scales were tipped in his favor. Coffees, shopping, lunches, drinks, endless conversation and, of course, the sex, were all too enticing. Skipping the odd class to spend time with Cameron was so much more entertaining than study and worrying about maintaining scholarship grades.

I sat at a desk opposite him in the library, stared out the window and down toward the road. Little rain had fallen in the past few months and the onset of winter was taking its toll on the landscape. The gardens were bare, the grass was scorched brown, and rich red dirt was visible everywhere. All the deciduous trees had turned golden, morning frosts were common and gale-force winds blew fiercely. Beanies, scarves and thick woolen coats were essential attire for everyone as they walked quickly to class to escape the dropping temperature.

"Come on!"

Cameron brought me out of my daydream by kicking the leg of my chair.

"No!"

"Yes," Cameron whispered. His eyes darted around, ensuring no one was near. "We've been studying for hours. We don't need to go to this tutorial. We've done all the work. We need a break. I want to give you a break." His eyes smoldered and a mischievous grin tugged at his lips.

"Now?" I blushed. *Hmm. Sex with Cameron or a two-hour tutorial with Mr. Barnes?*

Cameron gathered his books and bag, pushed back from the chair and wiggled his finger at me to follow. I couldn't believe I was contemplating this. He was right. I had done all the tutorial work and the extra review questions I could do tomorrow. But as I watched his butt in his jeans in front of me, there really was only one option.

We walked along the quadrangle pathway and headed for our residential college. I shuddered when Carlton Weber, my scholarship officer, came toward us.

"Wiley." He called out and blocked our way past. "Good to see you. Aren't you supposed to be going to a tutorial now?" His eyes glanced at his watch then darted from mine to Cameron's.

"Yes...but...um...I'm not feeling well. Cameron's making sure I get back to my room because I'm feeling giddy." I was such a bad liar.

"I see." He studied me with unblinking eyes, peering down the bridge of his nose and over the rim of his glasses.

"Well, Ms Cayton, I do hope you get better soon. I hope your studies are going well. Remember, you have your scholarship review coming up and I expect your grades to be outstanding as always."

Guilt strangled me around my throat, making it hard to swallow. Running into Mr Weber was the firm reminder I needed. My studies had to come first.

Cameron and I made it across the grounds and out of his sight before I stopped and faced him.

"I'll have to take a raincheck. I've got to go to class. I have my review coming up soon and I need to keep my track record perfect. I don't want to give the uni any reason to put black marks against my scholarship."

Cameron's shoulders slouched. I hated to disappoint him

and made a mental note to make it up to him later.

The look in his eyes made my innards ache. It was the first time since being together I was torn between my study and wanting to spend time with Cameron. It had always tugged at me beneath the surface, and until now, Cameron had always been the clear winner. But my future depended on my scholarship and my grades. With great reluctance, I turned and headed for my class.

***

"I'm going to The Club tonight to see a band playing. Do you want to come?" Cameron asked as we lazed in his bed. My skin was still blazing after making it up to him after having to turning him down yesterday and go to class. By the satiated look on his face, I must have passed with flying colors.

"But it's Wednesday!"

"So? One night won't kill you."

"But we went out on Monday, to the trivia night."

"Everyone's going. I'd love you to come."

"But exams are coming up."

"It's okay." Cameron rolled toward me and ran his fingertip up and down my breastbone, sending my nipples into hardened peaks. "I don't mind if you want to stay home."

I closed my eyes and clenched my teeth together. I'd already lost so many study hours over the past few weeks. It wasn't just The Club, but also the coffees, lunches, dinners, movies and the outings. Who knew a relationship could take up so much time. I hated the thought of being away from him. I still had insecurities about us being together and couldn't help the tinges of jealousy that flared up with all the female attention he attracted. That was one of my motivations for never leaving his side, another was because we had so much fun and he made me laugh. With his lips upon mine, his body here beside me, how could I resist? My constant distraction. I sighed heavily and gave in. "Okay, I'll come."

***

It was late when we arrived at The Club after having a few pre-going-out drinks. The dance floor was packed with students jumping and bouncing around to the blaring, vehement sound of the band. Cameron and I were full of laughs, tipsy from the alcohol we had drunk and joined them. The guilty feeling for being out the second time this week was washed away with kisses from Cameron. He swooped me around and around, making my head dizzy and my heart light.

"I'm going to the bathroom," he yelled over the band's pounding beat and disappeared through the crowd.

Kel was dancing nearby, trying her best pick-up moves on some guy. I let her be and continued to sway around to the music by myself knowing Cameron wouldn't be long.

Rick appeared before me, jumping around and sweating profusely. His squinting eyes were so bloodshot he looked like a vampire. I shook my head, knowing he probably had taken some kind of drug to come out for the night.

"Wiley! Babe. How you doing? Where's Cameron?" His voice boomed in my ears.

"Bathroom." I jutted my thumb in their direction.

"I'm impressed to see you out again this week. I like this party girl. Now would you like to let that hair of yours down even more? I've got something that will really blow your mind."

"No thanks. Cameron does that, I doubt if you have would compare. Thanks for the offer though."

"Not me, you goose. Try this."

He grabbed my hand, turned my palm upwards, held it

close into his chest and pushed what felt like a tablet into it, and forced my fingers shut.

I froze in horror.

"Babe. Trust me. Try this and you'll have the time of your life. This'll give you the energy to go at it all night." Rick said, his eyes all wild under the disco lights

"I don't do drugs. Take it back."

From out of the darkness, Cameron's hand grasped mine so tightly it hurt. He shoved Rick hard on the shoulder, forcing him back into a group of girls dancing behind him. "What the hell do you think you are doing? Get your drug-fucked ass out of here now."

Cameron was red with rage. I had never seen him look so terrifying. He still gripped my hand and I started to wince in pain.

"Cam, let go, you are hurting me."

He turned to face me, his eyes, like fiery daggers, stabbed me straight through the heart. "What the hell are you doing?" He reefed my fingers open, grabbed the pill and crushed it on the dance floor beneath the heel of his boot. "Ecstasy? You were going to take this shit?"

"No. Cam…I'd never…"

He glared at me, his jaw locked, then he turned and stormed off out into the beer garden.

"Cam, wait!" I chased after him as my heart thundered in my chest. I hated seeing him like this.

"What were you thinking?" Cameron turned to me when I caught him on the arm. Anger laced his every word.

"Rick forced it into my hand. I'd never do drugs. You, of all people, should know that."

"Do I, Wiley? We've only been together a couple of months. You want an upper to party hard all night? Am I not enough for you? I thought we had it good and trusted each other. Am I still naïve not to see this coming? Have I had clouds over my eyes all the time?" Cameron's cheeks flushed red and fury flared in his eyes, turning them a steely-gray. "How am I supposed to trust you now?"

Tears streaked down my face as I shook my head. "You're not wrong about me. You can trust me. I swear to God. I swear on my life I did not take that pill from Rick. He forced it into my hand, and regardless, I certainly would've never taken it. Ever. Even if he tried to ram it down my throat." Desperation clutched at me. How could I make Cameron see the truth? I flung my arms around his waist and held on to him. My tears soaked into his shirt as I trembled all over.

Cameron's arms hung limp and he barely drew breath.

I don't know how long we stood there. It could have been seconds, or it could have been minutes. Time was irrelevant. All I know was it seemed like a lifetime passed before he sighed, wound his arms around me and nuzzled his head against mine.

"I'm sorry. You scared the shit out of me. It's the one thing I can't tolerate. You know that. "

"Don't you ever freak me out like this again either." I blubbered over my tears. "Don't go jumping to the wrong conclusions, because you're everything to me. Can't you see that?"

"Yeah." He kissed me on my forehead. "Come on, let's go dance, but I need a drink of water first."

"You stay here, I'll go and get it." I slid out of his arms and headed back inside to the bar.

I weaved my way through the sea of people but was stopped in my tracks by someone standing in front of me.

Could the night get any worse? Obviously, yes.

"Hey! Wiley!" There before me, drunk out of his mind was Michael, swaying in the middle of my path. "I was hoping you'd be here."

A knot of contempt lodged in my throat. Glancing past him I could see his motley crew of friends buying drinks at the bar. *Why did they have to come here?*

"What? Why?" I tried to be civil but seeing him again made the pain in my heart resurface like a submarine coming up for air.

"I've missed you heaps, Honey, and...wanted to see if we could...I don't know, catch up like old times." He slurred and inched suggestively toward me.

Taking a step back from his advances, I put my hand up to stop him.

"You've missed me?" I shook my head and looked at him pathetically. Why did he have to take up space on this planet? "Yeah well, you should've thought about that before you cheated on me." I didn't want anything to do with this lowlife any more.

"Come on, you know that was nothing." He shrugged like he'd done nothing wrong.

"Are you insane?" My blood started to boil and race through my veins.

Without warning, from behind, familiar arms wrapped around my waist. I'd been on the verge of lashing out with more verbal abuse at Michael when the feel, sound and smell of Cameron brought me safely back down to earth.

"Hey. I was wondering what was taking you so long," Cameron said, concern evident in his voice and his eyes jumped back and forth between me and Michael.

"Nothing's wrong," I said, clenching my hands by my side.

"Who's this?" Michael swayed on his feet and snarled rudely at Cameron.

"Cameron, this is Michael."

"Hey." Cameron grunted at Michael, then reached for my hand and started to lead me away. "Come on, Wiley, let's go."

"Hey buddy, I'm talking to her." Michael put out his arm to

stop Cameron from passing.

"Don't touch me." Cameron flinched. "And I know for a fact she doesn't want to talk to you."

Michael nudged Cameron hard in his shoulder. "You don't speak for her."

My skin prickled all over as the tension in the air grew thicker by the second. I didn't want this to get ugly.

"Yeah, I do. I think you should leave." Cameron pointed toward the door.

"And who are you?" Michael jutted his chin at Cameron.

"I'm her boyfriend."

My knight in shining armor coming to my rescue was all very flattering, but the alcohol-infused situation was like adding fuel to a fire. I was about to leave with Cameron when Michael let one fly, landing a hard punch on Cameron's right cheek. The thwack against Cameron's face reverberated through my arm and struck me in the pit of my belly making me feel sick.

Cameron shoved Michael back. "You idiot." He cursed, rubbing at his inflamed cheek.

I was caught in the middle. Cameron and Michael stood facing each other, their chests puffed out like roosters ready to fight and their fists were clenched tightly at their sides. Within a flash, Michael's friends were at his side, ready for an all-out brawl. All hell broke loose around us as Michael lunged at Cameron. A flurry of legs, arms and heads knocked me to the ground. The security guards pounced and grabbed Michael in a stronghold and forcefully removed him from the bar. His friends followed him like little lost sheep. The onlookers let out a sigh of disappointment seeing the brawl broken up so quickly.

"Oh my God, are you all right?" I scrambled to my feet, rushed to Cameron's side and watched in horror as the bruise on his face swelled quickly.

"What was that all about?" Dave and Justin appeared out

of the crowd. Why did guys seem to swarm toward a fight?

"Nothing." Cameron shrugged. "Just Wiley's ex causing me some grief."

"Cam, I'll get you some ice." I offered. "I'm so sorry. Michael is such an ass."

"No shit. Ow!" he grimaced while feeling along the upper bone of his cheek. "Let's go outside."

Standing near a crowded table back out in the beer garden, Cameron held ice to his face. We witnessed the last of Michael and his friends arguing with the bouncers at the front door to be let back in. I was amazed we hadn't been escorted out of the place as well. Maybe it paid to be a regular guest here, the staff knew us all and knew we weren't troublemakers.

Guilt riddled through me when I glanced at Cameron's face knowing he'd taken a wallop from my idiotic ex-boyfriend. When the people at the table behind us left, Cameron and I straddled one of the bench seat and faced each other. Cameron held one of my hands while the other held a glass of ice to his cheek. I winced at the sight of the bruise, feeling every bit of his pain.

"Are you okay?" he asked while moving his mouth and jaw around to make sure it was all right.

"Shaken." My hands still trembled, even as they rested against his thigh.

What a night it had been. There was too much action and was way too emotional for my liking. My head was spinning with everything that had happened. I knew I shouldn't have come out.

***

I woke the next morning in Cameron's room. My head hurt, my mouth was dry. So much for staying out last night for only a few hours. I drank too much and left The Club with Cameron at closing time. I'd never consumed so much alcohol in my life as I'd done recently, and after last night I swore it'd have to stop.

Cameron was still asleep leaning the length of his body back against the wall, still fully clothed in what he'd worn out last night. I cringed at the bruise on his face, all shining and black, had had now spread all around his eye.

Seeing Michael made me aware of the reason why I didn't want to get involved with anyone this year. The thought of losing Cameron now was not an option. Seeing Cameron's searing anger last night when he thought I'd taken Rick's pill had torn at me. I never wanted to face a situation like that ever again.

This was all my own stupid fault for going out last night.

I snuck out of Cameron's room, leaving him to rest. As I crossed over to my block, I saw Kel trying to sneak back to her room undetected. My curiosity kicked into overdrive when I noticed she was still dressed in the gear she wore out last night.

"Busted! Where've you been?" I hollered out to her as she opened up the door.

Her face was flushed. Her hair was messy. She had a goofy smile on her face.

I gasped. "You've had sex! Get in here now and tell me everything." I grabbed her hand and dragged her into my room.

Her eyes twinkled and she laughed when she stretched out on my bed. I grabbed my desk chair, turned it around and sat waiting for her to speak.

"Last night," she said, "after the whole Michael incident, and we were hanging out in beer garden... I met Matt."

She let out a heart-fluttering sigh. I was afraid she was going to float away. What had happened to my Kel?

"Matt who?"

"Matt from McGregor College." Ah, so he lived at one of

the other residential colleges here at uni. "Oh no!" she gasped and put her hand over her mouth, "I don't know his last name."

"That wouldn't be a first, Kel. I'm actually impressed you know his first name."

"True." She shrugged, unable to wipe the grin off her face. "You want to know something funny? He's been going to The Club like us since first year and I can't believe I've never seen him before. He always hangs out in the beer garden, while we're usually always on the dance floor."

We were regularly lost in our own world dancing the night away, we often didn't notice much else going on around us. And lately, my world revolved only around Cameron. Seeing the happiness drawn across Kel's face was good to see. She hadn't had any luck recently in the boyfriend department. Especially with one who could put such a goofy look upon her face. "So what does Sir Matt do?"

"He's a final year engineer. You'll like him, I'm sure of it. He's a bit of a spunk bubble."

I giggled. "A spunk bubble? Where do you come up with these words? So...are you going to see him again? When do I get to meet him?"

"Now," she pointed out my window, "here he comes." She knelt up on my bed and hung out the window to wave at him.

I jumped up and rushed over beside her to see. Matt strolled toward with a backpack slung over his broad shoulders. As he spotted us gawking out the window, he lowered his eyes to the pathway in front of him, unable to hide the blushing in his cheeks. He had gorgeous olive skin and his shaggy black hair fell across his eyes. He was tall, dark and handsome. Latino, I think. And someone I never would have expected Kel to fall for. She usually liked surfer blonds.

Kel leaned over and whispered in my ear. "I've got me a good one. I'm gonna go and have some more of *that* before class." She kissed me on the cheek, stood up on my bed, jumped out of the window and raced over to meet Matt. The poor guy didn't stand a chance as Kel grabbed his hand and dragged him around into her room.

I waved goodbye and went for a quick shower before heading over to uni. Results for the law assignment I'd done with Cameron were due out today. Queasiness filled my stomach like never before. This submission was far from my best work and I didn't feel confident that the result would be good. I'd had a lot of distractions I was not expecting — although Cameron was a mighty fine one.

Trailing through the student board I found it; my student number. I held my breath as I read, "R730708 – C, PASS". Cameron would have received the same mark.

Oh shit! I gasped, clinging my hand over my mouth. I turned around and leaned back against the wall. Tears swelled in my eyes and my whole body ached. I had never received such a low grade in my life. I was an A-grade student who achieved Distinctions and High Distinctions. Now I had a C – Pass. Would this result affect my overall GPA? I tried to do the sums in my head but couldn't figure it out.

How could this happen? I gritted my teeth and wanted to kick myself for even questioning such a thing. I wasn't stupid. I knew exactly why this had happened.

Cameron.

He was a constant distraction and now my grades had been affected.

In a haze I stumbled back to my room, flopped on my bed and cried, burying my face into my pillow and filling it with salty tears. I was so disappointed with myself and I could only blame one person. Me. Too much going out and not having the willpower to say no. Too much drinking and too much sex.

The soft one knock tapped on my door.

"Wiley?" Cameron eased the door open and entered my room. When he saw me sprawled out on the bed, he rushed to my side. "What's happened? What's wrong?"

On top of not feeling well from going out to The Club, my devastating grade was not helping. My thoughts were reeling as the cause of my sorry state of mind sat beside me. "We got our result back on the law assignment. We got a C."

"And you're crying because…?"

"Cameron! Don't you understand? I don't get Passes. I've never got anything less than an A. I'm devastated."

Cameron rubbed my back. "Well, I for one am very happy with a Pass. I wouldn't have got that without you. It's only an assignment, and it was a bloody hard one at that! You can make up the grade in the exam."

I sniffled loudly and wiped my eyes on my sleeve. "That assignment had a fifty percent weighting. The best I could achieve would be a B. I've screwed up big time. What are my parents going to say?" I shuddered at the thought of seeing their disappointed faces.

"You'll be fine."

"No. It's my fault. I should've had the strength to say no to going out so much and spending so much time with you."

"I know. I'm sorry. It's just…" he sighed and wiped his hand over his face. "I really like spending time with you. You give me so much strength to face every day and a reason to get out of bed. Seeing you and Rick last night scared the shit out of me. I thought I'd been naïve again. But I trust you. Sometimes that frightens me."

Some days I forgot how much he struggled with the guilt over Gillian's death. It shocked me when he said I was his strength. Was I part of his coping mechanism, and was that a good thing? Childish as it was, I felt horrid over my assignment, but my grades were very important to me. No more distractions.

I needed to refocus on my studies and help Cameron understand he was not the one to blame.

"I like being with you too. But I can't go on like this. It's not your fault. It's mine for not been able to resist you."

"I think that goes both ways," he said, leaning to kiss me on the lips. "We have to batten down the hatches. Exams are in only four weeks."

With falling behind in my study and so much other work to get through, had I left my run too late?

Chapter 13

Keeping all of the Steele Rudd College residents sane during the stressful period leading up to exams was one of the social highlights of the year: the Winter Dance. It was held on the first weekend in June, two weeks before final exams, and this year's theme was "Arabian Nights".

Kel and I scouted every shop in Toowoomba for a dress, and at the eleventh hour found the perfect little numbers in a boutique shopping arcade store on Ruthven Street. We were set, and excited about the dance on Saturday night.

The day of the dance was freezing cold so my friends and I avoided the horrid weather by helping to decorate the hall. The boys hung purple and gold organza fabric along the curtained walls and filled hundreds of gold balloons with helium, tying them off with curling-ribbon tails. The final touch was in the foyer, where we mounted a harem-type tent covered in fairy lights at the entrance for everyone to walk through. Melinda, our residential college manager and chief social organizer, had done an amazing job at sourcing decorations that would create a fantastic atmosphere for the evening ahead.

After devouring lunch, it wasn't long before I kissed Cameron goodbye and Kel dragged me off to her room, with Ashleigh and Megan in tow, to prepare for the evening ahead.

In Kel's room, she made me sit down in her chair and proceeded to curl and pin my hair into some fancy up-do on top of my head. The bobby pins were already causing me grief digging into my scalp. Then Ashleigh insisted on painting my fingers and my toes. Seven girls ended up in Kel's room all laughing, changing our hairstyles around, and doing each other's make-up. The vibe was contagious and I started to bubble with excitement as the night closed in. Finally it was time to go and get dressed, await our partners to arrive and venture over to the hall.

Back in my room, I slipped on my new satin, fuchsia-colored dress. The cool fabric glided down over my skin like silk and clung to my slender frame. I looked at my reflection in the mirror, admiring the diamantes and silver embroidery encircling the bodice. But the long slit that ran up the front of the skirt from the floor to nearly my groin had me anxiously trying to draw the fabric together, it really was too high. With it near zero degrees outside, yes, I would potentially freeze my butt off in this thing, but I didn't care, I'd warm up once we got dancing.

With my hair done up and soft tones of make-up highlighting my face, I thought I scrubbed up okay. I sat down on my bed to buckle up my sparkling silver stiletto sandals when Cameron knocked softly on my door.

My heart skipped a beat knowing it was him.

"Come in," I called out.

My pulse escalated and the air rushed from my lungs when my eyes fell upon him. Cameron was stunning; dressed in a black dinner suit, black collared shirt and a shiny black tie. He was cleanly shaven and his hair was gelled to look a bit James Dean-ish.

I had to remember to breathe as my eyes took in every inch of him. His cologne filled the room, delightfully intoxicating my senses when he walked toward me with sparkling eyes. Taking me by the hand, I stood up and he twirled me around to make his inspection.

"Wow, Wiley, you have outdone yourself. You look spectacular. You do make it hard for me not to ravish you right here and now," he said mischievously into my ear when he drew me into his embrace.

"Oh I know, I can tell." I pulled his groin into mine and felt the bulge within his trousers. His warm brushed over my face when he kissed me, making my head spin.

"Delicious," he murmured, licking his lips when he took a step back. It took a few moments for me to regain my own composure. "We'd better be careful, or you'll get yourself into trouble before we even make it to the dance." I hated having to let go of him for even the briefest of moments.

He looked like he was about to ravish me when he glanced over me from head to toe. My cheeks flushed at his provocative assessment of my attire.

He stepped toward me again, slid his hand around my waist and turned me around to face my full-length mirror. Stepping in close behind me, his breath tickled my neck. "We do make a hot couple, don't we?" he whispered into my ear and kissed me across my shoulder line. "And I love this dress."

He spun me to face him again. With a glimmer in his eye he guided me back a few steps and pinned me up against the wardrobe door. The glass of the mirror was cool against my exposed skin, but I started to warm up when his lips found my neck. I tried not to giggle when he pressed his body hard up against mine.

"Stop!" I didn't even manage to convince myself as I grinned from ear to ear.

"I particularly like this split." His voice bewitched me as his hand slipped underneath the thigh-high split on my leg and curled around to rest on my bottom. "Oh wow," Cameron feverishly responded, pulling my groin toward his, "aren't you wearing any panties?" He rested his forehead against mine. "Wiley, you can't do this to me." His voice strained with want. His body responded with need.

This was not good. Why did he have to turn me on so much? His touch. His voice. I needed to keep my head clear so I could make it out the door before things went any further and I lost control. But when a hair pin dug into my head when I leaned against the door, it quickly brought me back from my steamy thoughts. "Yes I am wearing panties. It's a T-string."

His fingertips slid around to the front of my dress and searched for the edge of my panties. My knees grew weak and between my legs started to hum when he hooked his finger underneath the fabric and run them down along the silky edge.

"Just checking," he teased, his breath rushing across my face.

I trembled when his fingers explored further. I closed my eyes, my breath coming in short bursts. His lips pressed against mine and he slid his finger inside me. *Shit!* Cameron, my constant distraction.

"Wiley, you ready?" Kel's voice rang out from down the hallway.

"Okay, Cam. Stop. We have to." I gasped using all my strength to pull myself away from his sensual hold on me. I hated having to stop. I loved him seducing me, and vice versa, but there were other imperative activities to attend to tonight — the dance. "We'd better get going before the situation gets further out of hand. I didn't spend all afternoon having this

Tania Joyce

hairdo done to have you wreck it all before dinner."

He looked at me, pouting with disappointment and a cheeky sparkle in his eyes. "We could be quick and I promise not to ruin your hair."

"No. Come on, it's time to go." I was *not* going to give in. Breaking out of his clutches, I reapplied my lip gloss, took him by the hand and dragged him out the door.

We were joined by Kel and Matt, and arm in arm we walked with a skip in our stride over to the hall. Kel was dressed in a navy-off-the-shoulder ankle-length dress and Matt in a black dinner suit, white shirt and tie. He certainly was pleasant on the eye — as Kel called him, *a real spunk bubble.*

Our breath misted in the cold night air while we scuttled along the fairy-lit path to the hall. The foyer was full of activity with everyone arriving and dressed up ready to party. It was nice to see everyone out of the usual attire of jeans and t-shirts. The boys scrubbed up handsomely in their dinner suits and the girls looked fabulous as well, with only a few hideous exceptions in the gown department.

Flashes from cameras strobed everywhere while all the girls, boys, couples and groups of friends had photos taken. It was a blast of excitement and pre-dinner drinks began to flow.

"Where are Ashleigh and Aaron? Dave and Megan?" I asked. "They're late."

"Probably getting one in," Cameron smirked, tightening his arm around my waist. "We should've done it," he whispered in my ear. "My balls are killing me."

After a glass of champagne the missing couples joined us.

We stood in the middle of the foyer enjoying our drinks when Melinda, our residential college manager, finally came out and invited us in to the hall for the dinner to commence.

The dining hall filled quickly with students and their guests. As I walked in with Cameron, I glanced up at all the twinkling fairy lights and the balloons floating on the ceiling. Some pungent, aromatic scent wafted through the air, adding to the middle-eastern theming. Soft music drifted from the DJ who was set up on the stage at the rear of the hall.

The dinner was sensational; a warm Thai-beef salad entrée, succulent chicken and asparagus for the main, followed by chocolate cheesecake for dessert. Melinda made a quick speech highlighting events and noted some of the memorable pranks that had occurred in our past semester on residential college. But it was not long before tables were cleared away and the DJ started pumping out the tunes.

The bobby pins digging into my hair had started to give me a headache during dinner, so I stuck to drinking water while everyone else went to the bar to purchase other beverages.

"Wiley, what's with you tonight?" Rick slurred in front of me when I took a seat at one of the bar tables on the edge of the dance floor.

"I've got a headache," I rubbed at my scalp and tried to remove the reluctant pin buried deep within my hair.

"Don't worry babe, I'll get you in the mood to party. It's time to dance!" Rick swayed his hips and arms around like an over-energetic orangutan. *What was with him tonight?* "Come on, girl, it's time to loosen up. Let me buy you a drink. "

"I'm fine." I forced a smile and watched the growing crowd on the dance floor.

"I won't take no for an answer."

"Okay, I'll have a Coke." Anything to get him off my back.

Rick disappeared and Cameron returned to my side. "Want to dance?"

"Yeah, sure. Rick is getting me a drink. Let's go before he gets back."

"Rick?" Cameron's brow furrowed. "I would have got you one."

Rick returned with my cola and a plate of two mini quiches. "Here, these will make you feel better."

"Thanks." I was grateful for the food. I hadn't eaten much during dinner thanks to my headache. I quickly devoured the snack and drink, then hit the dance floor with Cameron and my friends.

The booming sound of the music was deafening and the strobing light was blinding. The dance floor grew thick with heated bodies cavorting and jostling around. The vibrant mood was contagious and I slipped into the swing of the party.

Cameron swung me round, never letting me go. His arms, his lips, his body always connected to mine somehow. I was in heaven.

As the dance track tempo picked up, my body started to respond to every beat of the music, my heart raced inside my chest and my ears rung with the intense sound. Waving my arms around up in the air, my energy levels skyrocketed and I jumped around feeling the beat vibrate through me to my very core. Glancing at Cameron, my insides swirled. He looked so hot and sexy, I wanted to make love to him right here in the middle of the dance floor. He was mine. All mine. I groped his groin and was disappointed when he promptly removed my hand.

"What are you doing?" He gasped.

My feet didn't want to stop moving. I wanted to dance. The music was intoxicating. As I panted to catch my breath, I put my hand up to my brow. It was hot. Feverishly hot. But the buzz coursing through me was too overpowering and I turned around to keep on dancing. I ignored the profuse shaking in my hand and swiped away my hair that had fallen across my face.

"Stand still. For just one second. Please?" Cameron placed his hands on my shoulders to stop me bouncing around.

"I need a drink. Water, please." I begged of him.

He lead me to the side of the dance floor and poured me

a glass. I sculled the drink down in two seconds flat and was back on the dance floor with the girls. Yet again, I felt my body temperature rise, but surprised I wasn't sweating. Squeezing my eyes shut I fought against the fever rising in me. I didn't know what was wrong because the rest of me felt so alive...no, euphoric!

Cameron came over toward me. "Wiley, you've been dancing for ages. Come and have a break." He put his arms around me and I tried to focus on his face. But he turned white with horror when he touched my skin. "Wiley? You're burning up. What's wrong?"

I didn't understand the question. Wooziness washed over me when I tried to look into his eyes and the world around me started to blur. The music muffled out to nothing but silence, and in my peripheral vision, the flashing lights faded to black. I took a deep breath, concentrating on Cameron's beautiful face. My hand wouldn't move when I wanted to reach out and touch him. What was wrong with me? I felt so hot. Unbearably hot. My blood felt like it was on fire, burning me from the inside out as it rushed through my veins. Blackness closed in around me and Cameron's face started to distort and disappear before me. Everything spun dangerously fast. I staggered. My knees collapsed beneath me and I fell hard on to the ground.

"Wiley? Wiley?" My body wouldn't respond to Cameron's desperate plea. People gathered around me as I lay upon the floor. Cameron propped me up in his arms. I could feel him trembling underneath me as the soft fabric of his shirt rubbed against my face. My eyes rolled back in my head. My stomach lurched and I violently threw up.

"What's wrong?" Kel was at my side, but I still couldn't move. My eyes wouldn't open. My body was limp and useless. I wanted to call out to them, but every attempt was futile. "Cam, she hasn't drunk tonight. What's wrong?"

Cameron stiffen as he held me in his arms.

"Oh Wiley. God no. Wiley, did you take something? What did you take?" He shook me in his arms.

"Quick. Get her on her side. Is she breathing?" I could vaguely feel Kel's hands upon my burning skin. Fire had consumed my veins. I wanted to scream but couldn't. I was so scared and my mind started to fog.

Kel? Cam? Help me.

Everything went black.

***

Blip, Blip, Blip.

Was that a heart rate monitor? My mind hazily made out the soft sound somewhere nearby. I couldn't open my eyes, my body wouldn't move. Surely I must be dreaming.

Voices. I could hear voices. Was that my mother? My dad? Where am I? Where was Cameron? Kel?

I couldn't concentrate. I felt like everything weighed a ton.

Everything went black.

***

"Did you do this to my daughter? You stay away from her. She would never have taken drugs before she met you. Now get out of my sight."

That was definitely my mother.

Drugs? What is she talking about?

"I did not do this to her." Cameron sounded hysterical.

Cameron?

"Get out. Get out of here!" my mother shrieked.

"Cameron, it's okay. Go for a walk. I'll talk to you soon."

Dad. Was that Dad?

Why couldn't I wake up? Where was I? What was going on? I was scared. I felt so tired and exhausted.

Everything went black.

***

"Hey sleepyhead. Welcome back!"

Blinking my eyes open, I found myself staring into the face of a nurse with frizzy blonde hair. Panic hit. Where was I?

"Wiley, my name is Amanda and I'm your nurse. You're in Toowoomba Base Hospital. You've had an allergic reaction to the drugs you took."

What? Drugs? When? I closed my eyes, trying to make sense of everything. Fear had me frozen still. Drugs? Hospital? What the...?

"Drugs? I didn't take any drugs. I don't do drugs," I mumbled, but my mouth was so dry it was hard to form the words.

"Your toxicology report says otherwise, Sweetie. Ecstasy to be exact. It's not good when you end up in here, now is it?" She looked scornfully down at me, shining a torchlight into my eyes. I was temporarily blinded by the bright light and when I blinked my eyes to refocus, a stabbing bolt of pain shot through the center of my head. The headache from hell exploded inside my skull. "I'll finish your observations and then I'll let your parents know you're awake."

My parents were here?

The hospital bed was hard and uncomfortable but I didn't have the strength to move. I became aware of the IV needle stuck in my arm and the adhesive tape pulled on my skin. An oxygen tube was hooked under my nose and somehow I was now dressed in an unattractive pale yellow hospital gown. How on earth did I get here?

Mum threw herself at me when she entered the room. Her Chanel No.5 perfume overpowered the sickly sanitized hospital smell that lingered in the air. "Wiley." She burst out crying. "What are you doing, you silly girl? I never suspected in my wildest dreams you were doing drugs."

"Mum, I'm not." My throat was parched and I felt sick in the stomach. "Water, please?"

She shoved the straw of the cup off the bedside table into my mouth and I guzzled it down as best I could. "Then how do you explain this?"

"I don't know." I trembled. I was terrified at not knowing what had happened and what was going on.

"We got a call from Kel at midnight to say you'd been rushed to hospital and we came up straight away."

"What? What time is it? Where's Cameron?"

"It's nearly ten o'clock on Sunday morning. You had an allergic reaction to...ecs...ecstasy." She struggled to the words. "Why didn't you come to me for help." Tears streamed down her face, and Dad, standing next to her, was ashen and shell-shocked as well.

"Because I don't have a problem. I don't do drugs." All I remembered was dancing and having a good time. I gasped. "Oh no! Cameron. Where is he? I need to see him. He will be so freaked out."

"Don't you worry about that stupid boy. We'll do whatever it takes to get you clean. Anything. Rehab. The best counselors. You name it."

"Mum. This has nothing to do with Cameron. It wasn't him. I need to see him. Is he here?" I frantically asked, trying to sit up, but was too weak to muster up the strength to move. The IV in my arm was as heavy as an army tank.

Mum glared at Dad and shook her head, her tears made glassy streaks upon her cheeks. Dad sighed, ignoring her. "I'm glad to see you're okay. I'll go find Cameron for you, he's sitting outside with Kel."

Dad dragged Mum out of the room when Kel and Cameron came in. They were still dressed in their formal attire. Kel dived for me and hugged me tightly, but Cameron just sat down stiffly on the chair next to the bed.

"OhMyGod! You're okay. We've been worried sick." Kel's eyes, full of concern, looked like a raccoon's from all her smudged make-up.

"I don't understand." I forced myself to hold back my tears. "What happened?"

"You passed out cold. Totally unconscious." Kel uttered. "I had to put my nursing studies in to practice last night. I never thought I'd have to use them on my best-friend to save your life. You scared the shit out of everyone last night. Melinda had to call the ambulance and Cameron and I came in with you."

"Thanks, Kel." I clutched at her, not wanting to let go, but then I saw Cameron, silent and still on the chair, not even looking at me. All I wanted was him to come over to me, wrap me up in his arms and tell me everything was going to be okay. "Cam?"

His eyes were full of pain. The worry etched across his face made my heart ache and I burst out crying.

"Kel, can I have a moment alone with Wiley, please." his icy tone made me feel sick and my chest heaved for every breath. I'd only ever seen him like this once before — not so long ago at the Club when he thought I'd taken drugs.

Kel nodded and silently slipped out of the room.

"Cam, please?" I held out my hand for him to come to me but he stayed in his spot.

"So this has been going on behind my back? I was right, wasn't I. I should've walked away from you that night at The Club. But I believed you. Trusted you. I thought everything was good between us. But I'm wrong again, aren't I? I'm obviously too dumb not to see you're in trouble."

"No. You've got it all wrong!" I desperately wailed.

"What on earth possessed you to take *E*. You could've died." A tear fell from his eye and I could see every muscle on his face tense with a whole concoction of hate, anger and hurt.

"I didn't take any drugs. Are you insane? You, of all people, should know me better than that!" I sobbed. What did I have to do to prove to him that I didn't do this. I despised drugs. Why wasn't he listening to me?

For a fleeting second I realized his trust issues were always hovering close below the surface, just like mine. What kind of hope did we have together if we could never trust each other fully? But I was telling the truth. Why couldn't he see that in my desperate pleas?

"I thought I did. Is this some kind of sick attempt to hurt me? Break up with me? What, Wiley? Because I don't understand why you did this." The vein in the middle of his head protruded as his temper flared.

"Don't say things like that. I'm scared and no, I never want to break up with you. Never! You're the world to me."

"Well, the fucking world blew to pieces last night, didn't it?"

I lay there for a moment, closing my eyes tightly, trying to make sense of everything. My lower lip quivered as Cameron's words cut into me like a shard of glass had been rammed into my heart. Remnants of Saturday night flashed through my mind. I didn't drink any alcohol because I had a headache. We were dancing. Rick bought me a drink and some food. *Oh shit!* I was drugged? By Rick? I ripped my eyes open.

"Rick. It must have been Rick. He must have slipped something into the food or drink he gave me. It's the only thing I can think of. I don't know how else it could have happened.

Cam, you've got to believe me." His icy stare and rigid posture tore at my heart. Why was he being so cold?

"Rick?" Cameron wiped his hand across his face and clenched his teeth. "Why should I believe you?"

"You know what he's like. You saw what he tried to do to me at The Club. Have I ever given you any reason to doubt me before?" Okay, maybe the incident at The Club would cause some doubt. But did he now question every time I was away from him? Surely he knew me better than that and could see the truth through all this fucked-up mess.

"I don't know what to think anymore. You're in hospital because of a bad reaction to an illegal drug. Do you have any idea what it was like when I saw you collapse to the ground last night? Any idea? It was Gilly all over again only worse, because I stupidly really care about you. I told you right from the beginning I can't tolerate drugs. And look where I am — right back at the start. I won't lose another girlfriend to this shit! I'm sorry, I can't go through this again. I'm done." He stood up and fled from the room.

"Cameron!" I called out to him. "Cam, please come back!"

With him he took the air that I breathed. My world disappeared before my eyes. The hole in my heart he had repaired, ripped violently apart, shattering it into a thousand pieces. I clutched at my chest as an excruciating pain exploded. I sobbed into the pillow to muffle my anguish. How on earth was I going to survive without Cameron?

Chapter 14

After much arguing with my parents, and the doctor had assured them I was not a regular drug user, I was discharged from hospital and returned to campus late on Monday morning. My mother had been prepared to pull me out of uni and admit me straight into rehab, but she finally came around. My parents reluctantly dropped me off at Steele Rudd College and headed back home to Brisbane after I had to promise to call them every day. Still lethargic from the reaction to the drugs and the nice red rash covering half of my body, I spent most of the day curled up in bed. I felt numb and needed Cameron by my side for comfort, yet he never came.

Melinda came to visit me after lunchtime and after entering my room, she closed the door behind her. *Oh, this didn't look good.*

"Hey, how are you?" She asked as she sat down on my chair to face me.

"Tired."

"I hate to be the bearer of bad news, especially when

you've been such a wonderful student, but it's college policy not to tolerate drugs and drug related incidents. Since this episode happened on residential college grounds and the paramedics were involved, I have to follow protocol. I have to administer a formal warning for inappropriate behavior. In addition to that, we need to go through some necessary steps and recommend you seek counseling. The uni faculty will be notified and the incident report will also go through to your scholarship review officer."

I gasped. "What? You can't be serious. I didn't do this. Someone drugged me!"

"If you know who did this to you, you can press charges."

I shook my head in spite of my suspicions.

"You're very lucky, not only to be okay after your ordeal, but the residential college director wanted to expel you. I managed to convince him otherwise. So here's your letter." She pulled the white envelope out from her duffle coat pocket and held it in her hand. "Let this be the first and last, okay?"

"What about my medical file from the doctor to show you I'm not a druggo? Doesn't that help with anything?"

"Not really. If you're clean, you'll have nothing to worry about. There's only a semester to go, don't give me another reason to have to visit you like this again."

She stood, handed me the envelope and left my room. I collapsed back down into the depths of my pillows and fought back tears swelling in my eyes.

Could this week get any worse?

Throughout the afternoon, visitors drifted in and out, glad to see that I was okay. But all I wanted was Cameron. No one had seen him around, which was starting to make me worry. I wouldn't accept what happened to me as a deal breaker in our relationship. I had paid the price for somebody's stupid antics. How could he not believe me? He didn't respond to my phone calls or texts. I desperately wanted to talk to him and prayed that he was all right.

The person I was most apprehensive about seeing arrived midafternoon.

"Hey, baby! How ya doing?" Rick slinked through the door. Uneasiness swept through me and my skin prickled all over at the sight of him.

"Not good, Rick. How the hell do you think I am? I collapsed from taking E, and considering I wouldn't even know where to get it in the first place, it's been a fucking nightmare. The detox has been hell. The headaches are skull-splitting, the tiredness paralyzing, and the cramps make PMS feel like a walk in the park. And on top of it all, I've got this ugly rash all over me that itches like crazy. I don't know why you'd want to do this on a regular basis."

"Man, I've never had a rash before." Rick scanned over the red blotches covering my arms, neck and legs.

"You freakin' idiot." I clenched my fists and shook my head. "You want to know the worst thing? I've been lying here, trying to recall everything that happened on Saturday night. The food, the drinks, everything. And it makes me sick when I can come up with only one valid conclusion." I gritted my teeth, trying not to shake with rage. "Did you do this to me? Did you slip something in to my Coke or the quiches?"

"What...no way... it must have been Cameron or someone else." Rick fidgeted and couldn't look me in the eye as he brushed the accusation aside.

"Don't be stupid. I'd bet my life on it, it wasn't Cameron. You don't know what damage you've done." My chest constricted at the horrific thought. "It was you, wasn't it? You did this to me." Anger hurtled through me as I pointed my finger at him.

"Baby, I... I...I never meant to hurt you." He confessed and hung his head in shame. "I wanted you to have a good time."

"I don't need that crap for a good time. And worst of all, you did it without my consent. You could've killed me, Rick."

"I'm so sorry, I never meant this to happen."

"Well, it did. When are you going to learn, Rick? Fuck up your own life, not everyone else's while you're at it. What you did was criminal. I could press charges against you for this."

His eyes widened. "I swear I never meant to hurt you. Please, don't involve the police. Baby, is there anything I can do to make this up to you?"

"Yes. You need go and find Cameron and tell him the truth. Then you can stay the hell away from me. If I so see you with a pill, I'll report you. Do you understand?"

Risk's face, white with shock, managed to nod and he carried his sorry ass out of my room. I was trembling all over from my outburst, I'd never gone off at anyone like that before. I'd never had any reason to. It had done little to relieve the worry still clouding my mind.

Where *was* Cameron?

He remained invisible. He wasn't in his room, he didn't answer his phone.

I was still overly tired and weak so Kel brought me dinner to my room and said she had not seen Cameron either. Surely we couldn't be over? He was just upset at the hospital. Wasn't he? Where the hell was he and why was he avoiding me?

It was late, nearly ten o'clock in the evening and he still hadn't visited. When I looked out the window I could see his desk light on, shining behind the drawn curtains in his room. With what little strength I had, I pulled on my UGG boots and duffle coat and made my way over to his block.

My legs ached from the small exertion. I knocked on his door. I tried the handle but it was locked.

"Cam, It's me. Please talk to me."

He ignored me, but I could hear him watching TV quietly

in his room.

"I swear. I'll stay out here until you let me in."

My heart ached when I heard no response.

There was commotion in the hallway as his neighbors cursed my actions, telling me to shut up. Feeling dizzy, I leaned against his wooden door and slid down into a curled-up bundle on the floor. I started singing and mumbling and knocking, insisting I be let in. It took every ounce of my strength but I managed to remain persistent.

I glanced at my watch and saw it was near midnight. My eyelids started to blink heavily as I rested my head against his door. If I closed my eyes for just a minute to recoup, then I would be able to resume my attempts at trying to gain entry into his room.

Blinking, I opened my eyes. Everything was on an angle and distorted. The beige carpet hallway extended out before me. The brick walls loomed up beside me. Fluorescent lights flickered above me. I wiped my eyes and couldn't believe I'd fallen asleep on the floor outside his bedroom. But underneath my head was a pillow and a blanket had been thrown over me. I drew it up close under my chin, smelling Cameron's scent upon the fibers. I missed him so much, but the small gesture gave me a glimmer of hope.

I reached up and tried the door handle, but collapsed back to the floor when I discovered it was still locked.

Against the reluctance of my muscles, I stood up, neatly folded the blanket, placed it on top of the pillow in front of his door and made my way back to my block.

I jumped out of my wits when Kel accosted me in our hallway.

"Where've you been? I heard you slept on the floor outside Cameron's room last night. What is with you? You should be in bed recovering. And what's with him at the moment?"

Yes, Nurse Kel. She was such a sweetheart and I loved her dearly, but I was gripped with desperation, in need a hot shower, food and a talk to Cameron to sort out this mess. I missed him and needed to set the record straight once and for all.

But he avoided me all day. I went to classes; he'd come in late and sit as far away from me as possible. At dinnertime, he'd sit looking away from me. He kept the curtains in his room shut so I couldn't see him from my window. All of a sudden it was like I didn't exist.

I was miserable without him. I had to do something.

***

At ten o'clock in the morning I glanced over to his room and saw him hanging out his washing on the line. This was my chance. I bolted out of my room, across the grassy mounds, through the rear door of the block and into his open room. Puffing and panting like I'd run a marathon, I tried to catch my breath while I waited for his return.

He loped in and his eyes widened when he saw me sitting at his desk.

"Hey." My heart pounded.

"What are you doing here? You should be resting," he said as he threw his laundry basket into the bottom of his wardrobe.

"I'm holding you hostage and I'm not leaving until we talk."

"There is nothing to talk about. Everything's fine." he said, folding his leg underneath him as he sat down onto the bed and leaned back against the wall.

"Well, I have plenty to talk about and you're going to listen to every damn word." His eyes looked bloodshot and bags under them from lack of sleep. "So enough of your nonsense." I hadn't really come up with any ideas of what to say to him and the pain in my chest made it hard to think straight. "What's going on with you? I've been going stir crazy. You up and left me when I've just been through one of the most scary situations in my life. Who does that?"

I trembled, trying to control my hurt, anger and frustration.

"Are you feeling any better now?" he asked, staring at the floor.

"Not really. I still feel sick, itchy and feverish." I paused. "Cam, you're scaring me. What's going on? Talk to me, please. "

"I'm sorry, but I haven't been able to. After seeing you in hospital, I flipped out. I needed time to process everything so I went to Gran's for a while and then locked myself away in here."

"What can I do to make you understand I didn't take those drugs? My toxicology report shows I'm not a user. You've been with me nearly every second of the day to know I haven't taken anything. You have to believe I was drugged."

His face winced in pain, making my heart ache. I couldn't lose him over this fiasco.

I fell to my knees in front of him, taking his hands in mine.

"You know me. You mean the world to me. I understand what you went through with Gilly but I'm not like that. Rick did this to me. He confessed and he was supposed to come and see you."

He shook his head.

Damn it! What a gutless, slimy snake Rick was.

"Are you going to press charges?" Cameron asked.

"No. I don't want to be the one responsible for kicking him off campus or getting into trouble with the police. I hope he's learned his lesson." I sat up on the bed beside Cameron, still holding his hands in mine. "I'm going to be okay once I get rid of this rash."

He turned my arm over and gently stroked one of the sore-looking marks on my skin. At last they were starting to fade.

"Walking away from you in the hospital the other day was one of the hardest things I've ever done in my life. I couldn't handle the doubt or the hurt I felt any more." Cameron's eyes glassed over with emotion. "I was terrified when you collapsed on the floor. I thought I'd lost you, just when I'd found you. When the doctor said you reacted to E, I freaked out. We haven't been going out long and I thought I'd misjudged you."

"You didn't believe me?"

"I doubted everything and wondered if I was the one that sent you over the edge. Was it me? Was it knowing who my family is? Or a combination of both? That's why I pulled away. I know it's bad, but I get withdrawn when upset. I needed some space to clear my head and tried to look at everything from every different angle. What I learned scared me even more."

Oh no...he was going to break up with me!

A tear fell from my eye and I quickly swiped it away with one hand. My whole body trembled like I was standing in front of the firing squad, waiting for the trigger to be pulled.

Cameron inhaled deeply and slumped back against the wall. "Analyzing every minute detail was hard and confronting. I was so afraid of losing you, but in the end I could only draw one conclusion. I was about to come over and see you." He squeezed my hands tightly as he shuffled on the bed.

I shook my head because I didn't want to hear what was coming. I placed my finger over his mouth to silence him.

"Do you understand I'm crazy about you. I don't know why, but I can't walk away from what we have together. You're the only drug I'm addicted to." I tried to smile but it was impossible. "You're not breaking up with me over something that was out of my control."

He closed his eyes, his brow furrowed. "I know you slept outside my door the other night ... that was kinda cool."

Tears trickled down my face. "I'll do anything to make this right. Please give us another chance."

"Wiley...I'm not breaking up with you. You're stuck with me. For some reason, I like you a lot. That's what I've come to realize; I can't let go of you either. I know I've handled this badly, but you scared the hell out of me. I really am sorry."

With lightning speed, I mounted myself across his hips, buried my fingers deep within his hair and planted my lips against his.

More than nearly losing my life, I was petrified of losing Cameron. With him by my side, I would make it through exams next week. It was highly likely within the next few days, someone else here at college would do something outlandish and crazy and be the new center of attention. I was looking forward to no longer having the spotlight focused on me. Surely if I lay low, this whole drug fiasco would pass by. Surely there couldn't be any other major consequences.

Chapter 15

Frost blanketed the ground and thick fog hindered our view every morning. When out and about, the chill factor on the wind was unbearable. Winter had truly set in. Exam time had me curled up under the blankets on my bed with the room heater softly humming in my best efforts to keep warm while studying.

I rubbed my tired eyes that were suffering from too many late nights and endless hours of reading. My head hurt from information overload as I struggled to cover all the material in time. There'd been too many distractions this semester. With one exam down and three to go, it was going to be a long week ahead.

It was nearing eight o'clock in the evening and I needed a break. Cameron was my reward after putting in some solid hours of work.

I shrugged on my coat, pulled on my UGG boots, grabbed my keys and phone and headed out the door. My face stung in the cold night air when I ran over to his block. I raised my hand to knock on his door but it swung open and I was confronted by a tall brunette. I jumped in fright and nearly stumbled into her. Her eyes widened as my knuckles almost connected with her face. My solar plexus took a dive when I noticed how pretty she was; bright green eyes, fair skin, long hair tumbling down across her shoulders over her bright red jacket.

"Hi," she said, "I was just leaving." She shuffled past me and I turned to watch her leave down the hallway and disappear around the corner.

I turned to face Cameron, his face one of pure innocence.

"Who's that?" I asked, shutting his door behind me and then sitting down next to him on the bed. I hated the wave of suspicion oozing through me, threatening to clog my veins.

"Melissa. She's in my accounting tute and we ran through some practice exam questions."

The thought of him studying with someone other than me, especially alone in his room with the curtains drawn, only added to my concerns.

Cameron 's eyes glinted. "Wiley Cayton, do I detect a hint of jealousy?"

I stared down at my hands, fumbling around on my lap. I hated that my insecurities flared whenever he was around other females...especially attractive ones like Melissa. Having my ex cheat on me had done some irreparable damage and the tinge of incertitude always lurked below the surface.

"That's kinda cool," he said, "but you have nothing to worry about." He swung his arm around my shoulders and kissed me, making my concerns disappear.

"You nearly made me forget why I came to see you. In the middle of the holidays it's my mum's fiftieth birthday and she's having a party. I was wondering if you'd like to come. They're going away for a week after it, so you could stay with me if you'd like."

"I'm not sure your mother likes me considering the circumstances in which we met." His brow furrowed as I had a vague recollection of her yelling and screaming at him while I was in hospital.

"You don't have to come. But it's a long three-week break and I'll miss you."

He laughed. "Of course I'll come. There's nothing happening at my place over the holidays, so it would be great. I've only got to catch-up with my shrink in the first week, but then I'm free to do whatever."

Cameron joked about visiting his trauma psychologist, but after witnessing his nightmares firsthand and seeing him flip out after my own close call with drugs, he'd have a lot to talk about in his next session.

"Oh, that's hot. A week with you in your parent's house without them being there, they're going to love that." Cameron chuckled.

"They don't know about you staying yet." I bit the corner of my lip. I dreaded the thought of my parents' reaction to me inviting my boyfriend to stay. Dad would be overly protective and Mum would overdramatize everything, insisting that I was the one causing her blood pressure to go through the roof.

"Let's call them now so I can organize my flights." He grabbed my phone out of my coat pocket, found their number, hit call and put it on speakerphone.

"Hi Mum." My voice scratched in my dry throat while Cameron waved the phone around in front of my face.

"Hey sweetheart, how are you? Good to hear from you. How are your exams going? Hope you're studying hard. What day will you be home?" My mother asked so many questions, as always, without taking a breath.

"Study is fine. Exams are going well — hey!" Cameron

nudged me in the side.

"Hi Mrs Cayton," His smooth voice could turn any rock into putty in your hands.

"That's Cameron, Mum. He's mucking around."

"Where are you?" Disapproval was evident in her tone.

"Studying in Cameron's room." I could feel the stress radiating out from my mother, rushing down the phone line like a seismic tidal wave. "The reason for my call is to ask about your birthday. Is it all right if Cameron comes up for it and stays for a few days with me?" I tugged at my loose hair, waiting for her response.

The silence lingered.

"Mum?"

She didn't like this one bit.

"I think you should ask your father." I could hear her tapping her acrylic nails.

"Mum, you know he will say yes," I moaned.

"But your father and I are going away. You want to stay here in our house by yourself, I mean, with Cameron?"

"I'm an adult now and Cameron is my boyfriend. I would really like him to come with me to your party."

"But...but."

My mother was not happy when she found out we were still together. She was convinced it was Cameron who drugged me and no amount of discussion would sway her opinion. Her shallow, quick-to-judge-people-on-first-impressions attitude was getting harder to tolerate as I grew older.

"Please Mum? If he can't stay at our house, we'll crash at Chris's for the week." Now there was a great idea. Why didn't I think of that sooner? My brother wouldn't care.

"No. No. You don't need to do that." She sighed heavily. "He can come, but while I'm in the house, you're to sleep in separate rooms. When I'm not here — well, I don't want to think about that."

"Thanks Mum. You're the best. I'll chat with you later. Bye."

I ended the conversation before she started lecturing me about focusing on my studies, my behavior and God only knows what else. I threw my phone down on the bed and cuddled into Cameron's shoulder. "Do you realize she's probably crying now at the thought of me coming home with you?" I did feel a little bad, but my mother really had to accept I was growing up, especially considering I was turning twenty-one in September.

Cameron kissed my forehead. "I'll have to be extra nice to her when I see her again. Now I'm looking forward to these holidays, we're going to have so much fun."

Now that, I was definitely looking forward to.

***

Cameron flew home to Sydney for the first week of the holidays and I worked at Dad's practice for a few days to earn some much needed cash.

Saturday, the day of my mum's party arrived and Cameron was due any moment. I was sitting on the deck at home, rugged up in a blanket and trying to warm up in the morning sun. Sipping on a hot cup of coffee, I gazed out across my mother's manicured gardens, over the surrounding rooftops, and admired the sun's rays glinting off the glass of the city's high-rise buildings in the distance.

I was about to go inside and watch some television, when I heard Cameron's Hilux pull into my driveway. Clapping my hands with excitement, I skipped out of the front door and down the stairs, taking two at a time, before I flung myself into his arms.

"Hey beautiful, I missed you." He swung me around hugging me tightly. "I can't believe it's only been a week since

I've seen you. It feels so much longer."

"Missed you too." Our lips locked and I savored the taste of his tongue against mine. His fingers brushed through my hair while he pressed his body against mine. I could feel him rise to the occasion.

Oh my, how I missed him next to me.

"Are you parents home? We better stop this or I'm going to have a huge hard-on. That won't be a good look for meeting them again."

I laughed over our kisses. "They won't be home until after lunch. Come on"

Before we gave the elderly neighbors something to gossip about, Cameron grabbed his luggage and I led him inside to my room for a good and proper catch-up.

We were watching TV in the middle of the afternoon when I heard my parents pull up in the garage. I squeezed Cameron's hand, needing some reassurance everything was going to be okay. I was not looking forward to introducing him again to my mother.

Mum walked in with her handbag hanging off her shoulder and her high heeled pumps hooked over her fingers. She struggled carrying a box of wine. She'd gone out this morning to get her hair done, now it was all neatly trimmed and a champagne blonde color instead of dark brown. Mum had lost a bit of weight over the past few months, and I couldn't deny she looked fantastic for turning fifty. She dumped her load down on the kitchen table and smiled at me, but it disappeared from her face when she saw Cameron.

Cameron and I stood up and walked over to her. "Hey Mum, you remember Cameron."

"Yes, I do." She put out her hand to shake it, but Cameron gave her a big hug instead. On release, my mother looked him up and down with startled eyes; I had to bite on my inner cheek really hard so I wouldn't laugh.

"It's good to see you again, Mrs Cayton."

"Please, call me Victoria," she flapped her hand at him, turning to put away her things.

Dad appeared at the top of the steps, dragging his feet after a morning of golf.

"Cam," I pointed in Dad's direction, "My dad, John."

"Well, hello there again." Dad greeted Cameron with a firm shake of the hand.

"How was golf, Dad?"

"Good. I was glad to avoid all the last minute party preparations for tonight, that's for sure. Hair appointments, picking up cakes, delivering stuff to the hotel, I would have only got in the way."

"Can I get you guys a drink? Let's have one before we have to get ready for tonight." I suggested.

"Sure." They both said together. I clasped my hand around Cameron's and headed over to the kitchen.

"How was your trip up today, Cameron?" Mum asked as I poured her a wine and Cameron popped open three beers.

"Good," he said handing my dad a beer, "The flights were all back on time after the heavy fog in Sydney this morning. Luckily, I wasn't delayed. I'm looking forward to spending the week up here in Brisbane. I'm going to make sure Wiley shows me all the sights because I've never really spent much time up here before."

My mother's face turned gray with nausea. She didn't believe we were going to leave the bedroom for the entire week Cameron was here.

"Good for you. Cameron, are you into rugby league at all?" Dad diverted the conversation. I sipped on my beer and watch them talk about team players and who was doing well for the season. The room started to fill with too much testosterone for my liking and most of the talk went straight over my head.

I watched Cameron in amazement; he seemed so relaxed and made pleasant conversation with my parents. There was something different about him. I couldn't quite put my finger on it. He seemed so much more relaxed and at ease. He actually looked happy. Conversation came naturally to him, he was charismatic to watch. He laughed, he joked; his comical facial expressions continually made me giggle.

"Okay, time to go get ready." Mum finished off her drinks and headed for her room down the hall.

I grabbed Cameron by the hand and led him downstairs to my room.

***

"Wow! You do own a dress other than that thing you wore to the Winter Dance. I was beginning to wonder." Cameron's eyes lit up as I slipped into my black silky box-pleated dress and sequined cardigan. He lay propped up against my pillows on the bed already dressed in his black dinner suit and pale blue button-up shirt, and oozed sexiness from every inch of his body. He'd give any Hollywood actor on the red carpet a run for their money. He threatened to take the spotlight off my mother at her party tonight and that was not a good thing.

I hitched up the skirt of my dress, climbed on to the bed and straddled his hips. "Wow yourself, look at you! Maybe we should skip Mum's tonight," I suggested then kissed him from the base of his neck, up along his throat and onto his lips.

My insides spring to life when Cameron placed his hands on my hips and drew me in closer. He groaned when he deepened our kiss, making my fingertips tingle when I ran them down across his smoothly shaven cheek. His metallic blue eyes locked on to mine and sent my pulse up a notch. Cameron's wandering hand ran up my back, across my shoulders and then down over my chest. He lingered on my breast, making my nipples harden beneath my bra. I arched into his hand, begging for him to fondle me more. Wrapping my fingers through his hair I drove my hips toward his. Feeling his hardness between my legs made my core clench with want.

"Wiley. No." I glanced at him. His eyes were tightly closed and the muscles in his jaw ticked. "You're very tempting. Too tempting. But your parents are upstairs and we have to go out." He opened his eyes and took a deep breath. "You're making it very difficult. We promised to be good while your parents are here."

I groaned in disappointment. He patted me on my backside for us to get up and make a move. "Come on. It's time to go."

***

Mum and Dad were waiting for us upstairs on the stools at the kitchen counter. Their suitcases stood packed beside them. They were staying at the hotel tonight and heading off on their holiday in the morning. Mum's eyes narrowed at the sight of me, then she looked at Cameron. Our cheeks were flushed and Cameron's hair was messed up thanks to me. She turned away, glancing at the clock, no doubt eager to get to the venue.

"Come on, the cab's arrived." She sprang up at the sound of a car pulling into the driveway. We all clambered out together and headed into Southbank.

We arrived ten minutes later at Rydges Hotel. People rugged up in woolly winter coats, scarves and beanies bustled along the street beside us and in and out of the venue. The CBD buildings, dotted with office lights, towered up to the heavens on the other side of the river. We climbed out of the taxi, shuffled into the hotel and walked upstairs into the private function room.

One hundred of my mum's closest friends and family filled the room. With her meticulous attention to detail, the party started without a hitch. As the meals were going to be served soon, everyone bustled around to find their allocated seats. Cameron and I were on the table with my parents and a couple of her closest friends. While Dad and Cameron went off to the bar for more drinks, I found myself alone at the table with my mother.

"It's obvious you like Cameron a lot. You haven't taken your eyes off him for a second. And he seems to be smitten with you as well. You've only got one more semester at uni to get through, you should be focused on that. There's no need to be so intense with him, you can worry about a relationship once you've finished. I don't want to see you hurt again, like you were with Michael."

"Mum, Cameron's different. He's nothing like Michael."

"Yes, but what's Cameron? Twenty-one? At that age, guys are only after one thing, aren't they?" She fumbled with her pendant on her necklace. Conversations about sex, the birds and the bees, were not her specialty. She was so prudish when it came to sex and I was too embarrassed to have this discussion with her right here in the middle of her party.

"All you need to know is we're being careful." I looked up to see Cameron gazing toward me from over at the bar. I couldn't deny the powerful connection between us; it was some weird force of nature. He'd become part of my very existence, the very air that I breathed. To some degree it scared the hell out of me, considering my past.

"Well!" She now played with the napkin on her table and fidgeted with the cutlery. "That's good to hear. But after your hospitalization a few weeks ago, can you be sure it wasn't him that drugged you? You haven't known him for very long. I've noticed a big change in you and I'm not sure it's a good one. I'm concerned Cameron is the cause of it. I hope being with him isn't affecting your study."

As I recalled my poor assignment grade and tough examinations, the dose of reality was a bitter taste to swallow.

"I want you to be careful," my mum continued, "because I'm not convinced he's right for you."

With every word that trickled out of my mother's mouth, knots of tension grew in my temples. I hated how she had misjudged Cameron and why she couldn't see what an amazing person he was.

"Here you go ladies." Cameron returned with drinks and broke me away from giving an evil glare in my mother's direction. "Everything okay?" he asked while he took a seat, placed his hand on mine and gave it a gentle squeeze. "Dare I ask what you were talking about?"

"You and how amazing you are," I smiled sweetly at my mother.

Mum took a quick drink from her champagne glass, then plastered a fake smile across her face.

There was a flurry of hugs and kisses as friends and family walked past our table to take their seats for dinner to be served. With all the chatter, music and laughter, it was hard to hear. I could barely hold a conversation with my parents sitting next to me and Cameron, let alone her friends on the other side of the large table.

"Cameron, Wiley says your dad works for a mining company, which one?" Dad asked as our meals arrived.

I shrank into my seat because I hadn't told my parents, or anyone for that matter, anything about Cameron's family. The majority of the time I forgot who Cameron's family were.

"Wilks Resources." Cameron looked at me quizzically; he

didn't know I hadn't told them either. I didn't see the point. To me, it wasn't an issue and didn't form part of any reason why I was with him.

"What does he do?" Dad asked while buttering his bread roll.

Cameron whipped his mouth on his napkin and grinned. "My father owns it."

My mother choked and spluttered on a sip of champagne, my dad dropped his knife with a loud clang. Their mouths dropped open like clowns at a fair and stared at Cameron with bulging eyes.

"I take it from your reaction, Wiley hasn't filled you in on any of the details." Cameron glanced in my direction, amusement was written all over his face.

"Is your father Robert Wilks?" my mother stuttered.

"Yes," Cameron replied then took a mouthful of his steak.

"Wiley, why didn't you tell us?" My mother whispered to me and kicked my leg under the table.

"Ow!" I rubbed at my shin. "I did tell you. I said his dad was in mining."

The look on their faces was priceless. But I wondered if now knowing who Cameron was would change my mother's opinion of him. It was one of the reasons why I never wanted to say anything. I wanted them to like him for who he was, not because of his father.

"Well, you have an exciting career ahead of you. You'll go straight into working with your father after uni, right?" Dad asked.

"I'm not sure, Mr Cayton, I mean, John. I know the opportunity is there but I still haven't decided what I'm going to do. I've got five months of university to get through first." Cameron replied.

"Your mother is admirable with all the charity work she

does. How does she do it all?" Mum poised her fingers against the side of her cheeks. "I could've used someone like her to help organize tonight."

Cameron nodded, "Mum does some awesome fundraisers, but I prefer the sports. Dad's company sponsors one of the Sydney rugby teams. When I'm home I usually get to go to the games."

Cameron certainly was connecting with my father with his love of sports.

"Oh, right. When you said before you supported your dad's team, I didn't know I had to take it literally," Dad's eyes shone when he took a drink.

Dinner passed without any more drama, but my mother had notably softened toward Cameron and spoke to him in a much nicer manner. It was good to catch up with family and friends, especially my brother Chris, who I didn't get to see very often. Mum successfully embarrassed me and Cameron every time she introduced us to her friends, always making sure she emphasized who his father was. So not cool! Regardless of that, Cameron and I had fun, sat through long drawn out speeches, toasts and, of course, happy birthday songs and cake.

By the end of the evening, both my parents were tipsy and twirled around the dance floor. Dad cut in on Cameron, asking me for a dance. My aunty swooped into grab Cameron's arms and swung him off in the other direction.

"Hey, princess," Dad slurred. He swayed too much as he tried to waltz with me. "Regardless what your mother says, I think Cameron is a nice guy and it's good to see you happy. But don't ruin the house while we're away next week."

I could hear him mumble *one two three, one two three* under his breath while he concentrated on keeping up the dance steps.

"We won't be silly. Cameron's great though, isn't he?" My

heart felt light like a feather as I watched him dance with my Aunty Jan who was giggling like a schoolgirl. "I'd better go and rescue him."

I dragged Dad over to where they were dancing and released Cameron from my Aunty Jan's clutches.

For the rest of the night, no one other than me was going to have their hands on my man. It was time to say good night to everyone and head for home.

***

Throughout the following week, I dragged Cameron around the sights of Brisbane and the Gold Coast including Southbank, the mall and a day at Dreamworld Theme Park. We went out for brunch nearly every day, played tennis and lazed about watching movies. It was a brilliant week and Saturday, the day he had to go home, came about too fast.

"I hate goodbyes," I said, burying my head into his chest and snuggling against his gray hoodie.

"We'll be back together on campus in no time. It's only a week away."

"Don't go. Stay." I pleaded and pouted.

"I wish I could, but I need to get going or I'll miss my flight. I'll talk to you once I get to Sydney." He took the breath from my lungs as he kissed me. His succulent lips caressed mine, making my knees feel weak. I gazed into his eyes and tugged on his shirt.

"Beautiful, don't look at me like that!" He pried my hands off his body. "I have to get going. I'll see you soon."

He opened the car door, hopped in and I waved goodbye as he drove off down the street. The minute he turned the corner and disappeared from sight, an emptiness opened up deep within my chest, it felt like he'd taken a piece of my soul away with him. I was incomplete without him here by my side.

Half an hour later, I was dragging my feet around the house cleaning up when my phone buzzed with a text message.

```
Thx 4 the lovers balls — they hurt like
hell! xoxo
```

I smiled with a small sense of satisfaction and went on cleaning, awaiting my parents return home in the morning.

Chapter 16

The last week of the winter break dragged by slowly. I could usually lose myself in a good book, enjoy playing golf and visiting friends or spend hours browsing useless information on the Internet and watching TV. But now all I did was miss Cameron. On top of that, I was worried sick about Semester One results being made available online at midday.

I paced the floor all morning and watched the minutes tick by slowly. As the clock struck twelve, I jumped in front of my laptop; my fingers clicked on the keys at lightning speed to log on to the student portal. My hands shook as I moved my fingers across the touchpad. When I found the page, I scanned over the details on the screen.

I froze. I had to blink several times to make sure what I was reading was correct. My lip quivered, then my hands, then my whole body. My eyes stung as they filled with tears. *Oh No!* Two B – Credits and two C – Passes. The worst results in my life. I know many people would have been ecstatic with passing everything, but it felt like the end of the world to me.

I burst out crying. Salty droplets fell upon the keyboard as I dared to read the screen again. I pounded my clenched fists against my head, then slammed the lid of my laptop closed. My stomach churned with bile and a foul taste started to loom in my mouth. I spun around as fast as I could and jumped off the office chair. With my hand covering my mouth I ran down the hallway, into the bathroom, and made it just in time to the toilet to throw up.

***

My parents arrived home after work and found me on the couch. I'd spent the entire afternoon curled up in a fetal position.

"Princess, what's wrong?" My mother dashed to my side. Her concern made the tears start all over again.

With shaking hands I leaned over, opened up the laptop I'd placed on the coffee table earlier and turned it around for her to read. I'd successfully managed to torture myself throughout the afternoon, rereading my grades over again and again. Each time I'd hoped they'd somehow magically get better. And like a low blow to the guts, I will never forget the look of disappointment in my mother's eyes.

"What happened?" she gasped.

Words failed me as I shook my head. Dad came over and read the screen over her shoulder.

"Oh, princess." Even worse than my mother's reaction was the look on my dad's face. I'd let them both down. I'd let myself down. "You still passed everything so don't worry, this shouldn't affect your grade point average too much. It's not the end of the world."

"Oh no!" Mum's hand flew up to her mouth. "What does this mean regarding your scholarship funding?"

"I don't know." Dread filled me. Could I lose my scholarship funding for not meeting the required GPA in a semester? My scholarship was performance based, had I done irreparable damage? The thought of ending up with a university debt to pay off was something I'd never had to contemplate before. I knew just about every student came out of uni with their tuition fee debt, that's why I'd never taken my scholarship for granted. I was fortunate to win it. How could I have been so stupid to lose focus on what was important to me and risk throwing it all away? I rubbed my fingers on my temples feeling my blood pressure skyrocket into the stratosphere. Had this one semester put me back down on to the slush pile?

Then my mother had to open her mouth.

"Do you think this is because you've been hanging out with Cameron? Is he the cause of this, pulling you away from your studies? You've worked so long and hard, don't throw it all away on some stupid boy."

The harshness of my mother's words dug deep inside me. I squeezed my eyes shut and told her it had nothing to do with Cameron, but deep down inside I knew it to be true.

Dad came and sat down beside me and gave me a big hug. "Come on now. It's final year and the subjects are hard. Don't be too tough on yourself."

"I'm so sorry I let you down." I whimpered. "I don't feel well so I'm going to go to bed. I'll have dinner later when I feel up to it." I stood up, grabbed my phone and went downstairs to my bedroom and cried even more. Luckily, my parents didn't disturb me.

I sat on the edge of my mattress, turning my phone over and over in my hands. It rang, startling me. I tried to smile when I saw the Caller ID flash with Cameron's name.

"I've got my results. Have you got yours yet? What are they?" He chirped happily. Pity I couldn't feel the same way.

"Yeah, I have them." I mumbled, barely above a whisper. He didn't pick up on how upset I was.

"Sorry I didn't call earlier but I was out catching up with friends and then went to dinner with my parents." For the first time ever, I was unaffected by Cameron's contagious energy. "I got a Distinction, two Credits and a Pass. Cool hey? Good results, all thanks to you. So, what did you get?"

I rubbed my eyes, wiped my damp cheeks and managed to blubber my results out to him.

"Oh, shit! ...They're okay, though. Don't be upset. I wish I was there to give you a big hug."

"You don't understand." I snapped.

"Understand what?"

"I can't afford grades like this. I could lose my scholarship with grades this low and affect my chance at getting the internship with Huntersville."

"Don't be silly, it's one semester."

"Huntersville are really strict on their performance requirements. My poor results could stuff up everything. It's all my fault for going out too much." I punched my pillow with all my might. "I can't afford to screw up any more. Things between us have to change next semester. For me, anyway. Okay?"

His silence scared me as it lingered on. But after a while he agreed. My head was aching, my heart was thudding and for the first time ever ... I doubted whether our relationship would survive the distance.

Chapter 17

On Sunday afternoon, with my mind in a haze, I survived the two-hour drive back to Toowoomba in my little red Mazda to start third term, second semester. I couldn't recall any of the journey along the Warrego Highway, past the abundant vegetable crops growing near Gatton or making in back to the top of the steep mountain range. I managed to put my bad results behind me, there was nothing I could do about them. But then I received an email from my scholarship review officer requesting a meeting at eleven o'clock tomorrow morning. There was no agenda listed in the message, only the time and the place. My main scholarship review wasn't until the end of the year, so this unexpected meeting request was making me sick with worry. Was it about my grades last semester, or the Winter Dance drama?

The bleakness of winter reflected my mood perfectly as I drove into the car park at Steele Rudd. As I stepped out of my car, I drew my scarf up around my neck to ward off the wild wind whipping against my face.

I didn't feel like being around anyone, so after Dave and Justin kindly helped me unload my car, they left to watch the rugby league on TV, leaving me alone to unpack my gear. After everything was away in its rightful place, I lay down on my bed feeling drained. Cameron wasn't back until tomorrow, so I had time to kill. I turned on my music to listen to Cold Play and before I knew it an hour had passed. Kel barged through my door and flopped down on my bed beside me.

"You made it." I hugged her hello.

"Sorry I'm late, but I had a the most harrowing hounding from my parents before I left. Dad's getting worse, he doesn't let up about anything anymore. They're so aggravating, annoying, and piss me off over the slightest thing. You think they'd start to trust me now at twenty-one, but no. I passed everything with flying colors last semester. You'd think they'd be happy for me, but no. It's all, *Study hard, you can do better, don't drink too much, don't have sex, be safe and don't do drugs* — yak, yak, yak. Do they think I'm stupid or something?" Kel ranted on and I lay there content to listen while she bitched about her parents.

"Oh, honey!" I gave her a big hug. "All parents are like that, yours are exceptionally good at it though." I rolled back on to my pillow and stared up at the roof. "Everything's all screwed up at the moment."

Kel turned to me.

"Wiley, what's wrong?"

I covered my eyes with my arm. "I've been called into see the review officer tomorrow and I'm freaking out about it."

"Why didn't you tell me sooner? Here I've been crapping on with my usual shit when that is so much more important." She snatched a tissue from the box on my bedside table and handed it to me. "What do they want to see you about?"

"It could be my grades. It could be the dance drama. Other than that, I have absolutely no fucking idea."

***

Eleven o'clock on Monday morning came around quickly. I sat on the uncomfortable green vinyl chair outside the administration office, tapping my feet nervously, waiting for my appointment.

The teak wooden door swung open with a loud squeek and the review officer, Carlton Weber, waved me into the room.

His small office was littered with piles of manila folders bulging with papers, stacks of in-trays overflowing with documents, shelves straining under the weight of books and a variety of notepads were flipped open on his desk beside his laptop.

I took a seat opposite him at his desk and tried to smile.

He sat down, crossed his hands and leaned forward.

"Ms Cayton. I have your results here. Would you like to explain what happened last semester?"

No polite conversation. No how are you doing. Just... Wham! I licked my lips and swallowed in an attempt to get moisture in my mouth so I could talk. "The subjects were hard and I struggled with the workload."

"Up until now, you've had exceptional results. With your hospitalization from an allergic reaction to illegal drugs you claim was not your fault, the sudden change in your behavior is cause for concern. Missing classes and lectures is out of character for you. We know there is a lot of pressure on you to perform and if you're having issues, we can provide you with the contact details for councilors that may be able to help."

What? Oh crap, he thinks I'm a druggie!

"You have no need for concern. I won't let you down again. I promise," I sat up straight and tall in my chair to show him I was perfectly in control of my behavior and not under the influence of illicit substances.

"It's more serious than that. Your GPA has hit 5.9. One of the requirements for your scholarship is that you must maintain a GPA of 6.0 above."

"But my overall GPA is calculated at the end of the year."

"I know that all too well, Ms Cayton. I'd like to reiterate your scholarship is based on performance. I want to make sure you're fully aware of what is at stake. It's not only the funding, but employment opportunities as well. You have your interview with the sponsoring organization at the end of next term and they will not tolerate poor results. You have to excel this semester, so consider this a warning for you to pull up your socks."

"Yes, sir."

"Okay then." He stared at me over the rim of his glasses. "That's all for now. I hope not to see you again before our final review."

I nodded. A numbness washed over me as I scrambled out of the office and shut the door behind me. My feet could not carry me fast enough out of the administration building. I was shuddering all over and headed to my safe haven in the library. I found an empty audio room, stepped inside, locked the door behind me and sunk to the floor. Curling my knees up tightly to my chest, I let the tears flood from my eyes.

Half an hour later, I struggled to put one foot in front of the other and headed back over to my accommodation. I jumped at the sound of thundering footsteps on the bitumen road behind me. I stepped off to the side of the road to make way for whoever it was in such a rush. I squealed when arms flung around my waist, picked me up off my feet and swung me over their shoulder.

Now this was a nice distraction.

"Put me down!" I shrieked and playfully smacked him on

the bottom. "What are you are doing?"

"I'm kidnapping you. What does it look like? And I'm not letting you go until I have my way with you." His grasp tightened around my legs, preventing any attempt at escape, and at the moment I didn't have the strength to even consider it.

Cameron bailed me into his room, lay me down on his bed and returned to shut the door behind him.

"You're back early." I said, adjusting the pillow behind my head. "I thought you wouldn't be back until tonight in time for Dave's birthday party."

He crawled on to the bed and lay down on top of me. I tried to wriggle free but every move I made was pointless as he had me pinned firmly down on the bed.

He drew back when he saw I'd been crying. I squeezed my eyes shut and turned away from his gaze. I was so over being upset. I was the only one who could pull myself together. No more brooding, no more crying and no more wallowing.

"What's wrong, beautiful?"

I relayed the details of my meeting with the review officer, appreciative that he let me blurt everything out.

He kissed my forehead. With his lips pressed against my skin and his heart beating next to mine I started to feel better.

"If the stupid scholarship program kicks you out, I'll pay your tuition."

I gasped. "Don't say things like that. I don't want your money. I haven't lost my funding yet, but...but I can't afford to fuck things up again. I hate to repeat what I said on the phone the other day when I was all upset, but things need to be different this semester."

A beautiful smile touched his mouth, making my heart flip over inside my chest. "I agree totally. Let me tell you what happened at my therapy session on Friday. I didn't say anything before because it didn't seem important at the time. Now, you need to hear it."

He shuffled off of me and lay the length of his body down next to mine on the mattress. He took my hand in his and ran his thumb across the back of it. The little shocks I got from his touch buzzed to life.

"My shrink said I've made progress with finally accepting Gilly's death. I've been through it all ... the denial, the anger and depression. He was relieved to see I was reconnecting with the world ... although he wasn't too impressed about my excessive partying." Cameron smirked, paused, then looked up at me from underneath his long eyelashes and smiled. "Wiley, you've helped me though it in a way I didn't think was possible. I'm in a good place now. For the first time I feel motivated and better about myself and I have you to thank for all of that."

My heart swelled in my chest.

"You've got to admit we did have some wicked fun last term. I know I was swept up in the craziness of moving out of home, campus life and you. I'm sorry you got caught up in all of that. I feel terrible you didn't do as well as you would've like to do last semester. I screwed up. We screwed up. I wish there was some way I can make it up to you."

"We have to set some new boundaries this semester, that's all?" I had to.

His brow furrowed. "I know and I understand completely. After the Winter Dance and seeing you in hospital, my whole attitude changed. I normally never want to fight for anything. I normally turn a blind eye to what's going on around me and you witnessed firsthand I can withdraw from the world when things go wrong. But your perseverance and determination to fight for me had a huge impact. I've never had anyone do anything like that for me before and I'm not going to risk losing you again. You've made me see things clearly for the first time in a long time and I know what I want in my life."

"What, you've had an epiphany?" Maybe we both had. Maybe everything that had happened, happened for a reason. It had made us both wake up and see what was important.

"Something like that."

"Cam, I hate myself for being so weak last semester." I rolled back onto the pillow and stared at the ceiling. "Going out and missing classes...I don't know what was wrong with me. That's not who I am. I'm normally so strong and focused. But for some reason I can't stay away from you. It's like you have me under a spell."

"Things are different now, I promise." He hooked his arm over my waist and nudged in closer. "I know your study means a lot to you, so we'll find a new balance. We won't go out through the week unless critically essential. We'll attend every lecture and tutorial — there'll be no leaving class to have sex. We'll spend two nights a week apart in our own rooms if you need some time away from me... no wait, make that one. Although I really would prefer none. I love sleeping next to you every night. And on weekends, we can unwind when we don't have exams or assignments due. I'll do anything you want. I just want to be with you any way I can."

"Are you really prepared to do all those things?" I turned to him and rested my hand against his chest. "You're making everything sound so easy. You don't have to change because of me, but I've got to pull my head in."

He slid his arm over my hip and rested his hand on the small of my back. "It's not because of you, it's because I want to."

Thoughts flashed through my mind of us being together and had sensed something different about him when he was with me on holidays. Was this it? He was becoming more responsible and mature? Maybe we both were. Life was starting to change at such a rapid pace, it made my head spin.

"Cam...you never cease to amaze me." I leaned forward and touched my lips to his.

"With our workload and our final project due, it's going to be a busy semester. If you think I was a bad influence on you before, wait until I pull you into line now.' He chuckled. "You've helped me and now I want to do the same for you and so much more. We're good for each other, trust me."

Was it a matter of trust? I'd had a rough time since receiving my poor grades last week and with my run this morning with my scholarship office. But Cameron knew exactly what to say to make me feel better. This beautiful man who entrusted me with so much when I seemed to give little in return. I gazed into his gorgeous blue eyes and felt like anything was possible. Now we were together again, everything felt right.

"Well then, I guess you're going to have to prove to me you've changed." I said, slipping my hand beneath the bottom of his shirt and sliding it up toward his chest.

I drew my leg over his and crawled on top of him. My lips found his. I brushed my hand down the side of his face over his soft facial hair. I deepened our kiss, slipping my tongue into his mouth. His gentle moan rippled through me veins. I craved him. Needed him. Didn't function without him.

"Oh I will," he said over our kisses. "But first—"

Clothes came off and we lost ourselves in each other. Mouth to mouth, skin on skin. Our connection filled me once more. With all our dramas behind us, I was now looking forward to the semester ahead. With renewed focus, nothing was going to get in our way.

Chapter 18

The end of July passed into August and the workload became daunting. Cameron was true to his word and we focused on our studies, sometimes apart, giving us a little diversification from living out of each other's pockets.

Friday nights became our date night where Cameron and I went off campus for dinner. Not once did I regret missing happy hour and all the drinking, and we still wound up at The Club later in the evening to dance the night away. Saturday night after work, we relaxed in the common room, played cards or watched a movie with everyone. Sunday morning I spent with the girls catching up or studying so I had free time in the afternoon to spend with Cameron.

Hours slipped away as we explored and experienced all the city of Toowoomba had to offer. Cameron drove me everywhere. He seemed enraptured to spend time with me, and I was a willing participant to experience anything he could think of to do and vice versa. We went go-cart racing, rock-climbing, borrowed bikes off our friends and went for a ride, played squash or tennis; went picnicking or on bush walks and ended up nearly every Sunday afternoon out somewhere having coffee or a beer somewhere. He loved going somewhere new all the time, insisting we never go to the same place twice. We tried all the trendy cafés on Margaret Street across the road from Queens Park, drove all the way out to Crow's Nest to visit the Cuckoo Clock shop, and even ventured to Murphy's Creek down the range one day and ate way too much SeatOnFire chilli chocolate from the local store.

I had seen more of the Toowoomba in the past few months with Cameron than I had in the entire past two years of living here. My confidence had been restored and uni was going well. Everything was thanks to Cameron.

***

One night after working at the tavern, I drove back to campus and managed to grab a late meal in the dining hall before the kitchen closed. Cameron waited with me as I chowed down crumbed fish and chips and cleared my dishes away.

As I was walking back to my block with Cameron, his hand felt clammy in mine; his stride a little off pace. I stopped and looked up at him with concern. "Are you okay?"

"Yeah. I was wondering if you had any plans for tonight?" he asked turning his hand around in mine and adjusting his hold.

"Nope. I need a shower and would like an early night. I'm stuffed."

"Do you want to come over to my room for a shower with me and then maybe watch a movie? I went shopping today and downloaded some new movies off the Net."

"That sounds nice. I'll grab my things and come on over. See you in five minutes or so."

"See you soon."

I let go of his hand and made my way into my block.

Veering via Kel's room, I made a quick stop to say hello before she went out with Matt for the evening.

"Where are you going tonight?" I asked, leaning against her built-in wardrobe just inside her room and watched her dart around getting ready.

"We're going to the movies." Kel bopped around in time to her music playing while she put on her make-up.

"This is getting serious, Kel. Do you realize, Matt is now officially the longest boyfriend you've ever had?"

Her eye's shone brightly. "Oh Wiley. I'm so in love with him. He's the best."

"Oo! The big *L* word!"

"Just like you are with Cameron."

I gulped hard and let out a half-hearted laugh. *Haha ha ha ha*. Me? In love with Cameron? How would I know if it was true?

"I have to get going, Sweetie," she said, gathering her handbag, phone and keys and started to shuffle me out the door. "I'll catch up with you sometime tomorrow. Okay?"

"Have a great night. I'm going over to Cameron's."

I hugged her goodbye and headed into my own room. Kel's comment about love played over and over in my head. I'd never said the *L* word to Cameron or him to me. How did you know if you were in love? I was crazy about Cameron, was that it? Had I been avoiding how I really felt?

I gathered my flannel pajamas, towel and toiletry bag and stuffed them in to my canvas tote bag. With UGG boots on my feet, I was ready to head over to Cameron's room and looked forward to a quiet night and a good night's sleep.

I headed over to his block, tapped on the door and heard his soft voice.

"Come in."

I opened it and gasped. The transformation of his room was breathtaking. My eyes whisked around, taking in the haven Cameron had created. Scattered around the room lay several large candles burning brightly; they flickered in the door draft and filled the air with the sweet scent of vanilla and musk.

He'd flipped his single bed up on its side and leaned it up against the wall. In its place, taking up nearly every inch of the bedroom floor, was a queen-sized blow-up camping mattress covered in sheets and a new queen-sized quilt. He had moved his little bar fridge right into the corner up against his wardrobe with his TV perched precariously on top. Cold Play music played from his iPod.

"Oh wow! What's all this for?" I closed the door and dropped my bag on to the floor.

Cameron stood up from his desk chair and stomped across the air mattress over to me, cupped my face with his warm hands and kissed me. "This is all for you. I'm glad you wanted a night in, otherwise my plans would have been shot to pieces."

"So this was what you bought when you went out on your shopping expedition today? I like the mattress." I smiled at his purchase splayed out on the floor.

"I'm sick of sleeping cramped up on a single bed. I thought this might be a bit more comfortable."

"Nice!" I had to agree. "All the candles are beautiful; definitely a nice touch. Let's pray we don't burn the place down or set the fire alarm off." I giggled, curling my arms around Cameron's waist. All of a sudden, I no longer felt tired.

"How about we start with a glass of wine and then have a shower." He took my hand and led me over to sit down on the mattress. The vinyl squished and squelched underneath us as we shuffled around trying to get comfortable. Over a glass of wine, we chatted about the day. I closed my eyes and licked my lips, savoring the taste of the cabernet. The berry aroma of the wine was decadent and the liquid warmed me from the inside out. We didn't even finish the first glass before Cameron took my hand and led me into his shower. How he scored a corner room with its own bathroom I do not know, but at moments like this I wasn't going to complain. We undressed and slipped into the flow of steaming water, the glass door of the shower clicking shut behind us. My head rolled to the side as Cameron massaged my shoulders to relieve the day's tension of work away.

Then his hands curled around my tummy and turned me around to face him. He looked so perfect in the soft candlelight and with the water hypnotically cascading down across his face and shoulders. Droplets of water fell from the tips of his wet hair, down onto his shoulders. Taking the shower gel, he proceeded to wash me all over. "I don't know what I've done to deserve this, but it's exactly what I needed at the end of a long work day."

"Good. I wanted to do something special for you and to show—" he stopped mid-sentence, closed his eyes and a grin tugged at the corner of his mouth as I kissed along his collarbone, down his pecs and licked his nipple with my tongue.

"Show me what?" I asked.

"Hmm, that's nice! You're distracting." His heart thudded beneath my touch. "I want to show you how special you are to me." He hooked his finger beneath my chin, tilted my head up so he could gaze into my eyes. "I'm crazy about you, Wiley, and fall for you more each day." My eyelids fluttered shut as he kissed my cheek and headed for my mouth. The sweet taste of wine lingered on his tongue.

"Really?" The biggest of all grins grew across my face and I entangled my hands up through his hair.

"Yeah." Goosebumps shot down my neck when he whispered in my ear, slipped his hands down my back on to my hips and drew me closer into his chest. His erection nudged at my belly and the heat escalated between us. The touch of his hot skin against mine sent tingles all over me as he tightened his grip. I was lost in his embrace; intoxicated after barely one glass of wine.

"Aaarrgghh!"

I screamed at the top of my lungs when the water spray turned ice-cold. Cameron laughed as he turned the faucet in his hand.

"It's freezing! You crazy son of a ..."

I leaped from the shower shivering and grabbed for a towel. Cameron was in hysterics as he stepped out after me. In one quick swoop, he picked me up and carried me out on to the mattress on the floor.

Naked and wet, we fell on top of the bed; the wall heater whizzing away to keep the room all toasty and warm. Cameron hovered above me propped up on his elbows, an arm on either side my head. My pulse quickened watching his eyes darkened with desire. His fingertips glided over my cheek, down my neck and on to my chest causing my blood to rush through my veins.

A glint in his eye appeared when small droplets of cool water fell from his hair and landed on my skin. "These have to go." He lowered his head and attempted to kiss every one of them away, making a trail from my face, down my neck and on to my chest. My back arched when he explored my nipples, circling each aroused bud with his hot, wet, tantalizing tongue. Shockwaves pulsed though me, making my whole body ripple with pleasure. His fingers slipped like silk over my skin, zigzagging this way and that as he wiped away the last few drops of water that dotted my flesh.

"Stay," he whispered, hunger burned in his eyes.

"I'm not going anywhere." I was only too happy to oblige and rubbed my hands over his bare lean shoulders and up through his damp, unruly hair.

"Oh, I won't let you." He shuffled down the bed, kissing my skin as he moved, leaving a path of blazing heat in his wake. His breath tickled me when he reached my stomach and teased along the line of my hip and across my groin. I bit my lip as he ventured down along my thigh; further areas for his lips, tongue, breath and hands to explore.

"What are you doing?" I giggled.

"Shh!"

Cameron's mouth lingered, nipping and licking with the softest of touches up and down each leg. His fingers taunted me with his soft, ticklish strokes and his breath sent goose bumps dancing across my skin. The teasing was driving me wild, but every time I tried to move he would push me back down gently on to the mattress and continue from where he left off. It was driving me crazy.

The soft rumbling groans resonating in the depths of his throat surged through me and nestled right at the peak of my legs. My arousal was growing and so was my craving to have him.

He nudged my legs further apart and feverishly trailed up my inner thigh with a line of kisses. His hot breath between my legs made me clutch at the bedsheets. He stroked his finger up the length of my slit, in between the folds of my skin and circled around my swollen bud. The air rushed from my lungs when he repeated the same action, only this time with his tongue.

Cameron and I had never done anything like this before. He'd felt me up, of course, but never anything so intimate.

My hips rocked as he continued to kiss and lick at my sensitive nerve endings and slid his finger inside me. *Fuck!* I was powerless and completely under his control with nothing but the titillating pressure of his tongue and the soft movements of his fingers between my legs.

My muscles burned. My body beckoned for more of his tormenting motions. All I could do was claw at the pillow while he made me quiver and quake in delight. I bit into my lip as hard as I could to avoid making any noise. I was conscious of the thin bedroom walls and didn't want to disturb Cameron's neighbor. I squeezed my eyes shut as Cameron's tongue went on unrelenting.

Panting breathlessly the pressure mounted in my body and begged for release. Cameron, sensing my need focused his sole attention on my clitoris. With his tongue swirling over me and his finger probing into my wetness, I gasped. My body quaked as a searing orgasm burst inside me. I'd never experienced anything so intense in all my life. My chest heaved and electricity charged through my veins.

I collapsed back against the pocket of air, the new mattress making me feel like I was floating on a cloud. Cameron grinned up at me, his face smitten with satisfaction.

"Wow!" Was all I could say, unable to wipe the smile off my face.

"You like that?" He kisses his way back up over me.

I nodded, maybe a bit too eagerly. He could do that to me every time we had sex. I'd never say no to that. Ever!

He hovered over me, lowered his hips against mine and slipped his erection inside of me. Tingles raced up my spine as he plunged into me and started to thrust. I rolled him over onto his back, straddled his hips, and with his slow pleasurable rhythm, he made me come again.

***

I lay embraced in Cameron arms, still in a daze in the

aftermath of lovemaking. He trailed his fingers up and down my spine while the flickering candles made shadows dance on the walls. Our heart beats had returned to normal and it felt like heaven to lie beside him.

"I love you," he whispered and kissed me on the forehead.

My breath hitched at hearing those three little words. Everything with Cameron seemed so right. We fit perfectly together, mentally and physically. It was though we were meant to be together. I snuggled in to him, even closer than before. It felt like the sun was shining right from the center of my chest. This...this is what it felt like. There was no doubt in my mind. "I love you, too."

Chapter 19

After a long, cold winter I was glad to see the first signs of spring. The warmth brought the gardens around the university, the college and the city slowly back to life. The bushes started to flower, the trees were covered with shoots of new growth and the grass showed tinges of green. Toowoomba was radiant in the spring and full of color once again.

Third term was flying by. Assignments were done and my final project was progressing. Skimming through the calendar on my tablet, I couldn't believe that mid-semester holidays were only one and a half weeks away, and my twenty-first birthday fell on the Wednesday before the end of term.

Cameron and I were lazing about on a blanket outside his room after lunch, having a short break before attending class. It was an unusually warm spring day and we enjoyed soaking up the warm rays of the sun. Glancing around the accommodation blocks, students attempting to be studious could be seen sitting at desks through their windows, while others drifted back and forth along the pathways heading to or returning from lectures and tutorials at uni. Music could be heard playing from up in someone's room in B-Block and laundry hanging on the clothes line near us flapped about in the breeze. It was a typical day in the life at residential college.

"Can you get work off this Saturday, and do you have any other plans I don't know about for this weekend?" Cameron asked while plucking at the grass with his fingers.

"Why?" I looked up from my tablet.

"Well, we've plans with your parents next weekend after your birthday at the end of term so I thought it would be nice if I could take you out this weekend to celebrate and ...well...my parents want to meet you."

"What? Your parents? Here?" Butterflies took flight in my stomach. "Are they coming up to Toowoomba?"

"You'll see. So can you get off work, please?" He asked while shading his eyes with his hand to avoid squinting in the sun.

"Sure, I'll call work this afternoon. Bruce should be able to find someone to fill in for me with a few days' notice."

"Excellent. You'll have to pack an overnight bag as well because we'll spend the weekend off campus." He flippantly added, like it was a passing afterthought.

"What? I sat up with a rush to my head. "Where are we going?"

"It's a surprise. We'll have to head off at midday on Friday."

"That early? But I will miss class."

"Oh no. You'll have to miss *one* class." Cameron poked me in the ribs. "It's only an auditing tutorial. I'm sure you'll be fine and, knowing you, you'll have blitzed all the work by then anyway."

"I like auditing," I mumbled. "we better be doing something really good."

Cameron rolled his eyes at me. "I'm hoping what I've

planned is much better than auditing. Just do this for me, please?" He tried to act casual but I could sense he was anxious about something. It made me all the more excited about what he had in store for me.

"Okay, whatever." I shrugged, but my mind was racing with endless possibilities, wondering what to expect. What was Cameron up to? I loved celebrating my birthday and now with this pending surprise, I was fired up and eager for the weekend.

"Do you think your parents will like me?" I wringed my hands together.

"Absolutely."

"What about your dad? I'm intimidated already. What do I wear? And...and your mum, she's going to hate me. She'll think I'm a slut because I'm sleeping with you, their only son! And ... and... I'm not good enough for you." I joked around, trying to cover up my real apprehension.

Cameron laughed. "Is that what you think? You have nothing to worry about. They'll love you, just as I do."

***

Thursday night I hardly slept a wink, anticipating my getaway with Cameron and meeting his parents. I tried not to toss and turn on the air mattress, but Cameron seemed restless too. He'd been evasive every time I asked for more detail about the plans for the weekend. I wanted more information on where we were going so I knew what to pack, but was only left frustrated when he told me to take whatever and something to sleep in — the latter being totally optional. I was going on a blind weekend, which didn't help with the quantity of clothing I'd have to take with me so I was prepared for the unknown.

My Friday morning lecture passed slowly, the minutes dragged on endlessly. I looked at my watch a hundred times, agonizing over and willing the time away. I played with my pen, checked email on my iPad and took down every note from the lecturer, but nothing made the time pass quicker. The minutes continued to creep by.

A permanent knot of apprehension had lodged itself within the depths of my stomach over the past few days. Meeting his parents was a big step in our relationship. Yes, he'd met mine — the first time was far from the ideal situation at the hospital, and secondly at my mum's party. I was terrified his parents would react like my mother. Oh, God forbid!

I ran through numerous scenarios and conversations in my head, trying to think of intelligent things to say and interesting topics to discuss with Cameron's father. I googled his dad's company during the lecture to read up on current news and press releases I might be able to ask questions about, but most of the information went way over my head.

Finally, after two long tortuous hours the lecture hall lights came up, class finished and I was first out the door so I could head back to my room.

Oh shit! Of all days to run in my auditing tutor. I had to take the upper hand. "Hi Mr. Gooding. Sorry I won't be in class this afternoon, it's my birthday and I'm going away for the weekend. I've done all the work, though."

He looked me up and down, his thinning gray hair flapped in the breeze. I stood up tall, straightened my shoulders and tried out my sweetest of smiles. I'd been the perfect student this term, but guilt rippled through me like I was doing something wrong.

"Uh-huh," he grunted. "Big celebrations, eh? Well, I still expect your tutorial work submitted by first thing Monday morning."

"Yes, Mr. Gooding. You shall have it before morning tea. Have a good weekend." I stepped around him and headed back to Steele Rudd College as fast as my legs would carry me. Why did I only run into my teachers when I was not on course for a class? Worry about my scholarship and pressure to do well was starting to do my head in. But all that dissipated into thin air when I walked into my block and saw Cameron. He was waiting for me in the common room, all dressed smartly in dark jeans and an oatmeal-colored long-sleeved t-shirt. My heart leapt with excitement as he stood to greet me and kissed me on the forehead.

"You ready to go?" He rubbed his hands together, eager to get the weekend under way.

"Yes." I bounced into my room and dumped my gear on to my desk. I loved surprises and being whisked away for the weekend had me peaking with fever-pitched adrenaline.

Cameron had been on edge since he'd asked me to go away with him. It was strange for him to be acting this way. I knew all of his mannerisms when he was worried, stressed or nervous. He would touch his hand to his forehead, run his fingers through his hair, his lip curled in the corner of his mouth or he would annoyingly tap a pen on a book at a hundred times a second when we were studying. All of these little things had been in overdrive in the past few days. Was he anxious about introducing me to his parents?

I quickly changed into different jeans and my favorite navy long-sleeved knit top and gathered the last of my things before we headed off. "We can cancel meeting your parents if you want." I offered him the chance to back out of the situation. If he was as nervous as I was, it was going to be an interesting weekend.

"That's not it at all." He furrowed his brow. "Come on, let's go." He grabbed my bag and started to headed out the door.

"Bye Kel," I yelled out while I locked my door behind me. "We're going now."

Her door swung open in a flash and she lunged at me, embracing me with a huge hug. "Oh have fun, I can't wait to hear all about it."

"I'll tell you everything on Sunday night. We've gotta go. So I'll see you soon. Love you."

"Love you too."

Cameron took me by the hand and scuttled me out of the block, down the pathway and into his car. We were heading along West Street and as usual, I was jabbering away about my boring lecture and feeling guilty when I'd seen Mr. Gooding, when I came to the realization that we had missed the turnoff . We didn't head up James Street that led to the road down the range. I had my suspicions and thought we might've be going to Brisbane for the weekend. Maybe we were taking the long way round to the highway.

"Um, Cameron, where are we going?" I was confused when he turned up the route to head out of town in totally the wrong direction.

He smiled, keeping his eyes on the road ahead of him. "You'll see."

The houses, shops and streets raced past my window. I didn't recognize anything on this side of the city. We never had reason to venture over this way.

A few seconds later his phone rang and he answered his Bluetooth connection.

"Cameron, how are you traveling?"

"Hey Scott. Yes, we're on time. We'll be there in a few minutes." He hung up and offered me no explanation of who was on the phone.

I tried to keep my excitement, and now bafflement, at bay. Who was Scott and what were we doing over this side of town?

Further down the road, my pulse rose to dangerous levels when he pulled into the airport terminal and parked in the car park. The airport, if you could call it that, was nothing more than a small beige brick building surrounded by a high wire fence overgrown with a creeping vine. "Cameron, what's going on? Are we picking up your parents now? Are they flying into Toowoomba? I would've dressed a bit better if I'd known."

"Nope." He raced around and opened my door for me, offering his hand. "Come on." I took it and slipped out of the car. He grabbed our bags, I could do nothing else but follow him into the terminal.

"Just wait here." He dropped our bags at my feet and walked over to the single check-in counter.

The building was near isolated; we were literally the only people in the terminal other than two lazy staff members who stood behind the desk. Cameron made a quick enquiry, returned to my side and collected our bags.

"Will you tell me what we're doing? What's going on?" The palms of my hands were sweating and I was flustered from the rushing about.

"Come on, we have to hurry." He collected our things, grabbed my hand and dragged me out the door on to the tarmac. I balked when we were confronted by a man dressed handsomely in a navy blue pilot's suit, complete with mirrored aviator sunglasses upon his face.

"Cameron, good to see you. I haven't seen you in ages. I hear you're enjoying Toowoomba." The man greeted Cameron with a handshake.

"Hey Scott. This is my girlfriend, Wiley Cayton."

"Nice to meet you, Ms Cayton. Are you ready to go? We have a tight clearance, so please climb on board."

"What?" I shook my head, trying to understand what was going on.

The overpowering fumes of aviation fuel hung heavy in the air and the sound of a jet engine roared with life directly in front of us. The tarmac was hot and the wind blew my loose hair in all directions.

"What's this?" I gawked.

Wilks One stood before us, glistening in the sunlight. It was one of the small, white and very sleek private jets I half-heartedly had noticed when we drove up to the airport.

Cameron kissed the top of my hand and led me toward the craft. I could barely put one foot in front of the other, he kept on having to tug me along.

"We're going to meet my parents." Cameron waved his hand about, coaxing me to climb up the metal stairway into the aircraft. After having to literally push me up into the plane, he then offered me a seat by the window in one of the lush, beige leather chairs. He fell into the one next to me and let out a huge breath. "We made it!"

"Can you please explain?" I'm sure my mouth was still gapping open.

"I might have forgotten to mention ... on purpose ... that we are actually going to meet my parents ... in Sydney, this weekend."

"Are you serious? Flying in a private jet. Holy shit! You can't do this, can you? What? How?"

Cameron's eyes sparkled "I made a few calls. I've been conspiring with my parents for weeks. Dad loaned me the plane. Mind you, this has never happened before, ever, so don't get used to it. There's also a cool band playing tonight I want to take you to see. So...surprise!"

"I knew there was something going on. But this!" My eyes were still popping out of my head. This was so over the top and the craziest thing that had ever happened to me. I felt like I could burst. Living with Cameron at college, you'd never know he was wealthy. He never splashed his money and was a down-to-earth type of guy. I was always adamant about paying my own way whenever we went out, so he never spoilt me. Not like this anyway! This was extreme and put him in the class of *not normal*. I couldn't believe he'd gone to all this trouble to make my birthday special.

"This is insane. I would've been happy to go out to dinner somewhere a bit nicer than McDonald's." I sprang into his lap. My heart was racing and I had to take a deep breath to try and calm down because I was shaking all over. Taking his face in my hands, I kissed him. His lips were warm and delicious as only Cameron's kiss could be.

"I know you would've been happy with a dinner out, but I wanted to spoil you rotten."

His lips met mine eagerly and his hand slid up along my thigh.

"Okay you two, not in the plane, please." Scott walked along the short aisle toward the cabin door. "We're ready to go. We have a short window to get into Sydney before air traffic control goes nuts during peak hour. So let's hit the tarmac. Brendan is in here, Ms Cayton. He is our co-pilot today and I, of course, am the all-essential and trusty captain. Cameron, the bar fridge is stocked with beer, rum and Coke as you requested. Seatbelts on, let's go."

"My parents are going to freak when I tell them about this and the girls are not going to believe me." I slid back into my chair and did up my belt.

"I'm glad I've managed to surprise you."

I shook my head in awe. "Is there anything you can't do?"

"Yes. That thing we tried to do in bed the other night." Leaning over, he tickled me in the side and kissed me beneath my ear lobe. "We will have to work on that."

The plane took off smoothly. As the craft leapt into the sky, the sound of the jet engines hummed through my body. I had been on planes before, but this was so much more exhilarating.

"I could get used to this kind of lifestyle, Cam." I ran my hand over the soft leather seats and snuggled in next to him while the plane crept above the clouds.

"Yeah. It's pretty easy to get used to."

Chapter 20

The plane arrived two hours later in Sydney. It had been ten years since I'd been here on a family holiday to see the popular tourist sites like Circular Quay, the Opera House, the Rocks and Taronga Zoo. It was long ago, but I do remember the stunning view of the clear harbor waters, the mighty Sydney Harbour Bridge and stunning the Opera House.

On the flight, I had resigned myself to the fact Cameron could not impress me anymore. I was all maxed out. But sure enough, when we departed the plane, a sleek black Lexus sedan awaited our arrival to drive us to Cameron's house.

"Hi, Cameron," the chauffeur said with a tip of his hat.

"Hey Gary, how's it going? I'd like you to meet my girlfriend, Wiley Cayton." Cameron introduced me, threw our bags in the car and off we set. Sitting in the back seat with Cameron, I refused to let go of him. He occasionally released my grip to wipe the sweat accumulating between our entwined hands off on his thigh, then wrapped his fingers around mine once again and gave me a reassuring squeeze.

"It's good to have you back around the traps, Cameron," the driver said. "But I don't miss driving your ass all over this city. How's the country bumpkin life up there in enemy territory?" He joked about the interstate sport rivalry between the two states of Queensland and New South Wales.

"Really good. How are the wife and kids?" Cameron asked.

Gary proceeded to update Cameron with his news. He was a tall and solid Asian-looking man, with graying hair and a cheeky grin. He was very friendly and had obviously known Cameron for some time.

Family chauffeur — I did not know they had one of those!

As the airport and city highways flew past, I stared out the window taking in the surrounds, trying to see if I could remember any of the sights looming in the distance. Only the Sydney Tower rising up in the middle of the city's skyline jolted my childhood memories.

"Depending on traffic, it should take us about thirty minutes or so to get home," Gary said. "Ms Cayton, I will drop yourself and Cameron off at the house in Vaucluse and then pick up Mr Wilks at the office. I'm sure Margaret is keenly awaiting your arrival."

I didn't know Sydney well. I knew Vaucluse lay out past the city CBD on the eastern headland, south of the harbor. It wasn't long until we wound our way past a splendid old Anglican Church and school and headed into Vaucluse. I was stunned by the magnificent and majestic houses lining the streets and occasionally caught a glimpse out to the harbor waters.

We entered a street where each house seemed more impressive than the last, overlooking Hermit Bay. I was speechless when Gary pulled the car into the large paved driveway outside a massive multi-tiered architecturally-designed house.

"Welcome home. Well, for the weekend anyway," Gary

chuckled. "Your flight is at two o'clock on Sunday afternoon, I'll drive you back to the airport about midday, okay?"

"Thanks, Gary. It's appreciated." We climbed out of the car, gathered our belongings and waved him off with a smile.

Cameron grabbed our luggage and steered me toward the house.

As we neared the door I hesitated, combed my fingers through my hair and brushed my clammy palms off on my jeans. I took a couple of deep breaths to settle my nerves as I glared up at the massive frosted glass doors looming in front of me.

"Come on, beautiful," Cameron grinned and took me gently by the hand to lead me inside.

"Don't you leave me for a second," I whispered.

"Not a chance. You'll be fine."

We walked into the ground floor of the house — actually, it was the middle floor of the three stories perched on the side of a steep hill. Stepping in to the huge foyer, bright light flooded down on me from the high ceilings above. Red timber flooring spanned the room and the walls were tastefully decorated with worldly artifacts. Cameron dropped our bags loudly on the ground and led me through into the open lounge, dining room and kitchen area. Elegant black leather and glass furniture filled the room. French doors led out onto a deck that gave way to the most spectacular uninterrupted view to the west and the Sydney skyline.

"Wow!" was all I managed to say. I didn't want to move. I wanted to seem cool, calm and collected, but I was mesmerized by the lavish home.

Cameron coaxed me along with a gentle pull. "Come on, silly."

The moment broke when I heard a scream of delight from within the kitchen. His mum — I recognized her from photos in

Cameron's room at college — rushed out from behind the doors of the butler's preparation area of the kitchen. She placed the bottle of wine in her hand down on the marble benchtop and raced over to Cameron and gave him the biggest of hugs.

"Yeah, thanks for that, Mum." His cheeks flushed. "I'd like you to meet Wiley."

"It's nice to meet you. I haven't stopped hearing about you for months. Wiley this, Wiley that." She gave me a friendly hug hello. "Happy birthday weekend." She gushed as she squeezed herself against me. "Look at you. You're gorgeous." She stroked my hair with her long red acrylic fingernails. "How was the trip? Did Scott moan about Toowoomba's airport at all?" She jabbered on, all the while looking me over from head to toe in what I hoped was a good way. "I was about to open a bottle of wine, do you want one or would you two like to freshen up first?"

Cameron looked at me and I think he could tell I was still overwhelmed. "Let's have a quick drink out on the deck and then we'll freshen up before Dad gets home. Is that okay with you?"

"Sure." I said. Yes, a drink might help me relax.

"I'm going to grab a beer, do you want one or a wine?" he asked me while wandering toward the kitchen.

"I'll have a wine thanks." I didn't want to look like a beer-swilling drunk in front of his mother.

"Cam, you grab the drinks, please. Wiley, you come on outside with me." Mrs Wilks looped her arm through mine and led the way outside.

The balcony deck was huge. It was nearly as large as the lounge room inside the house and was complete with a stainless steel gourmet barbecue and opulent outdoor furniture. Leaning against the balcony rail, the fresh harbor air felt cool against my skin. Towering above me loomed the top level of the house which I assumed to be bedrooms, while down below was more house, another outdoor area and sparkling blue pool.

"You don't need to go into the city for the fireworks, do you? You would have your own personal showing from here." I was struck by the beauty of the view, watching the sun set.

"No we don't. But we do go out on our boat for them occasionally."

Boat — didn't know they had one of those. Seeing this all around me made me realize how little I knew about Cameron's home life.

"Come on, come sit down." Mrs Wilks patted the cushion on the seat next to her.

"Okay, thank you, Mrs Wilks." I gratefully took the seat; I needed my legs to stop shaking.

"Oh gosh, please call me Margaret," she insisted and curled her feet up underneath her.

Margaret Wilks was a beautiful woman a few inches taller than me. She ruffled her fingers through her vibrant blonde hair, cut short and nymph-like; the style looked absolutely amazing on her. Her eyes were the same stunning metallic blue as Cameron's. Her face was perfectly made-up with makeup and her lips highlighted with vibrant cherry-red lipstick. Even as she lounged on the couch, dressed in casual cream linen pants, black singlet and cardigan she projected a refined elegance. "So, first and foremost," she said, "I have to say thank you."

"Thank me. For what?" I blinked.

"Since meeting you, Cameron is a changed man. He went through such a rough spot and it's good to see him happy again. We were really worried about him there for a while. Now he's a pleasure to hear from and is focused on his studies again. You are obviously a big reason behind that." She smiled. "I think I know what else is behind his continual good mood, but I don't need to know all those details." She winked at me and heat flooded into my cheeks. I'm sure they were scarlet red.

Cameron came outside and handed us our drinks. His brow furrowed when he saw my face. "Mum, what are you doing to my girl? Are you harassing her already?"

"Not at all, we were just talking," she said and took her glass of wine from him. "Cheers."

I took a long sip of my wine, licked my lips and savored the fresh, zingy taste.

"We're going to have a barbecue for dinner out here on the deck when Robert gets home." Margaret said. "He promised he wasn't going to be late since you were coming home. You remember how to cook, don't you, Cam?"

"Don't you have a cook?" I blurted out, grimacing once the words had left my mouth. I had to learn to hold my tongue when I was nervous.

Margaret's laugh chimed as she threw her head back a little. "No. We eat out most of the time. I insist it's home-cooked meals when we're here. We do have a housekeeper and a gardener though."

"Sorry. I didn't mean to—" I shuddered.

"Don't be silly, you're fine," she said before taking a sip of her wine.

Trying to redeem myself I redirected the conversation. "Cam tells me you're starting to work on your Christmas children's charity fundraiser for the hospital at Westmead — what are you going to do?"

Margaret rambled on about promotions, guests and entertainers she was planning to have at her gala charity dinner. I piped up with questions and continued to drink my wine, grateful the alcohol was starting to settle my nerves.

Cameron's eyes remained on me the whole time while I talked to his mother. The smile upon his face and the glint in his eyes reassured me I wasn't making a total idiot of myself.

"Well, that's enough of me going on about work," Margaret placed her empty glass down on the table. "I'm sure you'd like to freshen up before dinner. Cameron, why don't you take Wiley on a tour of the house first. I've put extra fresh towels down on your bed. Please let me know if you need anything else."

"I'm staying in your room? With you?" I whispered to Cameron.

"Yes. That all right?" He took my hand and we stood up.

"Everything all right?" Margaret asked.

"Wiley questioned sleeping arrangements." Cameron chuckled as he slipped around my waist.

"Make as much noise as you like," she laughed, waving her hands at us to get moving. Wow, she was the complete opposite of my mum. I loved her to pieces already.

"Come on, I'll show you around." With a nod in the direction of the house, we headed back inside.

He led me back through the house to the foyer where timber staircases with wrought-iron railings led either up or down. Tucked in behind the staircase was an office and access to the garage. A quick look upstairs revealed several large bedrooms — everything looked like it was out of a *Vogue Living* magazine.

We then wound our way down the flights of stairs to the lower ground floor to the games room, another bar, media room and a gym decked out with an assortment of exercise equipment.

"This way." Cameron walked backwards in front of me, holding my hands and leading me down the hallway that ran off the left-hand side of the games room. He stopped outside the first closed door and covered my eyes with one hand. I heard the door click open and he guided me inside. When he removed his palm, I stood before what could only be described as the ultimate bachelor pad — his bedroom. With a slight nautical theme, his room had a king-sized wooden bed, a couch, a desk and bookcase. Full-length windows and doors looked out over the sparkling blue pool. Even though he hadn't been home for weeks, the room smelt divinely of him.

"Nice." I walked around slowly checking everything out while Cameron stood in the middle of the room watching my every move.

"Do I pass?" he asked tentatively.

"With flying colors." I said while running my fingers over the suede material on the arm of the couch.

He came over to me, took me by the hand and drew me on to the lounge chair. "My mum is a bit full on, isn't she? She'll calm down now she has met you."

Maybe I will too.

"She's really nice." I added.

"How do you like your birthday weekend so far?" he asked.

"I keep pinching myself to make sure I'm not dreaming. This is beyond anything I could've ever imagined. You're the best."

"It's not over yet. I know it's not your birthday until Wednesday, but I want to give you your present now. You might want to wear it tonight when we go out. Stay here and I'll be back in a sec." He disappeared out of the room and I listened to his loud footsteps thump up the staircase and down again on his return.

He must have run at breakneck speed because he was puffing and all out of breath when he re-entered the room and sat down beside me again.

"Happy birthday, beautiful."

"Oh!" I gasped, my eyes widening at the sight of the gift bag. Not just any gift bag; a Tiffany's bag. I trembled as he placed it in my hands.

"Come on, open it." He wanted me to hurry, but I couldn't.

I peeked inside the bag to see a tiny box, tied up with the famous white satin ribbon and perfect bow. Carefully I took the box out like it was a fragile treasure and undid the bow. Opening it up I tipped the contents from the velvet blue pouch into the palm of my hand. A beautiful, round-linked, silver chain bracelet; complete with an airplane charm dangling from one of the links shone before me. "OhMyGod, it's gorgeous." I threw my arms around Cameron's neck and planted my lips against his. "Thank you so much."

His hands toyed with the back of my hair. "I'm glad you like it."

Tears swelled in my eyes. "Like it? I love it!" I settled back down next to him and he helped put the bracelet on my petite wrist.

"The airplane charm is to remember what we did this weekend," he said. "I will always fly anywhere to be with you and may we have many more adventures together."

"I'll never forget this weekend? Ever!" I sat there staring at my exquisite new gift, turning the little propellers around on the airplane charm.

"Do you want to have a shower now and get ready to go out tonight? We have to head off at about seven-thirty to go and see the band." Cameron noted the time with a glance at his wristwatch.

"Sure, but only if you come with me. I don't know my way around and don't want to get lost."

***

Once dressed we headed back upstairs to find his mum preparing salad at the kitchen bench. "Cam, your father rang, he's five minutes away. Would you go and turn on the barbecue please? Wiley, would you like to come and help me by doing the bread rolls, please?"

I perched myself on one of the stools and Margaret handed me a butter knife, bread knife and cutting board. "Oh and here, have a top up." She grabbed the wine from the fridge behind her and filled a fresh glass for me alongside hers.

"Did Cam give you your present?" Her voice was shrill with excitement.

"Yes, he did. It's gorgeous. Isn't it" I ran my fingers over the cool silver chain as I held my wrist out to show her the bracelet. "Did you come up with this idea or did Cameron?"

"I only acted as his personal shopper." She touched her hand to her heart. "He came up with the idea all by himself."

Mrs Wilks was easy to talk to; she was funny and obviously loved her wine. There she stood taking another long drink from her glass.

The front door clicked open and I froze. Before I could turn around on the bar stool, Cameron was at my side.

Here goes nothing. I hooked my lose hair in behind my ear and stood up from the stool.

Robert Wilks was a large character and very tall; a bit taller than Cameron. As he walked toward us I could see where Cameron got his good looks from. Robert was a handsome man, much better looking in real life than in the photos I'd seen. He had a head full of thick, graying hair, broad shoulders and a smile similar to Cameron's. He crossed the room in half a dozen long strides; his black leather shoes clacked against the wooden floor.

"Hey, my boy's home." He placed his laptop bag on the lounge before giving Cameron a welcoming hug.

"Dad, this is Wiley." Cameron introduced me and Robert embraced me, smothering my face against the shoulder of his plush black business suit.

Hmm, very friendly.

"Wiley, the ever-mentioned Wiley. Finally we meet. Gosh, Cam, what a stunner. You've done well, my son. Wiley, you're a little shorter than I envisaged. But height doesn't matter when you're lying down, now does it?" He winked and gestured toward Cameron. Yet again I blushed out of control. "Just joking with you kids. Needed to break the ice." He chuckled and turned to Margaret. "How about a drink, dear?" He walked around the bench and kissed her on the cheek.

Cameron certainly got his charisma from his father. Both personalities filled the room like an ever-expanding balloon. I was mesmerized in their presence. Robert's boisterous voice resonated, filling the air with his jokes and laughter. Cameron held his ground with his ever-present witty charm.

"I'll grab the steaks for cooking. Let's go outside, Wiley. Come on." Cameron gathered the food from the kitchen and off we went.

"What's with your parents and all the sexual innuendos?" I asked Cameron in a lowered voice.

"It's their poor attempt at making a joke and trying to embarrass us. Don't worry about them. They're fine with us being together. They know you mean a lot to me and are excited to finally meet you."

Margaret came out on to the deck and starting laying things out on the table for dinner.

"Would you like some help?" I offered.

"No, no, you stay here. Robert will be down in a second; he's just changing and then we will eat. Oh, and Lisa is coming around too, she'll be here in about fifteen minutes."

Robert joined us outside after showering and dressing into jeans and a polo shirt. Lisa arrived as Cameron finished cooking on the barbecue and we all sat down to eat.

"It's nice to finally met you after we've heard so much about you." Lisa, who was the splitting image of Margaret, said while she served salad onto her plate. "Took you long enough to get a new girlfriend, Cam."

I was surprised to hear Cameron had talked so much about me to his family. They made me feel welcome like they'd known me their whole life. It was so different to my place, where my judgmental mother always seemed to have her claws drawn, waiting for the moment to strike.

"Wiley's well worth the wait," Cameron replied. "Where's Peter? I thought he would have come too?" Cameron asked for the whereabouts of Lisa's husband.

"He's on the plane now, flying back from an IT security meeting he had in Melbourne. He should be home about nine o'clock."

We laughed throughout dinner, with Cameron's parents telling hilarious stories highlighting some of Cameron's misfortunes and adventures growing up. It gave me a great insight into his family and the good nature they all possessed. I'd worked myself in to a tizz over nothing.

Margaret jumped up out of her seat. "Oh, I almost forgot." She disappeared briefly inside before returning, holding something behind her back.

"Since I was out doing some shopping in the city the other day for someone," she winked at Cameron, then looked at me. "I thought I'd get you a little something for your birthday as well. So, happy birthday!" She handed me a brown gift bag and sat back down next to Robert.

"Thank you." My mouth gapped open when I examined the bag more closely. This time, the beautiful bold black type of *Louis Vuitton* blazed before me. "Oh my!" I couldn't believe it. These people hadn't met me before today, yet they were buying me Louis Vuitton!

Opening the present revealed a small, black patent-leather wallet. It was gorgeous and it smelled heavenly of fresh leather as I placed it up to my nose. I stood up and rushed around the table to give Margaret a heartfelt hug. "Thank you. This whole day has been amazing." I returned to my seat and struggled to hold back tears of happiness.

"Happy birthday," she smiled and raised her glass.

"Happy birthday," Robert added, joining in the toast with his bottle of beer.

Cameron's phone vibrated on the table and he picked it up.

"Sorry to break up this little party, but we gotta go. The taxi's arrived." Cameron drained the contents of his bear, stood up and put out his hand to help me stand. "Don't wait up for us," he said to his parents through a cheeky grin. "We'll be home late. See you in the morning."

Cameron entwined his fingers with mine and led me out the door. Yet again I was been whisked away for another exciting adventure.

***

The band was loud. Really loud. My ears were still ringing when we managed to hail down a taxi to take us home. "Thank you for the most amazing day of my life." I said as I curled into Cameron's side in the back of the car. "Should I expect any more surprises during the weekend?" If there were, I'm not sure I could handle it. I'd flown interstate, met his family, had received fabulous presents and met some of his friends tonight. Surly that was enough?

"That's it." He rested his hand on top of my thigh and drew circles with his fingertips. "Tomorrow we'll do breakfast with Mum and Dad and then we'll go down to Coogee Beach for lunch. I've no other plans."

Back at his house, it was late and his parents had already

gone to bed. Feeling tired ourselves, we freshened up and snuggled into bed. With no prying eyes from neighboring houses, I asked Cameron to leave the curtains open for a while so I could stare out over the beautiful harbor, watch the city lights twinkle on the water's surface and gaze at the sky above, blanketed with shining stars. He cuddled into me from behind, pressing his body up against mine, leaving no gap between us. The hairs on his legs tickled against the smooth skin of mine while he gently stroked his fingers up and down the length of my arm.

"It's nice not being on an air mattress," I said, enjoying the comfort of a real mattress beneath me.

"Yeah, but this one doesn't get that nice rocking motion, does it?" He started rolling around, trying to make the bed sway.

"I'll take this over an air mattress any day." I nudged his ribs to stop.

Curling his hand around my waist, Cameron started kissing his way up my arm and across my shoulder.

"I don't want this to end," I whispered.

"What to end?" He nuzzled into my neck. I'm sure he secretly enjoyed seeing me covered in goose bumps when his breath wisped across my skin.

"This weekend away with you. Today's been the best day of my life. How can I ever return to normality after this?"

"I'm glad you've had a great time, but it's not over yet. There *is* one more activity on today's agenda. Especially when you look this inviting lying in my bed." I smiled as his arousal nudged at me from behind. I rolled toward him as his breath and kisses on my neck intensified. Slipping my hands around his neck and entangling my fingers into his hair, I drew his face to mine. Our bodies connected. His legs against mine. His chest against mine. His lips against mine. Our hands gliding over each other's skin, taking in every inch of each other's bodies. A soft groan murmured in the depths of his throat. "I love you, Wiley."

Warmth spidered through my veins. Pajamas were quickly discarded, I rolled over on top of Cameron and straddled his hips. Taking hold of his erection, such smooth skin over firm hard muscle, and gently eased him inside me.

Making love to him while looking out over the spectacular Sydney skyline was something I'll never forget.

Chapter 21

Waking up and looking out over the harbor waters was breathtaking. Cameron's arm was draped over my waist, the sheet knotted around our legs and the rest of the bed was in total disarray. Snuggling in closer to Cameron, delirious contentment filled me.

It was eight o'clock when I snuck out from beneath Cameron's clutches, dressed and headed upstairs. No one was up so I grabbed a drink of water. When I walked around the kitchen bench, I noticed a pile of documents sitting on the end. I turned them around to take a peak. It was a detailed proposal for Wilks Resources to acquire a small mine in Mongolia. I eyed it with interest, scanning over the figures — the profit and loss statement, assets, expenses and sales forecasts; the numbers were absolutely mind-blowing. But something caught my eye. I flicked from the summary page to the detailed report, adding up the figures in my head.

"Morning." I jumped out of my skin, flicked the proposal shut, catching my hand in between the pages as Cameron's dad walked toward the kitchen.

"Sorry, I didn't mean to pry." Guilt knotted in my belly for snooping into the confidential documentation.

"It's okay. What did you think of the proposal?" He jutted his chin at the papers before me.

Mr. Wilks wanted my opinion? I quickly tried to form some kind of reply within my head. Had I been wrong at quickly calculating the figures? I didn't want to look a fool, but what I'd seen got the better of me. "Have you read this yet, Mr Wilks?"

"Briefly. I've looked at the summary. Why?"

"Um…" I grabbed the document and flicked open the pages I reviewed before. "I think there is an error in the P&L. They don't match the detailed reports." He came toward me and looked over my shoulder as I pointed out the mismatched figures. "If the detail is correct, then this Mongolian mine is running at a loss, not a profit."

"And you picked that up by quickly glancing at it?" He raised a questioning eyebrow at me.

"I'm good at math." I shrugged, without thinking much of it.

"I'm impressed. No one in the office noticed that. I better have them review this more closely. Thank you, Wiley."

"Thank Wiley for what?" Cameron rubbed his eyes as he crossed the floor.

"She noticed a massive error in this proposal. Saved me a lot of time, hard work and potentially money."

Cameron smiled, making me feel extra special when he wrapped his arms around me and kissed me.

Margaret came in through the front door after exercising. Well, I think she'd been exercising. Her cheeks were flushed but otherwise she looked amazing. Dressed in casual exercise clothes, her hair was perfect, red lipstick colored her lips but she wasn't out of breath and there was no perspiration in sight.

She darted around us and grabbed a bottle of chilled water from the fridge.

She insisted on making us breakfast, refusing our offer to help. Within thirty minutes it was ready; an assortment of fruit, croissants, bread, jams and juice lay spread across the kitchen counter. The smell of bacon and eggs wafted from the stove, making my mouth water in anticipation of having the hot food warm my belly. I looked at all the delicious options and didn't know where to start. Was it rude to take a bit of everything?

"Did you have a good night?" Margaret asked, loading the toaster with bread.

"Yeah, it was great." I said. "I'm finally coming back to the ground after yesterday."

Robert returned to the kitchen after fetching the morning paper from the front door. "I'm starving. Let's eat!" He made his way around the bench to help Margaret serve up the cooked breakfast she'd finished preparing.

"This certainly beats dining hall food," I eyeballed the feast before me.

"Absolutely," Cameron agreed as he handed me a plate. "Wiley, you want coffee or a juice?"

"Coffee, thanks." Cameron made his way over to the fancy stainless steel coffee machine and pressed a button; it ground the coffee beans, frothed the milk and filled a cup he held under the nozzle.

"What are you two up to today?" Robert asked as we all sat down with our food at the table.

"I thought I'd take Wiley down to Coogee for lunch." Cameron said, cutting into a strip of his bacon.

"Excellent. Margaret and I will be at the rugby this afternoon and go to the clubhouse for dinner. We'll be out from about midday and won't be home until late," Robert said then bit into his toast.

Margaret dabbed her mouth with her napkin. "Wiley, I forgot to ask you yesterday, how are you after your scary incident of being drugged at the dance? You must have been terrified."

What? Cameron had told them about that. Oh, I wanted to crawl under the mat on the floor and hide. I wanted to put the whole mess behind me. How much longer was it going to hang over my head?

"Yes it was scary. Someone's stupid prank went horribly wrong and I'm lucky to be okay. When you go through something like that, it certainly puts things in perspective and you realize what's important." That was the first time I'd said that, and I was struck by the truth in my words. Since the ordeal, I'd learned to reset my priorities around study and find balance with my relationship with Cameron. I winked at him when he looked up at me. Yes, he was definitely worth fighting for. "I was concerned for Cameron knowing what he'd been through with Gilly."

"Yeah, two girlfriends dead from drugs might start giving me some kind of complex." Cameron tried to make light of it but I could see pain reflect in his eyes. Even his parents' gazes turned solemn for the briefest of moments.

"Well…now…on a lighter note, you've only got two more months of uni, what are you two planning to do?" Robert said, waving his fork at us both.

His line of questioning hit me in the chest like a ton of bricks. I'm not convinced this was a better topic to discuss. My internship loomed ahead of me and Cameron and I hadn't talked about being together after uni. Maybe I had been avoiding it. I couldn't bear the thought of breaking up with him. The end of university was only nine weeks away and we lived in two different cities — one thousand miles apart.

"I hopefully have an internship at Huntersville." I stuttered.

"They'll look after you there; I hear they're a great company to work for." Robert nodded. "What about you, Cam? Have you decided what to do with yourself now the end is in the not too distant future?"

Cameron fumbled around with his croissant, shredding it into tiny pieces upon his plate. "Not yet. I need to get over next term and then I'll worry about it."

Margaret finished a piece of fruit salad. "You're right, Cam. Focus on your study for now, then everything else will fall in to place."

All past conversations with people over life beyond university never bothered me before; they were all blasé. But now reality was looming. It was confronting and scary, I had to cross my ankles underneath the table to stop my legs from jittering. Jobs, careers and officially moving out of home were items appearing on my To Do list and were needing to be addressed. Life decisions had to be made. My hand shook as I reached for my cup and sculled the remains of my coffee. My temples started to ache from all the mounting pressure.

The thought of losing Cameron was unbearable. I didn't want us to end. I wiggled about on the chair, unsettled by questions about our future. I didn't want to deal with them now. I didn't want to have my magnificent weekend away ruined.

We continued to eat in silence. I was thankful when the daunting topic wasn't discussed any further. After everyone finished eating breakfast, I helped Cameron clean up, washed the dishes and gathered our things together, ready to venture out for the day.

"Which car are you guys taking to the rugby?" Cameron asked his dad.

"Probably the Landcruiser. You can take whichever one you like for a drive. But remember, your life depends on bringing it back in one piece," Robert warned Cameron, but a sparkle glimmered in his eye when he winked. "The keys are on the hook in the office."

I didn't think anything of the conversation until Cameron led me into the four-car garage. I stopped in my tracks when I took note of the two vehicles beside the gold-colored Toyota Landcruiser. One sleek canary-yellow Maserati and one charcoal-colored Aston Martin. They looked like purring lions waiting to be unleashed from within their cages. A thrill ran through my veins at the sight of the magnificent machines. I was not by any means a car fanatic, but these two were beyond sleek. I'd watched enough James Bond to love the Aston, and the Maserati was just freaking sexy. Sheer elegance and class oozed off every curvaceous inch.

"Which one do you want to go for a drive in?" Cameron asked.

"Um...the Maserati! I thought you said the surprises were over. This birthday keeps getting better and better. Now I get to go for a drive in one of these!" A grin stretched across my face from ear to ear. "This is insane." I called out to him when he ducked into the office to grab the keys.

"Come on, let's go." He opened the car door for me like a true gentleman and waved at me to hop in.

I melted into the soft leather seats while Cameron ran around to the driver's side and slid in next to me. He started the engine and it purred. The vibrations shuddered through my body, thrilling me to the very core. The dash lit up with hundreds of buttons and display panels, making my eyes pop further out of my head. Cameron pumped his foot several times on the accelerator and revved the engine loudly. He put the car into gear, dropped the clutch and sped out of the garage, pinning me back against the seat. I squealed and clung on for dear life when he turned the corner and the tires squealed on the road.

The turquoise blue ocean water glistened with the sun's rays dancing on the surface. Coogee had certainly changed in the years since I had visited here on holidays as a kid. Modern apartment complexes lined the streets, the beachfront park was lush and green, while trendy coffee shops and restaurants ran up along the main streets.

Cameron parked at the southern end of the beach and we slid out of the car. While he was dressed smartly in cargo shorts and a black striped polo shirt, I felt grungy wearing jeans rolled up to three-quarter length and a plain white t-shirt. With no indication on what to pack from Cameron, my clothing options were limited. A weekend at the beach had never entered my mind.

With our shoes hooked over our fingertips, we headed north along the beach away from the rock pools. The sand was warm beneath my feet in the midday sun and tickled in between my toes. The sea breeze against my face felt glorious compared to the cold mountain air we experienced in Toowoomba.

Holding hands, Cameron and I strolled along the water's edge. I was rambling on about the Maserati but stopped when I noticed Cameron's mood had mellowed.

"What's wrong?" I pulled him closer to me.

"Do you want to have *the talk* since my parents brought it up this morning?" His brow furrowed above his sunglasses. "I mean about us and life after uni."

I gulped hard and my throat tightened.

"You look nervous. Why?" he asked, steering me up the sandy beach away from the water and sat down facing each other.

"I'm dreading a bad outcome to this conversation." I played with his hands resting in mine.

"Well, I hope it's not." Cameron said. "One thing's for certain is I don't want to lose you, Wiley. I may be crazy, but I know I love you and want to be with you."

Color still rose in my cheeks every time Cameron said those words to me. He inhaled deeply and looked out to the waves crashing on to the shore. "So, what do you think about living together? With your internship, I'm more than happy to move to Brisbane. Or do you want to delay working for a while and travel overseas? Maybe take some time out? What's going on in that smart little head of yours?"

He bombarded me with so many questions all at once, I shook my head, not sure if I heard him correctly. "Whoa. Whoa. What did you say?"

"Don't you want to be with me after uni?" His hand went limp in mine.

"Of course I do." I entwined my fingers around his for reassurance. "I'd do anything to be with you. You asked too many questions at once. Have you thought this through? Do you really want to live with me?"

"Yes. I know we're young and it's a huge step, but I don't care. I want to be with you and only you. I'm twenty-two in December, I'm in love with you and want to start living my life with you. It's all I can think of as the next logical step. So what do you say? Will you live with me?" He looked at me, searching my face for an answer.

My heart thundered like a Boeing 747 taking off. I lunged for Cameron, hooked my arms around his neck and planted my lips against his. "Of course I will. Yes. Yes. Yes."

"I know there's heaps of stuff to work out, but we have months to plan everything," Cameron hugged me tightly. "I can't wait. This is going to me awesome."

I continued to smother him with kisses all over his face.

"That wasn't too hard now, was it?" Cameron chuckled, his bright mood had returned. "Can you believe we're going to move in together? That's so cool! And hot!" Cameron rested his forehead against mine. "I want you so bad right now. Why did we have this conversation in a public place? That wasn't smart, now was it?"

"You're the one who brought up the topic," I tilted my head and kissed him again on the lips.

A crazy idea formed in my head. "I wonder if I can request a change in location for my internship. Huntersville are a huge national company, maybe I could be placed down here in Sydney. I've never contemplated moving before, but I would to be with you. There's more opportunity for you here rather than in Brisbane, even if you don't work for your dad. So ... how about it ... would you like me to move to Sydney instead?"

Cameron beamed. "You'd do that? For me? I will happily come to Brisbane, but down here would be awesome."

"This is so exciting. We're going to have to find somewhere to live." I was suddenly wishing for the next few months to pass quickly. The thought of having my own place and living with Cameron was mind-blowing.

"I know you probably won't have a bar of it, but I can afford a place. So don't worry about that."

"You know I don't want to be a kept woman or a leech. We won't be able to afford living in a penthouse on my internship salary, but everything is even when it comes to expenses, okay?"

"You're going to be my partner, Wiley. What's mine is yours and yours is mine." He bit his lower lip, trying to hide his grin after the words left his mouth.

"That sounds so freaky doesn't it? *Partner.*" I gushed. "Will you want me to sign something like a pre-nup ... living arrangement ... agreement of some kind, before we move in together? Does such a thing exist?" I laughed. "So you can protect your interests and whatever money and assets you might have. I want your family to feel comfortable about us being together."

"I hadn't really thought about that, but I suppose we'll have to sort out something. I'm confident you're not the vindictive or ruthless type."

I turned my gaze down to the sand and drew wiggles with my fingertips. "Cam, do you still not want to work for your dad?"

"The opportunity is there if I want it. My feet have only retouched the planet after a very long time. I'm taking it slowly to work out what it is I want to do. The only thing I am certain of is you."

"Well, let's hope my internship can be transferred to Sydney and everything falls into place." I linked my hands behind his neck and kissed him, then pushed him down on to the sand. I straddled his waist and continued with feverish kisses across his jawline, down his neck and back up to his hot, delicious mouth.

Cameron moaned softly under my touch. "As I said before, this is not a good place to have this conversation. You're going to end up in trouble soon if you keep on kissing me like this. Come on, let's go get some lunch, then I'll take you home to celebrate. My oldies will be gone soon, so we can tear up the house a little." His suggestive smile had my inner core clenching with anticipation.

"How about we get takeaway or skip lunch all together?" I whispered into his ear.

"You're bad." He playfully smacked me on the bottom. "But seriously, I'm hungry. I didn't eat much at breakfast."

Reluctantly I dragged myself off Cameron and stopped with our rather public display of affection. We stood up, brushed the sand off and headed up across the beach. Both of us unable to wipe the grins off our faces as we walked hand in hand.

***

Waking up in Sydney again was just as amazing as the day before. The thought of having to go back to Toowoomba and the reality of campus life was making it hard to get out of bed.

Breakfast was not as elaborate as the day before with Cameron and I opting for vegemite toast and coffee. His parents staggered down the stairs while we were standing in the kitchen making our cappuccinos. With heavy eyes, messed-up hair and sleepy looks on their face, they looked a little worse for wear after a late night out celebrating their team winning the rugby.

Morning greetings were said by all and Cameron made his parents coffee before we all sat down around the table.

"What did you two get up to yesterday, anything interesting?" his mum asked, wrapping her hands around the warm cup.

"We went to Coogee for lunch then came home." Cameron looked at me with the broadest of grins upon his face.

His mum caught our glances.

"What's up with you two this morning? Is there something I should know?" Her eyes narrowed, darting back and forth between us. "Cam, what's going on?"

She certainly was intuitive. I struggled to swallow the dry piece of toast in my mouth; it scrapped all the way down my oesophagus. Was Cameron going to tell his parents about us now?

Cameron leaned forward and rested his folded arms on the table. "We got chatting down at the beach yesterday about life after uni. We know we want to be together, so we've decided to live together." He held up a hand, splaying his palm forward to hold off his parent's protests. "There's a lot to sort out, but we'll work it out."

I froze, unable to move, watching his parents' reaction. Silence hung in the air as they took long sips on their coffee and looked at us. I wriggled on my seat growing more and more anxious by the second.

Cameron cleared his throat. "Mum, look at us. I'm in love with Wiley. She's the best thing that has happened to me and we want to be together."

"Cam, it's only been a year since Gilly died." Margaret ran her fingertip across her perfectly manicured eyebrow. "Only yesterday you hadn't discussed anything, now you want to live together. This is a big decision not to be taken lightly."

"We know that." Cameron sat back in his chair. "I can honestly say I never felt like this with Gilly. Wiley has changed my life for the better. Can't you see that?"

"Yes … Yes, I can." A smile touched the corner of Margaret's mouth as she raised her cup to her lips.

"We know it's a big step, but it's what we want. I've never been so sure about anything before." Cameron reiterated.

Robert rubbed the back of his neck, he'd been quiet all morning and looked like he was fighting off a sore head from drinking too much last night.

"Yes, I can see that." Robert mumbled. With a sparkle in his eye, he winked at me.

"We don't know whether we will be in Brisbane or Sydney yet, my internship will be the deciding factor." I added cautiously.

They nodded, accepting our decision.

"It sounds exciting." Margaret smiled. "We're happy for you."

I drew my shoulders back. This was not the reaction I was expecting from his parents. They were civil, calm and collected. Wait until we have to tell my parents. I was not looking forward to that. We'd have to go in wearing battle armor and holding up defense shields. Maybe if I drop subtle hints to them over the coming months it will soften the blow when the time comes.

The morning flew by filled with conversation. It wasn't long before his mum and dad hugged us goodbye and Cameron and I headed back to university.

The jet flew us back to Toowoomba; it was still a spin-out for me. We arrived in time for dinner. After my amazing weekend, I didn't think I could stomach dining hall food. As Cameron and I strolled into the hall, everyone was already sitting at tables eating. We headed straight for the serving area to grab our meals.

Over the past few hours, barely a second had gone by without Cameron and I connected somehow. Whether it was holding hands, cuddling, kissing or leaning in to touch each other. The world didn't seem right when we were apart. It now seemed daunting to separate from him to eat a meal because our tables were near full and there were no seats together. Plus I was bursting to tell the girls all the details from my weekend away.

"I suppose there's no chance of you toning down what we did on the weekend, is there?" he asked, looking at me through his long eyelashes.

"None whatsoever!" I beamed. "And remember, everyone will know what we did by the morning. News in this place travels fast."

His cheeks flushed and I turned away to go and sit down with the girls.

Kel sat on the edge of her seat. Ashleigh strummed her fingers on the table. Even Megan was wide-eyed with curiosity. Their eyes followed my every move, like a pack of wolves homing in on its kill, ready to pounce at any moment. I had texted Kel with a simple message on Friday night, simply saying:

You won't believe where Cam has taken me
— fill you in on Sunday. XOXOXO

I placed my food on the table and settled into the chair.

I took a deep breath while glancing at each one of them. Do I start telling them about the flight, my present or about living together. Oh what the hell, best get on with it. "Guess what Cam and I did this weekend?"

Chapter 22

I didn't want to open my eyes as I lay next to Cameron in his room, listening to the rain teeming down on the tin roof, splattering against the window outside. There was a chill in the air so I pulled the blankets up tightly under my chin, feeling unmotivated to get out of bed. Then I remembered it was my birthday. I was twenty-one! My eyes shot open and there, gleaming down at me, lying propped up on his elbow, was Cameron.

"Happy birthday to you, happy birthday to you, happy birthday dear Wiley, happy birthday to you." His deep voice was like angels singing in my ears. "Morning, beautiful."

Waking up next to his body was the best birthday present a girl could ever ask for. He was my addictive drug I couldn't get enough of. I could spend my days kissing him, touching him, being with him. My constant distraction. My skin starting to heat under his touch and my eyes narrowed with intent as I slipped my leg over his hip.

The wind howled outside and the window of the room

shuddered with its force.

"What horrible weather," I moaned.

"We could stay in here all day if you like." His hand crept underneath the sheets and drew me in closer toward his chest. I giggled when he tickled me, sliding his hand up under his old t-shirt I was wearing for pajamas and gently cupped my breast. His kisses brushed my face while he nudged his groin into mine.

But reality hit.

"I wish I could stay here all day but I have to finish off my assignment before holidays this Friday. I'll work on it this morning, go to my lectures and then be finished for the day at about three o'clock this afternoon."

"Are you still going out to dinner with the girls?"

"No, we cancelled it. Everyone's got too much on."

"But it's your birthday, we have to do something." He kissed my forehead, then my cheek, my nose, my eyes and my chin. He tweaked at my aroused nipple and fondled my breast. I was losing concentration and forgot what we were talking about as I wrapped my arms around him and pressed my lips to his. A rumble in his throat made my body hum. I was so easily distracted!

My mobile phone rang. I collapsed back against the pillow. *No! Not now.*

Cameron swore, reached over to grab the phone off his desk and showed me the caller ID. I would've been happy to let it ring out, but it was my parents.

He answered the phone and put it on speaker. "Good morning," he chirped.

I panicked and tried to grab the phone off him. My mother was not happy we were still together and my parents didn't need to know we spent *every* night in the same room. Cameron answering my phone at this early hour wouldn't go down well.

"Hi, Mum. How are you? Why are you calling so early —

it's not even seven o'clock?"

"Hello, princess. Happy birthday." Dad said and cleared his throat. "We wanted to call you before we head off to work. You probably have a full day and we had to wish you well."

"Happy birthday, dear." My mum joined in. "Is that Cameron with you? Where are you?"

"Cam came over to get me for breakfast." I winced. I was absolutely no good at lying to my parents, but there were certain elements of residential college life they didn't have to know about.

"Bullshit!" My dad coughed into the phone. Cameron chuckled next to me.

"Dad!" I gasped.

"Come on, princess, even you have to admit that was pretty lame. You even sound like you're still in bed."

"I don't know what you are talking about." My attempt at innocence was far from convincing. I bit down on my hooked index finger to prevent myself from giggling.

"Morning Cameron," my dad said.

"Hi John. Hi Victoria."

I could hear my mother suck in a deep breath. She still disapproved of Cameron for some unknown reason. "Well, dear, we hope you have a great day. I can't believe you're twenty-one. My baby's all grown up." Her voice shook like she was on the verge of tears and she sniffled loudly. "We'll see you at home on Saturday. Dinner's all planned. I know Kelly is coming, is ... Cameron?" She stumbled on his name.

I rolled my eyes, glad she could not see me. "Yes, he is. See you on Saturday."

Shortly after the call with my parents, my brother Chris called with well-wishes too. The phone calls with my family had killed the mood for getting it on with Cameron, so now it was best to get up and face the day. I'd have to pick up where we left off later in the day.

It was a freezing, drizzly day for mid-September and I spent most of the day entrenched in my assignment, pounding away at my laptop. At lunchtime my friends bound into my room with presents, cake and cheap champagne to celebrate. We ate, drank and I loved been spoilt with gifts. Evening fell, dinner passed and the rain hadn't stopped. Back in my room it was getting late. I was tired from traipsing through my endless assignment, I still hadn't finished it, it was taking so much longer than I thought. I rubbed my sore eyes, sitting in front of the laptop screen for most of the day was not healthy. My hands ached from typing hundreds of words and my head throbbed from information overload. It was time to call it a day.

As I turned off my laptop, Cameron knocked on my door. I loved it how we were so in tune.

"Hey, beautiful." He shut the door behind him, shrugged off his coat and dropped it on the floor. "You finished work yet?"

"I have now." I flipped the screen shut and closed my books. "I've nearly finished this damn assignment, it's taking forever."

Cameron flicked my bedroom light off, walked over and drew the curtains closed, pulled back the bed covers, removed his shirt and crawled on to the mattress.

"Have you had a good birthday?' he asked while he made himself comfortable.

"The best!" I said while kicking off my UGG boots.

"I feel bad I didn't take you out somewhere nice today."

I shook my head. "Don't. I've had too much work on. You took me to Sydney, that was more than enough."

I flicked off my desk light, walked over to the bed and straddled his hips. Our fingers entwined and I pressed my lips against his. Even just the smell of him made all the worries over my pending assignment disappear. I didn't understand the powerful connection we seemed to have together, it truly was unique. The tingling of my skin every time we touched, the dizziness in my head every time we kissed, the racing of my heart every time he walked in the room. If this was love, it was better than heaven and I knew nothing and no one would ever compare.

I ran my hands over his chest and across his broad shoulders, down the firm plain of his chest to his stomach and hips. My Tiffany bracelet swung on my wrist and shimmered in the dim light. He flinched when the cool charm brushed against his skin. His whole body felt warm and tantalizing beneath my fingertips and he smelt so deliciously fresh after his shower. He intoxicated my senses and my hunger for him ignited.

While Cameron's mouth was very delicious, tonight the rest of him looked more enticing and needed to be explored with my lips. Hovered over him, I slowly made my way down his neck with a trail of kisses, lingering and nuzzling into the small of his neck, sending goose bumps down his arm. Licking and nipping at his skin, I meandered across the line of his collarbone toward his chest. I glanced up at Cameron, his head sunk deep within my pillows. His eyes were closed and a smile was evident on his mouth. Seeing pleasure written across his face made me feel mischievousness and adventurous.

I shuffled further down the bed, pressing my lips against his searing skin, blowing softly and nipping at his flesh. His muscles contracted beneath my fingertips when I glided them across his stomach. I devilishly grinned when I slipped my hand under the waistband of his boxer shorts, eased them off of his legs so I had all of him exposed, ready for me to explore.

Nestling between his legs, I took hold of his shaft and rubbed my hand up and down the length of him and stroked the sensitive head. I inched forward and ran my tongue up along the vein that led from the base to the top and swirled round the tip. His breath hissed between his teeth when I drew him into my mouth.

"Wiley," he whispered and tangled his hand through my hair.

I loved driving my man wild. Licking and tasting and sucking at the salty taste of him was making Cameron pulse his hips. He clawed at the bedsheets, his thighs tensed, his stomach flexed and his jaw strained as I picked up the rhythm.

This certainly was turning out to be the best birthday ever, especially when I knew once he came he would return the favor.

Chapter 23

Following Friday night at The Club to celebrate the last day of term, everyone left campus on Saturday morning for the two week mid-semester break. Cameron in his Hilux, Kel in her Hyundai and me in my Mazda headed off, down the range in convoy and raced toward Brisbane. Kel was going home to her place for the afternoon and would meet us for dinner at the restaurant later in evening.

The one and half hour trip sailed by; Cameron and I pulled into my parents' driveway just before lunch. I hopped out of the car and glanced around the garden, taking in all the vivid spring color. Petunias blossomed in terracotta pots, azaleas flourished along the footpath and new growth burst on every bush. It caught me off guard knowing this place wouldn't be my home for much longer. My wings had grown so much in the past nine months. I was ready to leave the nest.

Much to my relief, my mother was polite to Cameron, but she still kept her distance. I often caught her looking down her nose or shaking her head in our direction when she thought I wasn't looking. Cameron was going to be a part of my life for the foreseeable future and I didn't want any animosity between them. Cameron was fine, it was my mother who couldn't let go of her ill-informed first impression.

Cameron and I spent the afternoon lazing about before getting ready to go to the Stamford Hotel for dinner. I fanned my face when Cameron walked into my room dressed up in a dark gray suit with a black button-up shirt. He lay down on my bed and flicked through a magazine while I continued to get ready. I didn't know what to wear but managed to finally settle on a short red halter-necked dress with embroidered flowers across the hem, a little black cardigan to keep off the chilly night air and a pair of black satin stiletto pumps. My Tiffany bracelet from Cameron never left my wrist.

"Nice." Cameron nodded, looking me up and down with approval.

"Come on, let's get going." I grabbed his hand, led him upstairs to join my parents and headed out.

At the hotel Kel was already waiting for us.

"Love the dress." I hugged her hello like it had been years since we'd seen each other.

"Thanks, I brought it this afternoon when Mum and I went shopping." She twirled around, showing off her new green floral dress.

"Come on you lot, the table is ready," Dad said and shuffled us all into the restaurant.

We had scored a table on the edge of the bistro, looking out over the Brisbane River where boats and City-Cat ferries kept on sailing by. The strands of fairy lights, wrapped around the pillars in the restaurant and across the ceiling, twinkled brightly and looked like stars in the night sky. Cameron and I sat across from my parents and Kel sat next to me on the end of the table. We quickly ordered drinks and food because Dad was overly hungry.

"Kelly, are you getting excited about finishing uni in eight weeks?" Mum asked her as the waiter poured our champagne.

"Absolutely. Has Wiley told you I'm going to travel at the end of the year and take twelve months off before starting work? I've been trying to convince Wiley and Cameron to come but they have other plans."

"So what are you going to do with yourself, Cameron?" she asked. "What's in store for you?" Although her tone was off, at least she was making an effort to include him in the conversation.

"Yeah, like Kel, I'm looking forward to finishing, but still undecided about what to do." Cameron replied, turned to me and gave me one of his drop-dead gorgeous smiles and squeezed my hand under the table. "I'm just looking forward to the future."

"And moving in together," Kel blurted.

"Excuse me?" My mother choked on a mouthful of champagne.

"Oh shit!" Kel touched her fingers to her lips. "Hasn't Wiley told you yet? Oh hell! Sorry Wiley!" She cringed and looked at me with sorrow written all over her face.

"No you're not!" Mum glared at me across the table, her eyes bulging in their sockets. "Are you?"

"Well, yeah, Cameron and I have talked about it and we want to move in with each other." I shrugged, trying not to make it sound like a big deal.

Mum and Dad glared at us. You'd think the world was about to end.

"But you're only twenty-one." My dad's voice shook. "Aren't you too young to move in together? You've only known each other for a few months."

"They basically live together anyway. They never spend a

night apart," Kel piped up again.

"Kel, you're not helping." I said through gritted teeth and gave her a kick under the table. "Mum, Dad, did you expect me to live at home forever?"

"Well. No. Maybe for a little while longer. We thought you would move into an apartment with a couple of girlfriends, not your boyfriend!" Mum jutted her chin toward Cameron. I closed my eyes and shuddered.

My parents would love me to stay at home after university. But I'd grown up so much over the past few years and now had a serious boyfriend. I'd found my feet and my future career was yet to unfold. Finding Cameron was an added bonus. I didn't want to disappoint them in any way, but I knew Cameron and I were meant to be together. Why couldn't I have it all?

"I can make my own decisions now. Cam and I have known each other for the whole year and we love each other. We know we have a lot to sort out and are not racing into this decision lightly." I said, managing to keep my voice steady, but their faces only burned with more fire. "You were together from this age and have been together forever. Why can't it work for us?" I laid the guilt trip on them, packing it on thick and tight.

"I don't approve." Mum said through tightly drawn lips. "Things have changed since we were young." She glanced around at the other patrons, making sure she wasn't causing a scene. Why did she have to make me feel so bad about something that felt so perfectly right? Why was my mother being such a bitch? My heart ached and Cameron gripped my hand harder underneath the table.

"Mrs Cayton, Wiley is right. I love her and care for her more than anything. She has changed my life for the better." Cameron's kind words didn't put them at ease.

"You are not moving in with my daughter. You should get some life experience behind you before getting so serious and settling down?"

"Mum, how many guys do you want me to sleep with before I settle down?" I bit the inside of my cheek, trying not to laugh. I had to say something humorous to lighten the somber mood. My mother's eyes flashed with horror. Cameron and Kel were trying not to laugh, even Dad had a chuckle. "We've talked about it and... I'm going to try to get my internship moved to Sydney."

Dad jolted back in his seat. Seeing disappointment wash over his face cut me to the bone.

"Sydney? Really?" he sighed.

"There's more potential there for Cameron to find work." Dad looked down and stared at his glass, the look on his face made me feel terrible. His little girl was moving away, out into the big wide world. But what else could I do? This was the right move for me, I could no longer live under their wing.

"Wiley is the one being grounded about everything." Cameron said. "I can look after her financially, but she won't let me. She wants to ensure she has a job, an affordable place and everything remains even. She certainly doesn't want to take advantage of ... my situation."

Mum sculled the rest of her champagne and instantly poured another.

Our conversation was interrupted momentarily when our meals came out.

"Cameron, it's not about money. I think Wiley can do better than you and find someone who doesn't misguide and lead her astray all the time."

"Mum!" I gasped, horrified at her outburst.

"It's all right, Wiley." Cameron eyes glassed over, clearly affected by my mother's rude remarks. "Mrs Cayton, I'm not sure whether Wiley has told you my full story or not, but I could not imagine finding anyone better than her. I'm sorry

Wiley didn't meet your high expectations last semester and her grades were effected. But I will be forever grateful she helped me through a very difficult time in my life following the death of a friend who died from a drug overdose. But we found the right path together and this semester she is blitzing everything again. You should be proud of her. We've become best of friends and she will always be my rock."

He was going to have to pick me up off the floor if he kept talking like that. My insides had melted like honey drizzled over hot toast.

"I hope, for your sake, it's true," my mother replied after finishing off another glass of champagne. She slumped her shoulders and sighed heavily. Was she resigning to the fact she wasn't going to win this battle. Not tonight. Not ever.

"At least she's not pregnant!" Kel chipped in.

"Cheers to that one." Dad raised his glass. "You're not, are you, Wiley?" He asked, glaring at Cameron in the process.

"No Dad, I'm not pregnant," I smiled, relieved to see normal coloring return to my parents' faces.

"Oh thank God," he sighed and took a long drink.

The worry of breaking the news to my parents was over. *Thanks, Kel!* They'd have a few months to get used to the idea before I moved in with Cameron. As I sipped on my champagne and let the bubbles tickle my nose, I tried to ignore the uneasy feeling still lurking around in the pit of my stomach. Why was it still there? Was it the stress of final exams in six weeks? Maybe the reality of moving in with Cameron was taking a hold. Maybe it was the fear of the unknown. I was on edge about something, I just didn't know what is was. Only time would tell.

Chapter 24

Holidays came to an end and my last six weeks of university was about to commence. I was busting to get out of the door after lunch to make the trip back to Toowoomba, but Mum and Dad didn't let me go without an excessive number of hugs, kisses and well-wishes. I finally escaped, leaving my mother crying and Dad warding off his own tears. I jumped in my car and took a deep breath. The next time I saw my parents, my studies would be complete and my university days would be over. How exciting! I started the engine and took off.

The next few weeks would be harrowing. I had my interview with my scholarship sponsor in two weeks, exams started in four weeks, freedom was in six weeks. What a rush it was going to be!

As I rounded the bend at the top of the Toowoomba range, I put down my window and inhaled the fresh air into the depths of my lungs. This all too familiar red soil haven wouldn't be my home for much longer.

Steele Rudd College was bustling when I arrived, students

were unloading their gear out of their cars and saying goodbye to parents. My heartbeat soured when Cameron bounded toward me from his room the second I arrived.

I jumped out of the car and his arms were instantly around me, his lips found their all too familiar place against mine. He nudged me backwards, until I was leaning against the side of my car. I could feel from the hardness in his jeans he was very glad to see me. I loved having that effect on him; the way he was instantly aroused had the reciprocal effect.

Jennifer's parents, who were sitting in her room right beside my car, got an eyeful as Cameron continued to kiss me, making up for the weeks we'd been apart. Their eyes widened and eyebrows raised when I gave them a cheeky wave.

I turned my attention back to Cameron. "I'm glad you're here early for once, now you can help me unload all my gear."

"So you *are* after me just for my body and brute strength?" He brushed his fingertips down the side of my face and kissed me once before helping me with my belongings. "Have your parents started coming around to the idea of us living together yet or does your mum still hate my guts?" he asked while dragging out my suitcase from the boot of my car.

"You could say that. They think we're too young to live together and think I'm throwing my life away. Yours?"

"I've been surprised at how well they took it, actually. They've been great. Mum is genuinely excited and is keen to help us set up house."

"Why didn't you go to the rugby grand final with your dad today," I asked, carrying another load into my room.

"Dad took friends and clients, I only had a chance of going if someone cancelled." Cameron placed the last of my things on the floor in my room. "There will always be other football games to go to but I won't get another chance at the first day back on campus again. So here I am."

I smiled, clutched the front of his shirt and drew his lips to mine. "We better make the most of it then."

***

Classes started the following day and I was instantly overloaded with final projects, assignments and study. My dreaded exams loomed ahead. While all this was going on, Cameron started to apply for jobs in Brisbane and Sydney. The employment market was tough due to the recent downturn in the economy and everyone in their final year was finding it difficult to find work or even get a bite. I was so grateful to have a job lined up; it was one less item to worry about.

The days grew longer and warmer as the year approached summer again. Long sunny days with crystal clear blue skies begged me to go out and enjoy them but I had to stay focused on my studies and remain in front of the books. Cameron was often by my side and he made the study breaks rewarding and well worth the effort. Before I knew it, the day Cameron, Kel, Matt and I handed in our last assignment arrived and was cause for much celebration. Tired, relieved and thrilled, I headed to The Club with them to have a drink.

"No more assignments," squealed Kel as she waved her arms up in the air.

"They're done!" I cheered and hugged her.

"Here's to that, my sweet!" Matt raised his glass to Kel.

Kel glowed when Matt gave her a kiss on the cheek. Her cheeks blushed, unable to hide how besotted she was. He made her happy and I couldn't have asked for anything more for my best friend.

"Can I still not convince you to come overseas with us? Both of you can afford it. Can't I twist your arm any further? Kel pleaded to Cameron and I as she placed her empty glass down on the table.

"Kel, you know I love you, but I don't want to travel now. Backpacking is not really my thing and I've got my internship lined up. You know I can't go."

"There'll be plenty of time for work," she pouted. "Come on, please. You've got years ahead of you to build your career."

While the thought of travel was thrilling, it wasn't for me. Not now anyway. "Sorry, babe. Career first!"

"Fine," she jammed her hands on her hips. "Let's have another drink. My shout." She waddled off toward the bar.

Cameron was distant this afternoon. I wasn't sure what was going on. He was quieter than normal and agitated. He didn't even want to hold my hand. Something was off. When Kel returned with drinks I caught him staring off into the distance. I followed in the direction of his gaze to see what held him captivated. There was Louie at the bar having a drink by herself. My stomach hit the floor. Even after all this time, remembering what she did all those months ago with Michael still hurt me profoundly. I swung around to face Cameron who remained oblivious to the fact I'd caught him ogling. I kicked his leg hard under the table.

"Do you like something you see?" I tilted my head and glared at him.

"What?" Cameron wiped his hand across his forehead.

"Would you rather go and join Louie for a drink than be here with us?" My jealous streak flared like a bad rash.

"No. I was watching the cricket on TV." He pointed to the flat-screen hanging on the wall at the far end of the bar.

I reluctantly nodded and let the moment slide. Kel and I continued to talk of our plans. I hated the fact in a few weeks' time we would be on opposite sides of the planet from each other. I knew we'd be friends forever, regardless where our paths may lead us, but the thought of not being able to see her, talk to her or wind up on her doorstep everyday made me miserable. What would I do without her?

I missed her already.

The remainder of the week disappeared with countless hours of study and on the weekend, with a heavy heart, I resigned from my job at the tavern. Bruce had been the best boss and it was sad to wear my tavern polo shirt one last time. I cried when I had to say goodbye to the great team of people I'd worked with over the past three years. But holding my shoulders back and my head high, I knew my future was bright and full of unknown possibilities. Everything was changing around me and a strange vibe hung in the air. Tomorrow was my interview with Huntersville, my scholarship sponsor. My future lay in their hands.

***

My bed was covered in nearly every item of clothing from my closet, and half of Kel's wardrobe as well. In the past half hour I'd tried on nearly every combination of shirt, top, blouse and dress pants the two of us owned. Nothing felt right. It was either too big, too small, too frumpy, too...ergh!

Kel was more flustered than I was as we tried to come up with the most professional looking outfit to impress the people from Huntersville. Looking in the mirror, I eyed off my final selection; Kel's black pencil skirt paired with my baby pink button-up blouse and black pumps. Rallying up my confidence I turned to Kel and gave her a big hug, ready to make my way over to the university's boardroom for my meeting.

As my heels clicked on the paved pathway, I concentrated on putting one foot carefully in front of the other, trying not to trip over and make a fool of myself in front of all the students passing by.

Cameron's withdrawn behavior over the past few days had started to concern me and provided me with a distraction from my nerves. He'd stayed in his own room last night, insisting I needed my beauty sleep for today. But I lay awake most of the night, tossing and turning with worry and woke up with bags under my eyes. So much for beauty rest.

He barely said a word at breakfast and gave me a fleeting kiss on my forehead, wishing me luck for my interview before he left to go and study. But he wasn't in his room when I walked past to see him and I wondered where he could be. For now, my concern for Cameron had to be put on hold, I had other priorities at the moment. I pulled the glass door open into the administration building, and stepped inside. In sixty minutes this would all be over and then I would be able to get to the bottom of what was eating at Cameron.

I greeted the receptionist and was asked to take a seat and I found it impossible not to fidget. I kept wiping my sweaty palms on my thighs and hoped it wouldn't leave marks on Kel's skirt. I had to stop jiggling my legs because the chair made an awful squelching noise every time I moved. Each time I stroked and touched my hair, I caught the receptionist looking at me; she probably thought I had lice.

Five minutes passed before Mr Weber came out to greet me and led me into the boardroom. Two gentlemen stood up at the end of the table and buttoned up their suit jackets when I walked over to meet them.

I remembered Cameron's pointers; firm handshake, eye contact, smile.

"Hello Ms Cayton, I'm Duncan Summerville." The larger man with the Donald Trump hairdo shook my hand first.

"Good morning, Ms Cayton. I'm Gary Hunter." The second man with gray-flecked hair and George Clooney eyes smiled politely. Trying to hide my nerves, I took a deep breath when they offered me a seat. I was surprised to see both gentlemen and Mr Weber had a file on me in front of them and it was as thick as a ream of paper. How could they possibly have that much information on me? I gulped, trying to get rid of the lump forming in my throat.

"Ms Cayton, thank you for coming in today." Mr. Summerville clasped his hands together and rested them on the table.

After some brief chitchat about how final term was going, I started to feel more relaxed. They were making every effort to make me feel comfortable.

"Now, Ms Cayton, we've kept a close eye on you during the program. Your first two years were exceptional. But this year..." Mr Summerville looked over a page of my results he'd drawn out of his folder, "hasn't quite met our expectations. Firstly, your hospitalization over the use of drugs was reported to us, and then we saw a significant downturn in your grades."

OhMyGod, I was going to be sick.

"It was evident in your exams and assignment submissions," he continued. "We have your current progress report for this semester, and although there is improvement, there are other areas to address."

Mr Hunter drew a sheet out from his folder. "Mr Weber has reported your attendance at classes last semester was only 65%."

What? But this semester my attendance was near 100%, surely they couldn't use that against me.

"The downfall in your grades and behavior has raised concerns for us. We understand there is a lot of pressure on you to perform well and we are sorry if you have struggled." Mr Hunter closed the folders and looked me straight in the eye. "Our business is in a very competitive environment where only the leaders survive. The industry has hit tough economic times and growth has stalled significantly in the past eighteen months for us. Like many organizations, we are having to downsize and look at refining our operations and service offering."

The pause. Why do they always have to pause and look at each other? My eyes darted from one gentleman to the next, trying to keep alert.

"Therefore, Ms Cayton, with all these factors mounting against you, it is with great regret we will not be offering you an internship at the end of the year."

A loud ring in my ear pierced my skull. My stomach lurched. "I'm sorry...can you please repeat what you just said?"

"We will not be offering you an internship at Huntersville." Mr Hunter repeated. "We will pay out your full scholarship, but we will not be providing you employment."

An invisible hand grasped seized my throat, squeezing me, choking me. I couldn't breath. *What? No employment?*

"But...but, I can explain. You have no reason to be concerned about my grades. The hospitalization was not my fault. I was drugged at a dance. I should not have to pay for something that I didn't do, my medical report shows that. Yes, last semester was hard. To top everything off, a friend of mine lost someone close to them and I did take time out to help them. That's the reason for my low attendance record. I still passed every subject, didn't I? I wanted to discuss the option of doing my internship in another city, specifically Sydney. Does that change things? Please, will you reconsider?"

"Ms Cayton, as we've explained," Mr Summerville said, "it's a combination of many factors, not all of them are to do with you alone. Our company has to take necessary steps to survive these tough economic times. We are facing other redundancies and downscaling, we cannot take on any new or unnecessary expenses at this time."

Great, I'm an expense!

Both gentlemen shook their heads, their eyes darkened with sorrow. Well, at least I hoped it was that, and not pity.

"We'll pay out your fees," Mr Hunter added. "We are truly sorry it has come to this. We wish you every success in your future career. You do have exceptional grades and you will be an asset to whoever takes you on board."

I sniffled, unable to hold back a tear, it trickled down my cheek. I brushed it away and tried to remain professional in front of the men. "Okay. Is that it, then? Is there anything else we need to discuss?" The gentlemen shook their heads and I glanced at Mr Weber who had this *"I told you so"* look plastered on his face. All that did was make me feel worse. "Right then, thank you for your time. I appreciate you paying my fees. I am, however, very disappointed I haven't met your expectations and hope you reconsider me for a job if any opportunities arises in the near future. I'm confident my final grades will restore your faith in me."

I don't know what dribble rolled off my tongue; I prayed it made sense and hopefully left them with a positive impression. I stood, shook everyone's hands and found my way out the door. The minute I left the building and entered the quadrangle, my whole body shuddered and I burst into tears. With trembling hands, I bent down, took off my shoes and gathered them up into my arms. Then I ran. Ran as fast as I could down the pathway. Through my blurred vision and stinging eyes, I dodged the odd student and crossed the road back over to my residential college.

I crashed through the doorway in to my block and stumbled down the hallway to my room. I slammed my door shut, cocooned myself up into a tight ball on my bed and let my tears consume me.

I sulked on my bed for hours. It was after midday when Cameron came to see me.

"Hey raccoon, what's up?" He sat down beside me and rubbed my arm.

I wiped my eyes. What a sight I must be. No doubt my mascara had run everywhere and streaked my face with ugly black lines. The make-up stains on my pillowcase, proof it had.

"I didn't get my internship." Those words managed to open up a whole new floodgate of waterworks. I mumbled and spluttered the entire time, relaying the story to him.

He nodded and offered a reassuring pat on my hand, "Everything will be fine."

I didn't feel fine. I was furious. Gutted all my hard work had mounted to nothing and my career disappeared before my eyes. Disappointment in myself didn't cut it. I was devastated and Cameron just sat there taking it all in like it wasn't a big deal. *It was to me.* Half the time he didn't look at me. He nodded occasionally. He jittered on the edge of the bed, like he couldn't wait to get out of my room. What the hell was going on with him? I needed his comfort. His cuddles and kisses. I needed his attention. Instead I got this cold, uninterested, lackluster person that was not like Cameron at all. It was making my blood boil and fester beneath my skin.

"How can you say everything will be fine? I've lost everything I've been working for. My whole life has fallen apart. First the drugging. Then my grades. Now my job has gone. I've lost everything because of you." My heart jerked violently in my chest as the hurtful words blurted from my mouth, but I couldn't stop. I was so angry and upset.

His eyes flared at me. "You're blaming this on me?"

"Yes... No... I don't know. Everything's so fucked up right now."

"Well, maybe you needed a reality check," he mumbled under his breath.

"A reality check. What are you saying?"

"Life isn't perfect, Wiley, you should know that by now. I'm not saying what happened to you regarding the drugs and losing your job placement is fair. But sometimes life isn't fair."

"Don't you think I know that?"

"Well, now you have to come down to earth and be like the rest of us."

"What? You, who's got money and a job with your father waiting for you on a silver platter. You're not even on the same planet as the rest of us."

Cameron lowered his eyes and stared at the floor. I hated myself for directing my anger at him and using him like a punching bag to let out my frustrations. Something inside me had burst and I'd lost all control of my emotions.

He stood up and the drawn look on his face sent a chill through me. His jaw was drawn tight and he clenched his fists. "You're angry and upset, I get that. I know what it's like when your world falls apart. I've been through it."

Why was it when he made reference to losing Gilly I felt like such a bitch?

I took a deep breath and tried to calm down, but I was too worked up at the moment. All my hard work had been for nothing. My career path set to zero.

"Why don't you go and have a shower and freshen up." Cameron made his way toward the door. "I'm going to go and do some study, we'll catch up later, okay?"

I nodded, afraid to utter another word in case I said something more biting or hurtful.

During dinner I apologized to Cameron profusely, but he was still in a solemn mood. He complained about having a headache and took off early saying he was heading straight to bed for an early night. Doubts continued to swirl through my mind and I couldn't put them to rest.

***

In the morning at breakfast, Cameron shuffled in and didn't look well. His hair was chaotic and tired bags hung heavily under his eyes. He sat down in the only spare seat at the table directly across from me and barely touched his food. My anguished looks at him were met with a half-hearted attempt at a grin and sullen-looking eyes. Where was my Cameron? Pain thudded in my chest. How could he be so distant and cold toward me after yet another rotten turn of events in my life? Weren't partners supposed to support each other through difficult times? I missed him — his kisses, cuddles and everything. We were so close, what had changed?

"Cam, wait!" I called out and followed him out of the dining hall. "We need to talk."

"About what?" he said as he headed along the path toward his block.

"About us. What's wrong?" I reached for his hand but he tucked his into the back pockets of his jeans.

"There's nothing wrong." He furrowed his brow. "Everything is fine. I told you, I'm just not feeling well, that's all. I gotta go. I'll see you later." Cameron strode off, leaving me standing in the middle of the pathway all alone.

His behavior over the past two days, however, had planted a seed of suspicion in my mind and it was growing rapidly by the hour. Confused and upset, I walked back to my room. Maybe he didn't think of me the same way now I didn't have an internship and no income after we finished uni? Was that it? No, it couldn't be that. He'd started to act differently even before my internship crashed and burned. Thoughts raced through my head as I tried to solve the mystery. I'd never doubted Cameron's love for me before, but his demeanor was starting to make me question everything.

From all the crying yesterday, I had a headache of my own and even after swallowing two Panadol, it continued to be violent throughout my day full of classes. By the evening, I was exhausted. After dinner I pleaded to stay with Cameron, but yet again he insisted on another night apart.

***

"Cam, do you want me to take you to the doctor" I asked at breakfast the next morning.

"No, it's not serious. I'll see you later." He stood up from the dining table, cleared his dishes away and disappeared out into the rain.

I was at the end of my tether with him and couldn't take much more of this nonsense.

I decided to check on him at lunchtime. When I walked into D-Block, I saw Louie trying to sneak out unnoticed. Her hair was disheveled and she was still realigning her clothes. My spine stiffened, like a metal rod had been rammed down my back, and my stomach churned at the sight of her. *Who* was she sleeping with in D-Block? I cringed as I crept past her to go to Cameron's room. I opened his door and peered in. There he was sprawled out on his single bed sound asleep. I desperately wanted to crawl in next to him. But if he wasn't feeling well, he needed his rest. I gently closed the door and left without disturbing him.

***

"What's wrong with Cam? He looks terrible," Kel said at breakfast the next day once Cameron took off yet again.

Kel graced us with her presence this morning for only about the fifth time this year, but I knew with exams only a week away, everyone was sleep deprived, restless and trying to study as much as possible.

"Maybe the dining hall food got to him," I shrugged. "I didn't stay with him last night so I'm not too sure." This was the third day in a row Cameron had been avoiding me and the stress was starting to get to me. I wasn't sleeping well and had lost my appetite. "I've got to get going, I'll see you at lunchtime."

I struggled through the morning tutorials and after lunch with Kel, I veered by Cameron's room before heading back over to uni. I found him slumped at his desk, staring out the window.

"I've had enough of this," I ranted, throwing my bag down on the floor. "You haven't talked to me in days. What's going on? Has something happened? Have I done something wrong?"

"Wiley, please. You haven't done anything wrong. We're fine." He rubbed at his forehead, not even looking at me.

I didn't believe him because if everything was fine, we would be in his bed and I wouldn't be acting like a crazy woman.

"Then why haven't you come to see me or let me stay with you? I've been in a living hell since Monday when my job went down the toilet and you started to ignore me. I'm starting to lose my mind here."

"I just haven't been feeling well." Cameron raised his voice, heat crept across the side of his neck. "There's nothing more to it."

"Then let me take you to the doctor."

"No. I'm okay." He stood up, walked over and kissed me on the forehead. But his lips were dry and his touch was cold and it made my skin prickle. Something was't right and it scared me. "I'm gonna go to the Pizza'n'Beer lunch at The Club with Dave and Justin," he said. "Maybe some greasy food will make me feel better. Are you heading over to class now?"

I nodded.

"I'll make it up to you later, I promise." He picked up his

phone and wallet off of his desk and shuffled me out the door. We walked in silence across the road over to campus and when I stopped to say goodbye, he continued on to The Club without even giving me a kiss.

The tutorial dragged on. The subject was interesting but the teacher spoke in uninspiring monotonous tones, making it hard to stay awake and listen. I was agitated and missed Cameron. He made classes so much more entertaining.

When the lesson ended, I stuffed my books into my bag, left the building and made my usual footsteps straight toward Cameron's room. When I entered D-Block, my nose wrinkled at the overpowering stench of beer and pizza filling the narrow halls. I wondered if the entire block of ten boys had been over to The Club for lunch. My day was over and I was finally looking forward to spending some time with Cameron if he was feeling better. Half-heartedly knocking, I opened the door to his room.

Nothing could prepare me for what I saw. An all too distant memory flashed like a bolt of lightning before my eyes. It was my nightmare all over again. Clothes were scattered all over the bathroom and bedroom floor. Cameron lay sprawled out on his single bed, eyes shut, bare chested and only wearing boxer briefs . And there, sitting beside and leaning all over him, stroking his hair and face, boobs jutting toward him and wearing nothing other than her bra and panties ... was Louie.

I screamed at her at the top of my lungs, my heart exploded like a bomb had been detonated. "No. No. No. You, you slut! How dare you?" Then I threw my bag with full force at Cameron. "You bastard! This...this is what's been going on for the past few days, is it? You're sleeping with Louie?"

My head spun and I stumbled back out the door, slamming it shut with all my might. Sprinting back to my room, my tear-filled, foggy eyes hindered my sight. Short, sharp breaths stabbed at my lungs. The small grassy hill that lay between our buildings suddenly seemed as big as a rough and rugged mountain. I couldn't run fast enough, my legs felt like they were weighed down with concrete blocks. It took every ounce of my strength to put one foot in front of the other. I was reliving hell and couldn't get away quickly enough from the horror behind me. I fought on through the pain. Faster. Clawing. Desperate to escape.

When I reached the main door into F-Block, I glanced over my shoulder and saw Cameron charge toward me in his underwear. I didn't stop. I made it into my room, slammed the door shut and locked it behind me. I fell on to my bed and buried my face into my pillow to muffle out the sound of my gut-wrenching bawling.

Cameron bashed on my door seconds later. "Wiley! Wiley, open up. It's not what you think. I wasn't with Louie."

"Go away!" I screamed, nearly raising the roof off the building.

"Goddamn it, open up. I was not with her." He yelled from the other side of my door.

"Do you know how pathetic that sounds? Leave me alone." Tears streamed down my face as I howled uncontrollably.

"Come on, please!" Cameron begged.

The pain in my chest tightened; I clutched at my shirt. I wanted my heart to stop beating because it hurt too much. My throat burned every time I drew air into the depths of my lungs. I couldn't believe it. Not Cameron. Not Louie. The horrid images flashed once again through my mind.

Cameron thumped my door again.

I gritted my teeth, the hurt inside me turned into a raging fire. I stormed over to the door and opened it to confront him, refusing to let him come in. "You lying bastard," I cried, tears streaked down my face. "Louie. You cheated on me with Louie. The one person in this world I can't fucking stand. How could you?"

"I didn't cheat on you!"

I raised my hands to silence him. I didn't want to hear any of his pathetic excuses.

"I don't believe you. I thought you were different, but you're just like..." I couldn't bring myself to say Michael's name, too much bitterness rose in my mouth. I couldn't go through this. Not again. "Go away. We are so over." I slammed the door with all my might, the whole building shook from the brute force.

Crumbling to the floor, tears saturated my cheeks. The heartbreak over Cameron was much greater than anything I'd ever felt before. I hated myself; hated myself for falling for him when I was so determined not to get involved with anyone this year. It sucked getting over Michael; and this time I knew my feelings for Cameron were so much stronger. I was in love with him, he was my world. Worst of all, I foolishly believed he'd loved me. He said he loved me. What an idiot I'd been for falling for his lies.

I wailed loudly, my heart shattered and a gapping hollowness took its place.

"Fuck." Cameron punched my door. "Let me in, Wiley. Nothing happened!"

"Go away! Please!" I bellowed.

I was causing a commotion throughout my entire block and half the college, but I didn't care at all.

There was a tap at my door, "Sweetie, let me in?" Kel's voice was full of concern.

"Has Cameron gone?"

"let me in, please," she begged and tried to turn the handle.

"Not until Cameron's gone."

Cameron gave the door another almighty thump. "Nothing happened, I'm telling you. You stayed at my door before, I'll happily do the same. Don't think I won't do it," he yelled.

"Leave now. I never want to see you again!" My throat burned as I screeched.

"Cam. Calm down. Go and put some clothes on, you're shivering. Let me talk to her. It'll be fine, I promise." Kel said.

"But she doesn't know what happened. I wasn't with Louie. I'm not leaving until she talks to me."

"You haven't talked to me all week, why start now?" I wailed.

I wiped my tears off on my shirt sleeve. When Kel confirmed Cameron had left, I let her into my room.

"What happened?" She gasped, seeing me in such a mess.

"He slept with Louie," I spluttered as we took a seat on my bed. She flung her arms around me, held me tight and let me cry. "Of all people, he slept with the bitch from hell."

"Cameron?" she gasped. "I didn't think he was like that. Come on, this has to be a big mistake. You two are so good together." Kel grabbed my box of tissues and handed me a handful.

"I walked in on them. They were in bed and she...she...she was all over him."

"Oh ... that doesn't sound good."

Now I knew why Cameron had been acting so strangely. The doubt in my mind had served me correctly. How could I have been so foolish not to see it sooner?

"Oh Kel. Why couldn't he just break up with me if he didn't want to be with me anymore? Instead, I have to find out like this." She hugged again and let me cry for what seemed like an eternity. Bawling my eyes out has been the only thing I have managed to perfect this week. "The last few days have been utter crap. Nearly dying from been drugged was fucked, but losing my career and Cameron sucks even more. I've lost everything I've worked hard for and someone I really cared about. Why is everything so screwed up at the moment? I can't handle this, Kel. I gotta get out of here."

"Don't be silly. You're just upset."

"I love you; you're my best friend. But I'm going. I gotta go somewhere before I go crazy. I can't face him. Or her. First Michael and now Cameron." I jumped up and grabbed my bag, phone and keys.

"Where are you going? What are you doing?" Kel stood up and tried to stop me.

"Home. Don't say a word to anyone." I kissed her on the cheek, fled from my room and headed for the hills.

Chapter 25

Mum took me in her arms when I fell through the front door at home, and my waterworks started again. Another headache raged in my skull and my eyes burned in their sockets. Dad made me a cup of tea while I curled up on the couch and clutched a cushion to my chest. I told them what happened. They nodded occasionally and barely said a word much to my relief. I was exhausted. I didn't think I could stomach food or anything else for that matter, so I excused myself and headed to bed for the night.

Unable to get out of bed the following morning, Friday started to slip away. When I turned my phone on late in the afternoon, there was fifty-three messages from Cameron. I threw my phone back on my bedside table and ignored every one of them. Mum and Dad came home after work, I picked at the chicken pasta Dad cooked for dinner, but headed back to bed early once more.

Lying in the darkness I stared up at the ceiling, trying

not to think, breath or feel anything when I heard a car pull in to the driveway. I froze. I knew that engine. *What the hell?* Seconds later, footsteps bound up the steps then there was a knock on the door.

I held my breath.

"What the hell are you doing here?" My mother screeched.

"I've come to see Wiley. She's got it all wrong. I swear to you on my life."

Cameron!

What was he doing here? Panic rendered me immobile.

"You need to leave, now."

"I'm not leaving until I see Wiley."

"John!" My mother shrilled hysterically. "Get out here."

"I'm on the loo! Who is it?"

"Wiley! Wiley?" Cameron's voice rang out. My mother screamed as I heard footsteps thunder down the wooden staircase. I flicked on my bedside light and sat up just as my door burst open and there he stood.

"Don't throw me out, I beg of you." Cameron pleaded, trying to catch his breath. "I swear to you I didn't sleep with Louie. I love you. Please. You have to listen to me,"

"How did you know where I was?"

"Kel finally relented." Cameron's eyes swelled with emotion, "Please, Wiley. You've got it all wrong."

Dad appeared at my bedroom door with Mum tailing close behind. "What's going on." He said, "Do I need to call the police?"

"Mr Cayton, I'm sorry. I didn't mean to barge in like that. I need to talk to Wiley. There's been a huge misunderstanding." He remained standing in the doorway.

Dad stood his ground while having to hold my mother at bay. Her eyes were wild and she tried to claw her way and get to Cameron. Dad looked at me, waiting for my cue. I couldn't believe Cameron had driven all this way to find me. Why would he do that?

In spite of the severe pain in my chest, I nodded. ""It's okay, Dad."

"You sure?" He hesitated. "All right. We'll leave you to it. Call me if you need anything."

"John, no." Mum shrieked and pointed at Cameron. "I want him out of the house, now!"

"Vicki, let's leave them to it." Dad placed his hands on her shoulders, turned her around, guided her down the hall and back up the stairs. Mum protested all the way.

Cameron shut the door behind him and fell on to his knees beside my bed. I shuffled back on the mattress and leaned against the wall. Curling my legs up underneath me and cuddling my pillow, I sat as far away from him as possible.

"I looked for you everywhere and was going out of my mind. Kel finally told me you'd come home after I begged her a thousand times to tell me where you were. You gotta hear me out." His voice rippled with anguish. "Yesterday, when I went out to lunch with the boys to The Club, I had too much pizza and beer. After not feeling well all week, it hit me hard. I was really sick. Dave helped me back to my room because I was giddy. Louie and Ben came out of his room when they heard the noise to help Dave."

"Ben? Louie?" I shook my head. This wasn't making any sense. "How come you were out of your clothes?"

"I threw up everywhere in my bathroom, my bed and all over Louie. Dave had helped me out of my jeans and got me into bed. Louie copped it on her dress when I retched over the side of my bed and I missed my bin. I didn't even notice she'd taken off her clothes because I was so out of it." I glared at him. As if he wouldn't notice Louie naked! "Dave and Ben hadn't left long before you arrived. Louie was being nice and looking after me because I was so unwell." He didn't draw breath as he relayed the course of events.

I didn't buy it. I know what I saw. I wiped away a tear with the back of my hand. "Don't lie to me." Hurt poured from my heart. "I walk in and you were naked in bed with her. Louie has been after you since the day you walked into the dining hall at the beginning of the year. You were eyeing her off at The Club not so long ago, I've seen her sneaking in and out of D-Block for the past couple of days and you've been ignoring me all week. Why couldn't you tell me we were over if you wanted to be with her, but no, I had to walk in and find you all over each other."

"She was not all over me, ever! I was not naked and neither was she. I told you what happened to our clothes." He scrunched up and twisted fistfuls of my quilt in his hands. "The evidence was right there in my room if you'd taken a moment to see – my clothes were covered in vomit and my bin was full of it. If you don't believe me ask Dave or Ben — even Louie."

"Why on earth would I ever talk to Louie?" I hugged my pillow tighter against my chest.

"Nothing happened. I would never do anything to hurt you."

"You're clocking up a pretty good scorecard this week!"

He flinched at my harsh words. His eyes were red, his face was pale and sweat appeared on his brow. Cameron looked as shattered as I felt.

"This is all a huge misunderstanding." Cameron shook his head, then rose to his feet and ripped his fingers through his hair. "This is insane." His voice lashed out at me like a whip. "You have one hell of an overly active imagination. You have concocted this whole mess up out of thin air because nothing... fucking...happened."

I closed my eyes, salty droplets soaked my lashes. My lip quivered. "Why did it have to be her. You could have picked anyone but her. She's so beautiful, all the guys fall for her. And you're obviously no different."

"Enough Wil. This has to stop because it's not the truth. Louie is with Ben in the room down the hall, they've been going at it like rabbits for weeks. You're the only one for me. For someone so smart, you're being downright idiotic over this." Cameron paced around my room several times before he knelt down in front of me again. He slumped forward and rested his head down on top of the bed. "Just give me a sec, I've had some kind of weird fever for days that keeps flaring up. I've never felt so crook in my life. I haven't been able to think straight, I keep getting giddy and feel nauseous all the time." His hands shook on top of the bedding and when he rubbed them across his brow. He really didn't look well.

"You were so upset on Monday about not getting your internship and I'm sorry I was all standoffish but I was seriously trying not to vomit. This setback you've had is only going to make you stronger and more determined to be successful. It's Huntersville's loss, and no doubt be someone else's gain. It has taken all my strength to keep away from you because with exams coming up I didn't want you to catch whatever it is I've got."

His gaze met mine and my heart lurched. Why was he here if he was sick? My head throbbed, my eyes stung and my heart ached. I licked a salty tear off my lip and wiped others away on my sleeve.

"Cam, I don't know what to believe anymore." Seeing him look like death was the only thing making me calm down.

"I swear to you I didn't sleep with Louie. You gotta believe me. You're everything to me."

"If you were so sick, why wouldn't you let me take care of you? I've been stressing for days that there's something wrong between us. Crap has been spun around in my head and combined with the stress of exams coming up, I've only been able to draw one conclusion. When I saw you with Louie...I...I..." I reached for a tissue and blew my nose.

"I'm sorry Wiley, I didn't know what to do. I haven't been myself with these fevers. They've been really bad. One minute I feel alright, the next minute I'm shivering, burning up and vomiting."

I hated seeing him like this. I sighed heavily and slouched my shoulders. I was exhausted and drained of nearly every ounce of energy left in my body.

"Why does everything keep screwing up between us?" I sniffled and looked up at nothing in particular on the ceiling.

"No. No, it's not. We're good together. We've had some rough patches and got through them, it's shown us how much we care for each other. What we have is worth fighting for and I won't lose you over something I didn't do." *Hmm...that did sound familiar.* "I can't wait to finish university, get away from the crazy mixed up bunch of people at res college, have no more study to worry about and start my life with you. Wiley, I'm yours, and yours only."

Cameron had weaved his way into my heart and I dared to trust him, only to have it all shattered to pieces. He'd fallen for me and had relived his worst nightmare with my drugging incident and now the same had happened to me. How can we be a good thing? How much more pain could we inflict on each other and survive? Would we ever be able to fully trust each other or would we be forever walking on shaky ground?

Were the good times enough? He showed me a life I dreamed about, enjoying everything from the simple things through to the lavish. He made me laugh, had restored my confidence and gave me balance in my life. Cameron had grown so much since I'd known him and he'd found a renewed inner strength. With common goals and ambitions, we made each other better people. It was why we were great together and why we wanted to be together.

But did any of that matter anymore? The anguish I felt tipped the scales way off balance at present.

"I don't know anything anymore, Cam. I need some time to think. I'm exhausted and you look terrible. I'll go get you some Panadol and you can stay in Chris's room for the night. We'll talk more in the morning."

"You gotta give me something, Wiley, you're breaking my heart."

"I'm not kicking you out. That's all I can give you at the moment."

***

My parents were not impressed with Cameron staying, but it was late when we finished talking and he was not well. Sleep eluded me throughout the night as I watched the digital numbers tick over on my clock before I dragged my feet upstairs for breakfast early the next morning.

"Hey, princess," Dad greeted me. "Coffee?"

"Yes, please. Where's Mum?" She was usually pottering around in the kitchen cleaning up and fussing over something at this hour.

"She's at golf. She was going to cancel her game today but I wouldn't let her. I thought you might need some space without her interfering." Wrinkles framed his eyes when he grinned.

After making me a cup, Dad sat back down at the table with me. "Sleep well?"

"Not a wink."

"What's the verdict?" he asked, then blew into his hot cup of fresh coffee.

"Cameron says he didn't do it. I don't know if I can believe him." Not so many months ago I hated him for not believing me over my drugging. Was this the same thing? What if he did cheat on me? He shouldn't get away with something like that.

"For a guy to come all this way, force himself into our house, grovel at your knees and beg for mercy, he must be pretty serious about you. Don't you think?"

"What would you know?" I stared at my coffee, not sure if I could stomach it. Just how much did my parents hear of our conversation last night?

"I'm a guy." Dad shrugged. "I went to university and I know how things can be extreme. There's so much happening all around you, emotions run high, your stressed with exams and you're still finding your path in life. Ups and downs are part of it. I certainly don't condone cheating if it happened. But I don't know, call me a sucker for romance, but he seems genuine to me."

"Dad!" I gasped in shock at seeing this side of my father.

"I've had a few good talks with Cameron over the past few months. He really cares for you, princess. I'm usually a pretty good judge of character. Relationships are tough and it takes a lot of work to keep it strong."

"I don't know what to do, Dad." I whispered as turned my cup to and fro between my hands. "If he did cheat, I can't forgive that. If he didn't do it, I'm the biggest fool on the face of the planet."

"One is easier to forgive than the other, remember that. We all make mistakes too." Dad scratched at his unshaven cheek. "Do you love him?"

This was such a weird conversation to be having with my dad. I didn't think he would want me to have such strong feelings for anyone at my age.

"Everything feels numb at the moment."

"Sometimes the truth can be hard to see."

I shuffled uncomfortably on the chair.

"Dad, we have to head back to university this morning. I've got exams next week and somehow need to get my head straight so I can get through them."

"I know, princess. Just want to let you know I'm here for you regardless."

"What about Mum?"

"I'll deal with her. You let me worry about that."

***

With hardly a word exchanged between us in the morning, I took Cameron to the medical center and he was prescribed some antibiotics. We then drove in convoy back to campus. The whole time, wild thoughts kept running through my head, still not knowing how I felt about the situation or what to do about it.

Study had to be my sole focus for now. With the warm sun shining, I pulled my blanket off my bed and decided to work outside underneath the shade of a tree. Deep in concentration, I jolted my head up in surprise when a pair of the longest, most perfectly shaped, tanned legs appeared a few feet away from me.

Ergh...Louie!

"What do you want?" I snapped.

"To see if you're okay?" She bubbled like a glorious fountain. It was sickening. "Everyone's talking about you losing your internship."

"Why do you care?"

She flicked her hair back over her shoulder. "I wanted to say sorry. That's got be really tough on you, considering you've worked so hard for it."

"Yeah well, I've learned shit happens."

"Yes, it does." She faked a smile, turned to leave, but stopped. "Oh, is Cameron feeling better, now? He was so sick the other day."

"You should know, you're the one who slept with him. You've done it again. Does that make you happy now you've had two of my boyfriend's?" I glared at her, my tone cutting.

"What?" She gasped. "I didn't sleep with Cameron. Is that what all the screaming was about the other day? You thought I was with him." She threw her head back and laughed, making me feel the size of a pea. "Oh, you're so wrong! Best to get your facts straight before you make such accusations, Wiley."

"Why should I believe you? Did Cameron put you up to this?"

"No, he didn't. He's too *Mr. Goodie Two Shoes* for my liking. I like the bad boys, *you* of all people should know that."

"Michael wasn't bad until you dug your claws into him."

She laughed again. "Wiley, I'd see Michael out at the nightclubs in town with someone different all the time. You weren't ever there to know. The night I was with him, he said that you weren't together anymore. I would never have slept with him otherwise. I'm sorry you had to find out in such an unpleasant way he was not the faithful kind."

Feeling like a worm, I wanted to dig myself into the earth and disappear. I didn't care about Michael anymore. Karma would come back and haunt him in the long run. But my thoughts wheeled to Cameron and I back-pedaled from my outburst. "You swear on your life you didn't sleep with Cameron?" *Oh shit!* Cameron *was* telling the truth. What have I done? I dragged my fingernails down over my cheeks. My heartbeat hit panic mode. How could I have been so stupid? Why didn't I believe him?

My jealousy had blinded me? My insecurities got the

better of me? Me fear had taken over me? I was such a fool and hung my head in shame.

"No, I didn't. He vomited all over me. That's what I get for trying to be nice." Louie screwed up her nose in disgust.

I flipped my book closed, threw it on the blanket, ran as fast as I could to Cameron's room and burst in through the door without even knocking. He was sitting slouched at his desk, morbidly trying to study. He turned to face me, his eyes wide and alert.

Panting from the short sprint to his room, I lunged for him, flung my arms around his neck and fell on to his lap. "Forgive me! I can't bear another second without you. I love you so much."

Feverishly my lips were on his. His arms clutched me around my waist and drew my chest flush against his.

"I'm so sorry too." He cupped the side of my neck. "For everything. You're my life. You know that, right?"

He scooped his arms beneath my legs, lifted me off the chair and lay me down onto his bed. My body ached to have him close to me again. Kissing him started to ease the pain. Peeling away each other's clothing, I couldn't get close to him quick enough.

"I've missed you so much," I grabbed a fistful of his hair and pulled his mouth to mine.

"I'm not going anywhere. You're stuck with me," he whispered and started to taunt my breasts. Licking and kissing one nipple then the next, making my back arch, wanting and begging for more.

His mouth reclaimed mine. His hands were all over me. His skin blazed against mine. He groaned when he thrust inside me and whispered in my ear. "I'm yours. Don't ever forget it."

Chapter 26

All the jacaranda trees were in full bloom; vibrant lavender bell-shaped flowers filled their canopies and the sweet sickly fragrance filled the air. Seeing these trees in flower was a telltale sign it was nearly the end of the year and exam time. Summer was inching closer and Christmas decorations started to appear in the shopping centers once more.

Two weeks of my exams stretched before me like a treacherous mountain road with no map. Sleepless nights, stress and fatigue caught up with me and I walked around the place in a zombie-like state. After my poor efforts last semester and the last couple of weeks of emotional turmoil, I wasn't looking forward to these finals.

I rolled my eyes when I read my exam timetable. It was horrid. My last exam fell in the final week on Thursday. There'd be no escaping off campus early for Cameron and me.

Most of my friends finished their exams at the end of the first week. There were many tearful goodbyes and heartfelt hugs before my friends departed campus for the very last time.

Saying goodbye to Kel was hardest of all. Life was about to pull us in all different directions, literally across the globe. We were about to be unleashed into the unknown and I wondered if we'd stay in contact and remain friends throughout the course of our life.

When I put the final stroke on my last exam, I put my pen down, closed my eyes and took in a huge deep breath. It was done. My last exam was over. My whole body prickled with elation. When I stood up and walked out of the examination hall, my feet felt like they weren't touching the ground. No more study. All I could now do was pray for good results.

Cameron and I drove back to Steele Rudd Residential College, big smiles drawn across our faces. But it was sad when I packed up my room for the very last time and loaded my gear into my car ready to head home in the morning. After I'd finished, we walked hand in hand over to The Club for a few drinks and to bid our old stomping ground farewell.

"Three years of uni over. This is our last night in Toowoomba for a very long time; maybe even forever." I'd become attached to this little metropolis on top of the range. My life had changed so much during my time here. All the experiences, the good and the bad, had led to meet this amazing person sitting across from me.

"We'll have to come back and visit Gran. And graduation is in February." Cameron took a swig on his beer and placed it down on his coaster. "It's been one full-on year," Cameron reflected. "Who knew college life could be such a roller coaster? But I found you and aim to hang on to you for a very long time." He took up his glass again and raised it. "Here's to new adventures!"

***

Cameron left his car at my place and headed home to Sydney for two weeks. He was then coming back to Brisbane and we were going to go camping up the coast. Spending a week on the beach sounded like a great way to start summer holidays and celebrate the end of uni. Just Cameron and I, by ourselves for a few days would be bliss.

We still hadn't sorted out our living arrangements.

The weeks Cameron was away, I spent endless hours a day at home in front of the computer, traipsing through and applying for jobs in Sydney. Since losing my internship I'd no desire to stay in Brisbane, and there seemed to be more opportunity for employment in the capital of New South Wales. I insisted on finding a job before moving in with Cameron so I could pay my share of the bills. I'd even started applying for jobs outside my qualifications just to get an income so I could move in with him. With my work experience and good grades, I thought finding work would be easy, but I was delusional. Each day that passed I became more disheartened but never gave up. I flicked through endless job sites on the Internet, submitted countless résumés to companies via recruitment sites and dragged my feet around the city into numerous agencies that did placements in Sydney. All to no avail.

If not looking for work, I was Skyping and messaging Cameron. Hearing his voice made everything better, even if we were only discussing our latest rejection emails from potential employers. With his father's connections in business, I thought Cameron would have walked straight into a job; but this had not been the case. Maybe we were too cocky about the whole job front. The time and effort it was taking to find work was frustrating. I wanted to be with Cameron and hated the delay.

My parents tolerated my moodiness and kept me sane by giving me a few hours work at the practice. I was glad to get out of the house and earn some money to keep my bank balance growing to aid my move to Sydney. Mum loved having the shorter work days so she could flit around town, run errands, go shopping and catch up with her friends.

Each morning at breakfast I sat toiling with two frames of mind. The first, excited: one day closer to seeing Cameron. The second, daunted: the prospect of more job applications. Today was no different as I hauled my feet upstairs to the kitchen, and plonked down at the table to indulge in some good strong coffee.

"Morning," I greeted my parents, rubbing my thick, sleepy eyes.

"There's some decent jobs advertised in the paper today." Dad said over a mouthful of cereal and pointed to the newspaper next to him on the table. "Why don't you apply?"

"Because they're in Brisbane and you know I want to move to Sydney."

"Then why haven't you?" Dad smiled and spooned another heap of cereal into his mouth.

"I want a job before I move. I want my own financial independence. I don't want to sap off Cameron."

"Have you two considered the cost of everything like rent, utilities, food, phones and other everyday expenses? You'll not survive very long on your savings. Sydney is expensive. Cameron's family is well off, but what actual access to funds does he have? Is it all tied up in some kind of trust fund and the company? I want to make sure you know what's involved in moving out on your own."

"Dad, we'll be fine." I rolled my eyes at him but, in fact, I was dreading reality. I must admit I'd never really considered what Cameron himself was worth or how much money he had to his name. It was never had been an issue between us. But now we were moving in together, these were elements we had to discuss. I had no idea what we could afford in Sydney.

If we were going on the amount of my money I had in my bank account, living in a caravan park might be our only option.

My parents raised a good point, making me doubtful of my plans. I folded my arms and hugged myself, stooping lower into my chair. I hated it when they were right.

"Sydney's so far away. We'll never see you," Mum wailed sadly and tried another of her guilt trips on me to stay. Dad had talked her around about Cameron but she was far from happy about us being back together — again.

"Stop trying to talk me out of it." I folded my arms and hugged myself tight.

"You've only known Cameron for the past year and it hasn't been all smooth sailing." Dad said. "Why not try Brisbane? Cameron could move up here." He threw the job section of the paper across the table, letting it land right in front of me.

"Come on, guys! We've talked about this already. I'm moving to Sydney with Cameron and that's it. It will be great, you'll see." I tried to sound convincing and kept my mind focused on my goal: Cameron and work. No distractions; not even my parents.

***

The day to camping arrived. I woke up, jumped out of bed and changed out of my pajamas into my bikinis, a denim mini skirt and a black shoestring top.

Cameron was due in at the airport right in the middle of morning peak hour so I had to leave early enough to allow for the traffic. I packed the last of the camping gear and food for our five-day trip into his Hilux, kissed my parents goodbye and took off. The freeway was bumper to bumper as I crossed the arch of the Gateway Bridge. The sun was already scorching hot as it climbed in the eastern sky; its rays sparkling and dancing off the murky waters of the Brisbane River below.

Twenty minutes later, I veered into the passenger zone at the Brisbane Domestic Terminal. With a huge grin upon his face, Cameron rushed to greet me. I opened the door, slid out and flung my arms around to kiss him.

"I'm not sure I like you driving my car." He said with a beaming smile. "Although, you do look mighty sexy behind the wheel." He nuzzled into my ear; wrapped his arms around me and swung me round.

"I missed you so much." I inhaled his delicious scent, kissed him and savored having him back in my arms. Pulling back from his clutches, my cheeks flushed when I saw all the people standing nearby were staring at us. I straightened my singlet and skirt back into place and helped Cameron with his luggage.

"How was the flight?" I asked as we hoped in the car.

"Good but couldn't get here soon enough," he smiled, did up his seatbelt and starting the engine.

"You're here now and that's all that matters. Let's get going, we have a long drive ahead."

***

Two hours later we were driving along the sandy beach up to Double Island Point. The sand whizzed under the wheels of the Hilux as we sped up the wide, open beach and the briny air tickled my nostrils. Seagulls squawked as they darted about and dived for fish out among the crystal-clear ocean waves. It was so good to be back on the beach.

I gazed across at Cameron driving, his eyes directed on the beach ahead while his hair dancing frantically about in the breeze with the windows down. I was one lucky girl to have such a sexy guy.

We entered the designated beach camping grounds at the northern end of the island and found a flat, grassy patch of ground tucked in behind a low sand dune. A clump of scraggly casuarina trees would provide shelter from the sun. For the next few days it would be the perfect campsite for the two of us. School holidays hadn't started yet so it wasn't busy and there were no other campers nearby.

In the heat of the scorching sun and while sweating profusely, we squabbled over which way to put up the tent, pumped up the air mattress and set up our portable canopy. Wiping my brow after setting up the chairs, our campsite was complete.

"Let's go for a swim." Cameron said, his body glistened with sweat. I didn't need much convincing to go and cool off. The air was stifling with not even a hint of breeze.

"Sure." I striped down to my bikini, took his hand and let him lead me down to the shoreline.

Looking up and down the beach, there was not another soul around. No cars. No campsites. No fishermen. It felt like Cameron and I were the only ones on the face of the planet. The gentle waves lapped at our feet, the cool water refreshing against our hot skin as we made our way out deeper.

"This is amazing," Cameron said floating out over a wave. "We won't ever get the beaches to ourselves in Sydney."

"We'd better make the most of it." I swam into his waiting open arms.

We drifted over the gentle swell together and I swept his wet tousled hair off his face. Gazing into his eyes, I brushed my fingertips down along his jawline and over his moist warm lips, wiping away droplets of the ocean. Placing the tip of my index finger into my mouth, I licked the salty water away, making soft moaning sounds as I sucked on it and rolled my tongue around. When Cameron's gorgeous eyes darkened, I grinned, successfully achieved the desired effect. His arms tightened around me and his arousal pressed against me. My heartbeat escalated as our lips found each other's and our tongues tasted each other.

"I want you," I whispered, kissed his lips and enjoyed the sweet briny taste.

"Here?" Cameron glanced up and down the beach.

"There's no one around."

"You're so bad." His lips left mine to explore, he made a trail down the side of my neck and across the rim of my shoulder. His kisses made me quiver like a leaf caught within the breeze. As his fingertips brushed over my arm, shivers ran through me when he gently blew his warm breath in their wake.

I closed my eyes when his hand slid to my breast and cupped it gently. With his sturdy thumb, he skimmed over the surface of the wet fabric of my bikini top and circled around my erect nipple. A deep rumbling murmur resonated in his throat.

"You turn me on so much," his gasped, his heart pounding beneath my touch. He gently slipped his fingers under my top and pulled the material aside to reveal my naked flesh. With one arm around me, he lifted me up out of the water so his mouth could suck, lick and tantalize my nipple further. With the ease and buoyancy of the water, I wrapped my legs around his waist and pressed my body toward him. Heat started to swell between my legs.

Threading my fingers through his hair, I pulled his face back up to mine, wanting more of his delicious kisses.

Placing my feet back on the sand, I lowered my hand down between us, teased his stomach at the top of his board shorts before gliding my hand down over his hardened shaft. Rubbing him up and down, feeling him in the palm of my hand. On the next stroke up, I found the cord of his shorts, pulled it undone, ripped open the velcro, shimmied them down off over his legs and pulled them clear of the water.

"Fair's fair." He ducked under the water and removed my bikini bottoms.

With our clothes gripped in one hand, Cameron pulled my legs back up around his waist. He kissed me, nudged his erection at my opening.

"I love you so much," I whispered, let him enter me. Cameron smiled as he rocked his hips and thrust deep inside me. I gasped. I loved the feel of him inside me, there was no other sensation like it. He fit perfectly and sent fevered tingles dancing all over my body.

Floating through the waves, the waters swirled around us and caressed our skin as we connected. His smile glorious. His laughter infectious. His touch magical. Just Cameron, me and the ocean all around us. But his little thrusts were starting to make my insides coil with too much heat and I needed more. Gripping onto his shoulders, I encouraged him to go deeper. Breath hissed between his teeth and my own quickened as he sank into me further. I gripped my legs tighter around his waist and pulsed in time with his rhythm, up and down on his shaft.

His body flexed and responded to mine.

With a new fervor we kissed. Hot air rushed between us as he drove into me. His eyes closed and jaw locked. He was all mine. Every inch of him. With one deep thrust I lost all control. Fire exploded within me and my body quaked.

"You're so mine — forever," he whispered into my ear. His body shuddered when his orgasm coursed through him, he curled his arms around me and nuzzled into the base of my neck. "There's one thing for sure though, we won't be doing this on the crowded beaches in Sydney. We'd be arrested."

***

For the next couple of days we attempted to fish, but caught nothing. Sunbaked, but Cameron got burned and it really was too hot. We played card games, but I always won. We bushwalked, but the flies were annoying. We read books in the shade of the trees, ventured around the island to see the sights and the colored sand cliffs, and dipped in and out of the water to stay cool.

On our third evening away, Cameron and I strolled along the beach; cold beer in one hand and linked together with the other. We stopped a short distance away from our campsite, sat down in the sand and looked out over the ocean while we had our drinks. A gentle breeze brushed against my skin while the faint moonlight danced upon the waves and a million stars filled the night skies.

"This has been the best holiday," I said, resting my head down on his shoulder.

"We'll have to go camping again." He hooked his arm around me and rested his head against mine. "But for now, my goal is to get you to Sydney." Cameron rubbed my arm. "You still want that, don't you?"

How could he ever question how much I wanted to be with him?

"Yes! It's frustrating I can't find work though."

"Why don't you just move in with me? You know I can afford it."

"I want to have a job so I can help pay all our expenses. I don't want you to waste your money on me," I said, staring out over the ocean waters.

"I don't think you have to worry about me wasting my money. I'm not the frivolous type. Just move in with me." He nudged against my side.

"I will." I rubbed my forehead, trying to think logically and reasonably.

He removed his arm from my shoulders, turned to face me and rest his hand on my bare thigh. "Screw the job. I can cover the cost of things. Just move in with me, please."

"Not yet."

"Why not? Stop making excuses." Frustration filled his eyes.

"I'm not making excuses."

"Then why not? Has something changed?" He furrowed his brow. "We're going to live together, and I want and need to understand why you won't let me look after things for a while."

A gust of breeze whipped hair across my face. He was quick to brush it away and tuck the strand behind my ear. The usual shivers ran down my side at his touch. He ran his finger down the line of my cheekbone, turning my chin to face him and pressed his lips to mine.

Before I got lost under his spell of intoxicating kisses, I pulled away and stared out over the waves and tried to collect my thoughts. I grabbed at handfuls of sand and let the cool grains fall through my fingers.

"Nothing's changed. Other than the fact I have to face something I thought would never happen to me. I never wanted to be one of those girls who'd wind up with someone wealthy looking after them. Yet here I am in the same situation. I want to be able to look after myself, be independent and be able to stand on my own two feet. I want a career and earn my own money. On one hand, the thought of your offer thrills me to pieces; on the other hand, I feel like I don't deserve it because I haven't earned it."

Cameron didn't say anything, he stared at his fingers making little swirls on my thigh. *Oh shit!* Did I say something hurtful by being so pigheaded?

Glancing at him sideways, I saw him bite into his lip. Damn him. He was trying not to laugh. He could be so infuriating sometimes. I resisted the temptation to thump him. He wanted to know what was on my mind and I was doing my best to jostle through the thoughts jumbling about in my head.

I placed my hand on top of his. "I didn't have any concerns at all about moving until it became difficult to find work. A job will give me...how shall I put it so you don't take it the wrong way...security. Half the time I feel like I'm in a fairy tale when I'm with you. It's too good to be true. I'm scared one day soon I'm going to wake up and you'll be gone and I'll have nothing. No job, no home, nothing. I know you have money, that doesn't bother me. It's your money. I want to earn my own."

In the soft moonlight his facial expression changed with so many different emotions; from laughing, to concentrating, to trying to be serious while he listened to me talk.

"So it's all right for you to get a job and look after me, but not vice versa?" He said with a glint in his eyes.

"I would consider the situation differently if you had a job. But you don't. I don't want to eat into your savings."

"Trust me, you won't be. So stop worrying."

"But I do. We can't live forever on having no income. We have to look at this realistically."

"I have an income, enough for the both of us. It seems like I know you better than yourself at the moment. You're definitely not the type of girl who wants to be a kept woman. I wouldn't be with you if you were. This will only be for a little while until we land jobs. I want to work and I know you do too," Cameron weaved his fingers around mine. "Wiley, not everything in life has to be difficult. I hope now university is behind us, we can have a few easy steps toward establishing our life together. Don't you think we deserve a break after all we've been through? I know moving in together is a huge commitment but I for one can't wait. Things will be different in Sydney, you'll see. What else can I say other than I love you and want to be with you?

Nothing else matters."

Cameron was right. We'd made it through some difficult times, it had made us stronger and bound our souls together.

"I've had my own concerns, too." He said. "You're so smart and savvy, I'm concerned one day you'll land some hotshot job and want to leave me to pursue your career. I'll support you in anything you want to do, but I'd follow you. Anywhere. So no more excuses. Please, move in with me."

His plea was hard to resist. I hated being away from him. I missed him so much it hurt when we weren't together. We sat in silence, listening to the sound of the waves break on the shoreline. My heart beat in time with them crashing on to the sand.

"You can be so stubborn," he chuckled and leaned over to kiss me on the forehead.

He was right. I was being stupid. We'd talked about moving in together for the past few months and knew it was right, but hadn't set a date. I'm glad he was giving me a kick up the butt. Here's me, with trust issues, about to put my life in his hands.

"Okay, here's the deal." I shuffled around on the sand to face him and gazed up into his heavenly eyes. "Why don't we keep looking over the next few weeks and if nothing comes up ... let's say by the end of January, I will finally let you have your way. I will pack my bags and move to Sydney, I promise."

Cameron eyes lit up like the brightest of stars. His lips engulfed mine, his kiss raw and full of emotion. His hands clasped around my neck and weaved up into my hair.

"Thank you. Finally. Together." He gasped, resting his forehead against mine.

Relief. Finally our plans were set in concrete; the end of January was only six weeks away.

Drawing my hair to the side, his lips found their way to

my neck and kissed me softly beneath my lobe. His deep voice rumbled in my ear. "Can I corrupt you somehow and convince you to move down sooner?" His hand ran down my arms, onto my ribcage and found home on my breast. He cupped and massaged it gently, arousing my nipple into a harden peak. I was losing the ability to concentrate as his hand ventured up under my shirt and connected with my bare flesh.

"You can try. I'm starting to falter, especially if you keep doing this to me. But no...no more distractions. I'll be there by the end of January." I smiled, brushing my hand down his cheek. "I'm coming to Sydney after Christmas for a few days and New Year's Eve anyway, we'll be able to look for a place then."

"I don't want to wait that long. Is there anything I can do to persuade you to come sooner?" He gently pushed me back to lie back down on the sand.

The cool grains felt soft against my skin in the evening breeze. Cameron hovered over me while his kisses, breath and tongue danced with mine. I wrapped my arms around on to his back and ran them up his muscly back, felling his muscles ripple beneath my fingertips. *Hmm ... maybe I should move to Sydney sooner.*

My phone buzzed in my pocket.

I slapped my hand down on the sand beside me and Cameron rolled off of me with a disgruntled groan. Why did my phone have to ring now? I pulled it out to see who was calling. I cursed when I read my brother's caller ID and swiped my finger across the screen to answer it and put it on speaker.

"Hey Chris. What's up?"

"Sorry to interrupt your holidays, Sis, but it's urgent. It's Dad. He's in hospital."

Chapter 27

"Dad? In hospital. What'd he do? Break a finger playing golf?" I sat upright so I could hear Chris properly.

"No ... he had a stroke."

My body stiffened. I closed my eyes tightly, surely I had misheard him. It is mind-blowing how the world can change in a split second. How quickly the mind and body react. One minute I was souring through the sky, deliriously happy, the next brought back down to earth with a crashing blow.

"A what?" Nausea flooded into my stomach and the blood drained from my face. "A stroke. When? How? Is he okay?" I started to tremble all over, Cameron's arms were instantly around me.

"It happened at home after dinner." Chris said, his voice wavering. "I don't know the full extent of it yet. Mum's with him at the hospital and I'm on the way there now. Can you come home?"

"Chris, tell me he's all right." Tears fell on to my cheeks and my hands shook uncontrollably. Cameron took the phone from me so I wouldn't drop it in the sand.

"Sis, we don't know yet. Just get your ass home now," Chris pleaded.

"Hey Chris," Cameron said, his arm rubbing up and down my back. "It's really late and we've both been drinking so neither of us can drive yet. We'll pack up now and leave first thing in the morning. We'll be there as soon as possible. Keep us informed with what's happening and if anything changes."

"Sure mate, no worries."

***

The long drive back to Brisbane was a blur, my mind clouded like thick fog as Cameron headed for the Mater Hospital. The smell of the sterile hospital environment assaulted my senses when we flew through the doors into the emergency ward. My belly swirled and my throat ran dry. My last hospital visit still fresh in my mind. Chris was in the waiting room when we arrived. His hair was a mess, bags hung under his eyes and he was still in his business suit he'd no doubt worn yesterday to work. He stood up, rushed over and hugged me when he saw us walk toward him.

"Where's Dad? Is he okay?" I clutched on to him tightly.

"He's down the hall in room 103. He's doing okay after surgery. Mum's in with him. Come on, come and see him."

We walked down the hallway, past other rooms in the ward. Chris opened the door and waved for me to go inside. Cameron squeezed my hand before letting go and waited outside with Chris. I took a deep breath and slipped into the room.

Teardrops escaped from my eyes when I saw Dad lying on the bed. I winced at the sight before me. His eyes were tightly closed. His head had been shaved and bandaged. A drain ran down the side of his neck. I covered my mouth and swallowed hard, trying not to throw up at the sight of the bloody fluid trickling down the pipe. Other various tubes and cables hung in all directions from his body and an oxygen tube lay under his nose. Monitors and machines blipped away beside him and a nurse was sitting in a chair writing on her clipboard. Mum sat on the other side of dad's bed.

I rushed to dad's bedside, grabbed his hand tightly; kissed him on the cheek and burst out with a loud sob. "Oh Dad. I got here as fast as I could." I didn't know whether he could hear me or not, or even knew if I was there, but it gave me comfort to finally be by his side.

Mum looked exhausted. It was the first time I think I had ever seen my mother look drained of energy.

"What happened? How did this happen?" I begged her for answers.

A tear slipped from her eye as she pulled her cardigan around her to ward off the chill of the air-conditioning. Her voice was barely audible. "We were having a quiet drink out on the deck last night after dinner. John walked back into the kitchen to refill our glasses. That's when I heard glass shatter all over the floor and the thud of him falling to the ground. Oh Wil, I was so scared. I thought I was going to lose him."

I squeezed my eyes shut, not wanting to think of how close that possibility might have been.

"We've been so busy at work trying to organize Christmas and worried about you moving out of home; everything has been stressful lately." Mum ran her hands across her weary face.

I wobbled on my feet. Could I have been part of the cause?

"How bad is he?"

The door swung open and the doctor walked in.

"Whoa!" The doctor's eyes widened. "It's a party in the Cayton room. Sorry ladies, but there it to be only one person in here at a time. Would you please wait outside while I check up on our patient and then I'll come and talk to you."

The hallway was full of commotion as doctors and nurses rushed about in all directions on their morning rounds. Machines and trolleys and carts of all various shapes, sizes and contents were wheeled up and down, in and out of patient's rooms. Chris and Cameron joined Mum and I while we waited outside dad's room. Cameron drew his arm around my waist.

"So, Doctor, what's the latest?" My mother asked, rounding her shoulders forward and hugging her arms across her belly when the doctor came out again. Seeing mum like this was hard, so different from her usual up-straight, perfect posture.

"The surgery last night was a success. We managed to clear the blockage and inserted a stent to hopefully prevent this from happening again. All in all, everything was textbook, even considering the emergency situation. He was very lucky. How he pulls through is now up to him. He's going to be groggy for most of the day, but we should see improvements in the next twelve to twenty-four hours. Providing there are no more complications, he should be out of here within a week. Until he wakes up we won't know the full extent of any damage, if any, and what physical effects there may be."

"Like what?" I shuddered.

"After the severity of his ischemic stroke, he will most likely have a partially paralyzed face and his speech may be slurred. Some of his motor skills may be affected, especially the use of his left arm. These are all hopefully temporary and will be regained through rehabilitation. John also has very high cholesterol and will have to go on medication. Tied in with a rehab program, we'll do everything we can to ensure he recovers as quickly as possible."

"How long is recovery? When will he be back to normal?" Mum asked, touching her trembling fingers to her brow.

"I'll get a better indication of that once he wakes up. We have to run some more tests to make sure there are no other blockages or areas for concern. I have scheduled these over the next couple of days. We'll have to await the results."

Mum, Chris and I slumped our shoulders, helplessness set in.

"And no more than one at a time in to see him, okay?" The doctor reiterated with a point of his finger. "John needs his rest. I'll catch up with you this evening; if not, tomorrow morning. He's in good hands. He'll sleep most of today so I advise you to go home and get some rest." The doctor bid us farewell and took off to continue his rounds.

Cameron and I offered to stay with Dad, while Mum and Chris went home to sleep after we'd promised to report to them if there was any change in his condition. After a long agonizing afternoon waiting around there was no change with dad. Mum came back in the afternoon so Cameron and I went home for the night and returned to the hospital the next day. The doctor had been accurate about the after-effects of Dad's stroke. When I walked into see him, he was awake but his eye drooped, his right arm lay limp by his side and he had difficulty talking.

"Hey, how you doing?" Sitting down in the chair next to Dad's bed, I took his hand in mine. My stomach still wanted to alleviate itself of my breakfast at the sight of all the tubes and machines blipping and buzzing away while attached to my father. Dad's eyes were sunken and black while his bald head looked swollen and sore.

"Fine." He whispered. "Don't cry, princess. I'm going to be okay."

"Oh Dad, I was so scared when Chris rang. We'll get you back to normal in no time."

Family had always come first for me. I loved them so much, even if I did have my moments with my mother. Seeing

Dad lying in the hospital bed made me realize how close we'd come to losing him. It was going to take months for him to recover. Physiotherapy, rehabilitation and countless doctors' appointments. We didn't even know yet if he'd ever be able to work again. Harsh reality hit me. My parents had a business to run. I could help out with it and with looking after Dad.

I grimaced and a pang lurched in my chest. There goes my plans of moving to Sydney with Cameron. I had to stay and help my dad. There was nothing else I could do. The universe was doing its best at trying to keep Cameron and I apart, and this time she may have succeeded. I took a deep breath to steady my voice. "I'm not going to go to Sydney. I'm going to stay here to help you for as long as you need me. You just concentrate on getting better. I'll do whatever it takes."

His closed his eyes and squeezed my hand.

"Are you in pain, Dad?" I stressed as he mushed my fingers into the palm of his hand. "Do you need the nurse? She's right here." The nurse glanced up from observing one of the monitors.

"No. Just tired."

"We'll get you back on the golf course in no time."

He tried to smile but it was all lopsided. "How was camping? Is Cameron still here?" I turned away, how was I going to break the news of not going to Sydney to Cameron.

"Cam's here, waiting outside." I sniffled loudly and wiped my nose.

""What's wrong? Tell me?"

"I haven't told him yet I can't go to Sydney." I put on a brave face while my heart broke in two. I needed some fresh air. "Dad, you look tired and need rest. I'll come in and see you later." I kissed him on the cheek and left the room.

Putting on a strong front, I walked toward Cameron. The thought of canceling our plans sickened me. The thought of losing Cameron again even more. His life was in Sydney. I'd seen it. I couldn't ask him to give all that up for me. What else could I do? My family needed me now more than ever.

Cameron stood up when I approached him. Hugged me and I let the tears flow. It was going to be so hard to let him go. I had to find the strength.

"Come on," he said and took my hand. "Let's go and get a coffee."

***

My eyes strained as the sun glared in through the café windows and filled the room with warmth. It was such a pleasant change compared to the cold, stale ward. The aromatic smell of freshly brewed coffee and toast filled the air but did nothing to tempt my appetite.

"You okay?" Cameron asked over his cappuccino. With so many thoughts racing through my head, I hadn't been very talkative.

"Numb, is the best way to describe it. I can't believe this has happened. It's so unexpected. He's fit, moderately healthy and never seems to worry about anything."

"I'm sure he's going to be fine." He reached out and rubbed my hand.

"Mum's a wreck and will fuss over him to the nth degree. They've got the business to run. Staff to look after. Bills to pay. Christmas is in three weeks. Dad doesn't need all this stress, especially at this time of the year. I couldn't bear to lose him, Cam. You don't know what it's like."

"Yes, I do." He stared vacantly at his cup.

I squeezed my eyes shut. "Shit! ... I'm so sorry. That's awful of me." He'd been through much worse than this, how could I be so self-absorbed? "Thank you for staying. It means the world to me."

"There's nowhere else I'd rather be. Well, I would much rather not be in a hospital, but I'm with you, and that's all that matters." He reached for my hand and stroked his thumb across my skin.

My anguish consumed me. The thought of messing up all our plans made every cell in my body ache. Why did loving someone have to hurt so much? How was I going to tell him Sydney was off?

I took a deep breath, my throat felt like it was lined with razors when I swallowed. "Cam, what has happened to Dad changes everything. I have to be here for my family. I can't move to Sydney now." Salty droplets formed in my ducts, I used all my strength to told myself together. Breaking up with Cameron was the hardest thing I ever had to do.

Cameron froze, the only movement was the tick of a muscle in his strained jaw. His eyes drew away from mine and he stared outside at the pathway. "Your dad's going to be fine. The doctor said so. Let's wait and see what happens over the next few days. Please don't worry about anything."

"Your family is in Sydney, I can't ask you to leave them for me." My lip started to quiver.

I clutched at my chest when his face flitted with a combination of anger, frustration and concern. He let go of my hand and stood up abruptly, scraping the chair loudly on the tiled floor. "I need some fresh air. I'll see you up in the ward in a bit."

When he walked away from me and out through the door, I covered my face with my hands and sobbed. I desperately wanted a life with Cameron, but I couldn't see how it was possible.

I returned to the ward and ran into my mother as she walked out of Dad's room.

"How's he doing?" I asked while giving her a hug.

"He seems to be doing well. He's sore and tired but the drain in his head should come out today." She glanced at her watch. "I'm going to grab a coffee. Where is Cameron?" She looked about with concern.

"Getting some fresh air."

She touched my arm and gave it a rub. "You go in see your father, I'll catch up with you soon."

After a quick chat with Dad, I walked out toward the waiting room and found Cameron and my mum deep in conversation. It was the first time I'd seen them speak to each other in a civilized manner. I sat down beside Cameron and he instantly took my hand in his.

My mother stood up slowly, the exhaustion from the past few days setting in. "I'm going back to see John. I'll catch up with you two soon."

"What did Mum say to you?" I wriggled around trying to get comfortable on the hard plastic waiting room chair when my mum disappeared.

"That we've spent too much time in hospitals." A grin tugged at the corner of his mouth. He turned to face me, raised my hand up and pressed his lips onto the back of my hand. "Wiley, about before. I'm sorry I walked out. I was just pissed off our plans at being together are upended once again. But I am not going to lose you over this. That's ridiculous and you know it. We'll change everything around and I'll move up here instead."

"I can't ask you to do that. There is nothing up here for you. Sydney is your home."

"No it's not. My life is with you. You don't even have to ask. I want to be wherever you are. If Brisbane is it, I'm happy to move."

"Really? You'd do that for me?"

"Yes. Of course I will."

I flung my arms around Cameron's neck and hugged him. My heart started to beat again. I don't know what I did to deserve him or how he put up with all my dramas — and there'd been enough of them lately — but I thanked my lucky stars every day that he did and he was mine.

***

The clock above the nursing station ticked loudly and medical staff scuttled back and forth all day long. Shifts changed, one emergency came in after another and visitors came and went. I was exhausted from watching it all.

"Cameron, John wants to see you." My mum, placed her hand on his shoulder when she came back out to see us. Her expression was blank and gave me no indication what it was all about.

"Really?" Cameron hesitated. "Are you sure?"

My mother nodded. "Yes. Go on in."

Cameron stood, kissed me on the forehead and walked off. Mum sat down in his place and said nothing to me for a few moments. Her not saying anything was weirding me out. "Cameron's a good young man." She finally said. "I can see how much you care about each other."

I nearly fell off my chair in shock.

"You know I've had my concerns and I'm not sure they've entirely gone away. But I have a feeling he's going to be around a while so I'd better get used to it. Put it this way, I'd sooner put up with him rather than risk losing you."

My mouth fell open, I was lost for words. All I managed was to smile and nod my head.

Twenty minutes ticked by before Cameron stuck his head out the door of Dad's room and waved me over to join him.

"Your father wants to speak to us. Come on."

Wondering what this was all about, I snuck into the room, sat down next to Dad on the uncomfortable hard hospital bed and took his hand in mine. Cameron took the chair next to me and held my other hand. A beautiful smile let his handsome face.

"What's up?" I looked back and forth between them. My father and Cameron conspiring together held me intrigued.

Dad spoke softly as if it was an effort. "What are you doing, princess?"

"What do you mean? Doing what?"

"Why are you trying to change all your plans around and not go to Sydney? Holidays? Moving? Everything?"

I glared at Cameron. He didn't need to stress my dad out with all this information.

"I need to be here to help look after you."

"Wiley, stop! No you don't. I have your mother to do all that. She's an organizational time management freak. You know that."

I nodded. It was true.

"Princess, you can't put your life on hold because of me. You have a whole new life about to start. So many exciting new opportunities and experiences await you. I don't want and will not let you give up your plans for me. The practice runs fine without you and always has. The girls in the office will manage. And your mother ... she'll have me back on my feet in no time. So no more silliness, okay?" He pointed and waved his good finger at me. "It's time to think about you and what you want first for a change. I've had a chat to Cameron and when I heard he was going to change everything to move up here I knew it was time to intervene. I know you're having troubles finding work, but something will come up. Enough is enough. Please go to Sydney with Cameron. Enjoy your holiday. There's no need to cancel it. Get yourself organized and move in January as you've discussed. I don't want to have to officially kick you out of home, but I will if it means you will go."

Dad cracked a smile but he had tears swelling in his eyes. I leaned down and hugged his burly chest.

I really did have the best dad in the world. My unknown future frightened me, but I was ready to take the jump with Cameron by my side.

Chapter 28

Dad came home from hospital a week before Christmas and Cameron left the following morning for the long drive back to Sydney. My father was recovering well and was jovial about enjoying time off work and missing out on the busy Christmas period. My mum monitored his every move, every second of the day. She was ruthless ensuring he changed his diet and got him to all his doctor and physiotherapy appointments, handled all their business affairs and organized Christmas functions. Mum took it all in her stride with endless phone calls, filling her diary with engagements and drove Dad everywhere ... including up the wall!

A few days before Christmas, exam results came out. Finally some good news. Three A's–Distinctions and one HD– High Distinction. I danced around on my bed, ecstatic to be back at the top of my game. I called Cameron once I calmed down and recaptured my breath. He scored two A's–Distinctions and two B's–Credits. Our great results had given me the confidence boost I desperately needed.

Christmas Day was quiet this year. There was no big boozyy family catch-ups or wild parties with dad at home recovering. I looked around the room, taking in the four of us sitting by our Christmas tree opening up our presents. Mum, Dad, Chris and me. Maybe it was my intuition, or maybe it was wishful thinking now Cameron was part of my life, but somehow I knew this would be the last time it was only going to be the four of us.

Three days after Christmas, I jumped on a plane and hightailed it to Sydney. It was now where I belonged. I had a week's holiday with Cameron to celebrate New Year's and find somewhere to live before I moved interstate permanently. But today was a day to forget about daunting tasks like job applications and interviews and house hunting, because it was December twenty-eighth and it was Cameron's birthday.

"Happy birthday. I have presents," I sang while digging into the depths of my suitcase down in his room. "Twenty-two today, twenty-two today. Geez, it must suck having your birthday straight after Christmas?"

"Nope. Now, give me my presents." His eyes sparkled at me while he sat on his couch and rubbed his hands together in anticipation.

I pulled out a red gift box tied up with ribbon; his birthday present, and a Christmas gift bag. "I hope you like them." I hesitated before handing over the packages. I'd spent hours traipsing through the shops in Brisbane, trying to decide what to buy the man who has everything and seems to want nothing. Cameron smiled as he tugged them free from my grasp. I sat down next to him and awaited his reaction.

"What's this?" he laughed, pulling a bottle of fragrant massage oil from the bag.

"That's for a bit of fun later on." I rolled my shoulder and did my best attempt at making sexy eyes at him before I burst out laughing. "Come on, there's more."

He delved into the bag again. "Nice." He beamed, holding up two new pairs of silky red boxer briefs. "You, buying me sexy underwear — that's kind of hot!" He leaned over and kissed me. "Would you like to see them on now or later" He hooked his leg over mine and his kisses became more zealous.

"Stop," I giggled, "you have one more present."

"Mmm ... I forgot." He picked up the second present, untied the ribbon and opened up the box. Tearing away the tissue paper was a wooden-framed photo of us together lazing in the sun on the grass at Steele Rudd College. I was going to put one of the photos from our Winter Dance in it, but quickly changed my mind because that was a night we both wanted to forget.

"And what's this?" He waved a red envelope in front of his face. I'd hidden it inside wrapping with the photo frame. He ripped it open to read the card, and two tickets fell into his lap. As he read the print, his eyes widened, then he hollered. "Holy shit! Tickets to Cold Play! This is incredible."

His excitement was contagious and I laughed as he stared at the tickets in his hand. "Their concerts have been sold out for months, how did you get these?"

"On the website, Viagogo."

"Best ... present ... ever." He hugged me tightly and kissed me all over my face. I love you so much."

"I'm glad you like them. Sorry about the other stuff, I really suck at getting presents." I sulked, because it was the truth. "I didn't know what to get you. You seem to have everything already. Think of the photo as an early housewarming present. And the underwear, well, you needed those. Now you can get rid of some of your old ones with holes in them."

"The holes are only from you manhandling me and tearing them off me all the time." He chuckled, nuzzled into my neck and kissed me.

"Would you like me to stop doing that to you?" I giggled as he nibbled on my earlobe.

"Never!" He pushed me gently back down on the couch. Paper and presents fell to the floor. "You can manhandle me any time you like. How about right now?"

***

The following summer evening was stifling hot and humid. Margaret, Cameron and I sat outside on the deck lounge, trying to capture and enjoy the harbor breezes and having a cool drink of wine. Cameron had his laptop open and we were sifting through the real estate sites trying to find a place to live. His mother sat quietly, smiled a lot and nodded when we asked questions. All she contributed was "Ah-ha", "Yep", and "That sounds good." Not very helpful at all. The sun was well past setting and we were on to our second glass of wine when his dad arrived home from work.

"Evening all. "He said when he came through the doorway. "Cam, are you heading out this evening?"

"Nope, we're staying in and watching a movie tonight. Why?" Cameron asked while placing his glass down on the coffee table.

"I want to talk to you and Wiley about something. I'll grab us all a round of drinks." Robert said and disappeared back inside the house.

"What's this all about?" I nudged my elbow against Cameron.

"I don't know. I've no idea."

Robert returned with a fresh bottle of chilled wine and topped up everyone's glasses before taking a seat next to Margaret on the lounge opposite Cameron and me. He took a long sip before his gaze locked on to us and sat swirling the glass stem around in his fingertips. I grabbed Cameron's hand and felt the tension in his fingers when he entwined them with mine.

"Okay, here goes!" Robert started. "Margaret and I know you've being going to great lengths to sort everything out so you can start living together and also in applying for jobs." Robert glanced at Margaret, she smiled and touched his arm. "It's tough out there in the marketplace at the moment, so here's the deal... I want to offer you both work within our company."

My mouth gapped open and Cameron was about to interject when his dad put his hand up to stop him. "Please hear me out before you say anything."

I couldn't say anything if I tried at the moment. My heart was dancing around inside my chest to the sound of *Saturday Night Fever.*

"If you are going to be successful in business, you have to learn to identify and take opportunities, and sometimes risks, when they present themselves. I have two jobs available — the first is for a graduate Commercial Accountant in our Drilling and Exploration company; and the second is the same role in the Mining Projects division. The two of you can discuss who takes which one. In spite of being in the same building, you won't be working together; they'll be on different floors in our CBD office. This'll give you some separation and focus. This is a great opportunity for you both. You can get into the workforce, gain experience and learn all about our business. " Robert's gaze was directed straight at Cameron. But he was focused at some point on the ground in front of his feet.

Robert cleared his throat. "We're lucky our business is still growing and I think you'd be foolish not to take advantage of the opportunities available to you. I'm not saying do it for life, but it's a start. Do some time, maybe a few years then you can move on to other things if you wish. No strings attached." Robert's eyes jumped between Cameron's and mine as he grabbed his glass of wine and took another drink. I knew Robert would love to have Cameron work with him at Wilks Resources, side by side, but would never want him to do it if he wasn't interested. "So what do you think?"

"Are you for real?" I asked, while Cameron slumped back in the chair.

"Yes. Your mother and I have talked about it and we want to give you both this opportunity." Robert smiled. "Wiley, I know you have some work experience and have achieved excellent results in your studies. Your résumé came through to our HR department. You'd be nothing but an asset to my organization — especially with your quick eye for detail. And Cameron, you have done so well this year and your grades improved drastically. I'm really proud of you. I could think of worse things than working for your old man, hey?" Robert chuckled. "I know you may want to do other things for a career and I'm all okay with that. But until it happens, I want to help out where I can, and how I can help is by giving you this start in life."

"Oh wow!" I gushed. "I don't know what to say. I mean ... I don't expect ... you don't have to ..." I was stuttering and stumbling over my words like a bumbling fool.

"Wiley, I know you don't expect anything," Robert added. "But what good is being this successful if I can't help out my own family ... and girlfriends?"

Cameron toyed with my hand in his. "Dad, Can I think about it and let you know?"

Robert nodded, hope loomed in his eyes."Sure. Here are the job details and position descriptions." He reached inside his jacket, pulled out two envelopes and pushed them across the table toward us. "I had Amy in the office draw these up. Have a look through them. Ask me any questions. Can you let me know what you decide to do by New Year's please? Otherwise, I'm going to have to advertise to fill these positions."

"Sure," Cameron grunted and poured another drink.

"There is one more thing," Robert added, "about your living arrangements. Margaret and I have tried not to overhear too many of your conversations; but sorry, you are not staying here with us. If you take the jobs, I'd like to offer you the pick of one of the unsold units down in the apartment complex we have just finished at Coogee. There are three to choose from; they are all three-bedroom apartments on the second floor. Sorry, there are no penthouses left." Robert sighed and held up his palms, then with a glint in his eye he continued. "Your age group all want to live down near the beach and I know you love it there too, Cam. The agreement is I will own it, for at least the first year anyway and you will have to pay rent...if you want to call it that." He winked at me. "And of course, you'll have to cover all your own expenses. It's not a freeload by any means. Cam, I know you could buy it outright but I think it would be a good experience for you to live off your salaries so you can see how the majority of the nation lives. If after twelve months you like it, great, then you can buy it or look for your own place elsewhere. We can sort out all those details later."

"You're offering us an apartment as well!" I squealed, wriggled around on the lounge and stamped my feet up and down on the ground. This was better than winning the lotto.

"Mum. Dad." Cameron's knuckles were turning white from gripping around the stem of his wine glass so tight, I was afraid it was going to shatter in his hand. "You don't have to do this. I can afford our own place."

"We know. But this gives you a chance to get some life experience before you jump into anything. Twelve months. That's all we're asking." Robert placed his hand on Margaret's leg beside him.

"You two probably have a lot to talk about so we'll leave you to it," Margaret said and she stood up to leave with Robert.

I jumped up and hugged them both. "Thank you."

Robert and Margaret smiled before turning around and headed inside the house. I sank on to the lounge beside Cameron and held on to the side in fear I'd float away. But the sullen look on Cameron's face brought me back down from the clouds. "What's wrong?"

"This is exactly what my dad has always wanted."

"But it's a start and we can move in together and do other things later on. This will give you some much needed work experience that may help you to land a different job if and when you want one. All the work placements we've been applying for all want professional experience, you'll get it with this. This is amazing. Don't you think? It's not a life sentence; it's a start. It's an awesome opportunity we can't afford to miss."

"Do you honestly think he will let me leave once I start working for him? He'll make sure he embeds me in there somehow. It'll be a life sentence for me." Cameron shook his head, not sharing in my excitement at all.

"I don't believe that." I leaned back against his shoulder. "You're dad has always supported you and let you make your own decisions. Of course he'd love you to work for him, but he'd never stop you doing something else. I firmly believe that."

Cameron tried to smile but it failed to reach his eyes.

"You really had no idea about this, did you?" I quizzed him.

"Nope, absolutely none."

I snuggled against him. "You don't have to take up your dad's offer if you don't want to. We'll be fine if you don't. But it's a no-brainer for me." I leaned forward, grabbed the envelopes off the table, stood up, grabbed his hand and hauled him to his feet. "Come on, grumpy pants. Let's go downstairs and watch a movie."

***

Before I opened my eyes when I woke the next morning, I reached out to cuddle into Cameron. But the sheets were cold and the bed was empty. My eyes shot open and I sat bolt upright. His room was empty and he wasn't jostling about in the bathroom. I jumped out of bed, quickly showered, dressed and headed upstairs to find him. He was sitting at the kitchen counter, reading the paper and drinking coffee; he smiled as I walked toward him and cuddled into him for a morning kiss.

After breakfast he was keen to get out for the day, so we ventured down to Coogee Beach. The waterfront was crowded, we had to continually weave around the holiday goers enjoying the summer sun as we walked along the water's edge.

"Sorry about last night," Cameron said when he took my hand. "I had no idea about Dad's offer and it blew me away. So much has been going on in my head with applying for jobs and trying to sort out being together, it all came as a big surprise."

"It was a *massive* surprise," I reiterated. "I was totally caught off guard. I hope I didn't make a fool of myself in front of them, but I was so excited." That was a massive understatement. Maybe losing my internship with Huntersville was the best thing that could have happened. "What are your thoughts now you've had a chance to sleep on it? Or are there other underlying issues you have with your dad I don't know about?"

Cameron adjusted his sunglasses on his face and gazed up the beach in front of us. "My dad is a great businessman and I know I could learn a lot from him. My issue is ... I don't feel like I deserve the role he's offering me. I haven't earned it or worked hard for it like you have. I barely scraped through the first two years at university and my grades were shit. All I did was party, drink and hang out with my friend. The only work experience I've had is from helping out at various charity events. I've had no goals, ambitions or career aspirations until I went to Toowoomba to finish my degree and I met you. You drew me out of the darkness and everything changed.

With my track record I don't understand why dad wants me to work with him. He seems to have this faith in me I don't have in myself. I'm afraid I will let him down or be a huge disappointment. He's so good at what he does and I'm worried I won't live up to his expectations. He sets the bar so high."

"I have faith in you." I snaked my arm around his waist. "We're all afraid of failing, but you learn from your mistakes and move on, right? You're the most amazing person I've ever met. Going by your gene pool, you're going to succeed in whatever it is you decide to do. To top everything off, you're family, and your dad wants to do anything he can to help you. We all went stir crazy during uni, experienced so many things but came out of it alive and better people because of it. I know you want a career and will work hard at whatever it is you end up doing. You don't have to accept your dad's offer if you don't want to, but I can't refuse his offer."

I briefly had to let go of Cameron's hand while we diverted around children digging holes in the sand and several others that ran at full speed in front of us and splashed into the waves. We continued along the beach enjoying the sand squish between our toes and the water wash over our feet. "Did you read the job offers in the letters your dad gave us?" I asked when I took his hand in mine again. "The salary is incredible, it's nearly twice the amount compared to anything else we've applied for." The staggering figure still danced before my eyes. "The jobs are to start in mid-February which suits us perfectly. Cam, please, tell me what you're thinking? Don't go quiet on me."

He stopped walking, tugged on my hand, drew me toward

him and rested his hands on my hips. "So you really want to do it? You want to work for my father?"

I nodded. "Yes, I do. This is an incredible opportunity I can't afford to miss. I'll be happy working for a great company and will be living with you. I won't ever need anything else." I ran my hands over his chest and across his shoulders. "What about you? Yay or nay?"

A smile crept on to his face. "I knew from the moment I met you there was something special about you. You've helped me in so many ways, I will be forever in your debt. It's taken me a long time to work out want I want to do and your enthusiasm, determination and aspiration helped me to find it. I'm not going to deny I'm scared shitless but I'm ready for the challenge ... and yes, I will take the job with Dad."

I squealed and threw my arms around his neck. We laughed as he picked me up and swung me around in circles.

When my feet touched the ground again, I grabbed his hands and spun him around in circles while singing. "We've both got jobs. I'm moving to Sydney. I'm moving to Sydney."

He threw his head back and laughed along with me.

With giddy heads, he stopped me and drew me into his embrace. He turned me around to face the road where hotels, cafes, restaurants and apartment complexes filled the streets and surrounding hillsides.

"What?" I giggled as he cuddled me from behind.

"Do you think you could handle living up there with me?" Cameron pointed toward a new apartment complex on top of the hill to the north.

"Is that...? Oh my gosh! That's the apartment complex your dad owns?" My mouth gapped open at the sight of the curved charcoal-gray and white structure with large balconies and floor to ceiling glass windows on the crest before us.

"Come on. I have the keys. Dad gave them to me this

morning before he went to work. Do you want to go and pick one?"

"Now?" My heart raced.

Cameron nodded, took my hand , guided me up the beach, across the parklands and up the short, steep hill to the complex.

We pulled open cupboard doors, gazed in bathrooms, and peered in and out of all the bedrooms as we looked through each of the apartments. All had amazing water views. The one I particularly liked, because it had an extra-large balcony. Two bedrooms lay at the rear of the apartment; it then angled out in a triangular shape, broadening out into the lounge and kitchen area, with the master bedroom off to the right. Glossy cream-colored tiles lined the floor and thick luxurious beige woolen carpets lay throughout the bedrooms. The apartment was stunning. It felt like it was a hundred times bigger than the single bedroom I lived in at residential college.

"Well, which one?' Cameron asked me while we stood outside and leaned back against the balcony railing.

"This is so much more than I was expecting, but I really like this one. It has a nicer outlook over the beach. The walk-in robe is huge and I aim to get a lot of use out of the spa bath in the main bathroom. You?"

"I'm a guy. I'd be happy in any of them." He shrugged. "But you're right. This one has better storage space, too. We might have to learn how to surf living this close to the beach. What do you think about that?"

Me? Surf? Good luck with that! Learning to surf wasn't on my bucket list, but now living at the beach I suppose I'd have to give it a go.

He folded his arms and his brow creased. "There's one more thing you're going to have to do when we start living together. It's critical to the survival of our relationship."

"What's that?" I squinted in the bright sunlight, wondering

what the hell he was going to throw at me.

"You're going to have to learn how to cook."

"Cook?" This was cause for concern. My current skills didn't equate to much more than canned spaghetti on toast and two-minute noodles. Luckily Cameron knew how to and I looked forward to fun in the kitchen with him trying to teach me. "I'll learn how to cook only if you learn how to clean. I like things neat and tidy so you have to improve on the skillset you had at college. You room was always a mess. It drove me crazy."

"Deal." Then he tilted his head. "What if we hire a cleaner instead?"

"No, not for a small place like this." I said, thumping him in the arm.

"Spoil sport," he frowned.

I stepped over to him, stood up on my tippy toes and kissed him on the cheek. "You'll be fine. I promise. I can't wait to see you get all … sweaty and dirty."

He drew his arm around my shoulder and kissed me on the forehead. "You're so bad."

I cuddled against his ribs and looked back inside the apartment. "How much would a unit like this cost to buy?"

"To buy? These lower level apartments are around the million dollar mark and the penthouses all went for about two million." The color drained from my face when I heard the exorbitant figure. "I haven't worked out how much dad wants to charge us for rent yet. Around this area of Coogee in new apartments like this, rent is around one thousand dollars a week. But we'll easily be able to afford it."

"Holy shit!" I gasped. "We certainly aren't going to be roughing it, are we? What happened to slumming it after university, surviving on baked beans and living in nothing more than something the size of a cardboard box?"

"Wiley, Wiley, Wiley." He sighed, turned to face me and

tugged on the bottom of my shirt to pull me into his embrace. "Let's hope and pray we *never* have to slum it. You might have to start getting used to some of the finer things in life now."

As he kissed me, my head filled with delightful images of the home we were about to start living in together. Everything was finally falling into place after a hellish year. We had landed great jobs. We had a home. We had each other. It couldn't get much better than this.

He slid his hand on to my butt and drew my hips hard up against his. "Do you wanna christen this place as ours now?" he said with a glint in his eye, his lips hovering an inch away from mine.

"But there's no furniture."

"There's a kitchen bench, the floor, the bathroom. I certainly don't need furniture." He kissed me, getting steamier by the second.

"Who's the bad one now?" I said over our kisses, feeling his hot skin on his back beneath his shirt. "I think the kitchen bench is calling to us. I'm sure of it."

Cameron picked me up, I wrapped my legs around his waist and we headed on indoors.

***

Later that evening we were sitting by the pool at his parents' house having a thirst-quenching beer. As I played with the bottle in my hands, I toyed with the idea of approaching a sensitive subject I'd never wanted to or ever needed to ask Cameron before. But now we were going to live together I had a niggling curiosity. "Cam, I want to ask you something and I don't know how to approach the subject properly because I don't want you to take it the wrong way. You should know by now it doesn't bother me one way or the other...I trust you completely... But since we're going to be living together —"

"Geez, Just ask me." He abruptly cut me off short from rambling on any further. "What do you want to know? I will tell you anything."

I hated asking, but managed to blurt out the questions. "So how much money do you have? What are you worth? Not your dad or the company, but you, yourself?" I winced, waiting to hear his response and see his reaction.

He laughed, making me question his sanity...or maybe my own. "Do you really want to know?"

"Well, yeah. I want to know everything about you. I don't want to have any secrets between us or skeletons hidden in the closet. I've about twenty thousand dollars in my bank account which I've been saving since I started working. It's not much, but it's every cent I own."

"I don't mind you knowing about my financial situation."

"Cam?" I pleaded while shuffling around on the sun lounge.

"Sorry, beautiful." He swigged on his beer, swallowed and licked his lips. "Well ... I haven't looked closely lately, but most of my wealth ... if you want to call it that ... is all tied up in the family trust and the companies Dad owns and operates. It's not like I can get my hands on it. So not taking into account Lisa and I are the heirs to a multibillion dollar company—" He sat up and spun around to sit on the side of his seat to face me. "Do you know how much that actually freaks me out? I try not to think about it too often." His eyes widened and his shoulders shuddered. "Sorry to digress," he inhaled deeply, "so my current income from trust payments, some other shares I own, money from Pop's death several years ago, working with Mum, a bit of this and that — there's probably more somewhere I haven't got my head around yet — but I think it's up around twenty million.

I coughed, spluttered and spilt beer everywhere. "Holy crap! Are you for real?"

Chapter 29

Standing on the back deck of the house, I watched the sun set over the harbor while I waited for Cameron to finish getting ready. This New Year's Eve was going to be spectacular. I was in Sydney with Cameron and going to see the best fireworks in the world for real, not just telecast on TV. I tingled all over, like a party popper ready to explode.

My conversation with Cameron about money had made my head rattle. I liked to think I wasn't totally naïve; I'd read enough business articles to know how well off his father was and what the company was worth. It was hard to fathom that *my* Cameron was part of it, had a significant shareholding in the Wilks Resources empire and I was now part of his life. It was very comforting to know we would never have any financial concerns in our life together... hopefully. How much of an idiot was I when a few short weeks ago I was stressing about not having enough money to survive on? No wonder Cameron wanted to laugh at me when he said we could survive on his money alone.

Over lunch today Cameron and I told Robert we would accepted the job offers and were grateful for all his help. I didn't know how I was ever going to repay Robert for this amazing opportunity — maybe with all my blood, sweat and tears when I started to work for him. Robert and Margaret were clearly moved by Cameron starting in the family business; there were lots of hugs, tears and kisses.

I closed my eyes and drew the warm evening air into my lungs. These past few days in Sydney with Cameron had been amazing. I turned when I heard Cameron's footsteps approaching and called me inside. Everyone was ready to head out for the evening. We were joining his family on board a boat to venture up closer to the Harbour Bridge and watch the midnight fireworks. Cameron and I piled in to Robert's Landcruiser, along with Margaret, and headed down to the marina. Lisa and Peter were already there awaiting for us.

I swore under my breath when I saw the sheer size and monstrosity of the luxurious super-yacht we boarded. It had three huge levels and two massive decks; it should be in the French Riviera, docked alongside other similar celebrity-owned craft. What fantasy world had I landed in?

"Nice boat," I muttered, looking around in awe. "This is incredible."

"This isn't ours," Robert said as he led us into the living area on the main deck. "We only have a little one for cruising around the harbor. A friend of mine owns this and said we could borrow it tonight while they're overseas."

I nodded, trying to not gawk at the extreme opulence around me. Shining chrome, leather lounges, plush carpet, silver mirrors and every item on board was embossed with gold monogram logos.

"Is this one of the finer things in life you said I might have to get use to now I'm going to be living with you?" I tugged on

Cameron's hand when we walked out onto the rear deck.

"Just one," Cameron whispered in my ear and drew me in for a kiss.

"This boat is freaking crazy!" I had to glanced down at my feet to make sure I was on solid ground. Then I gazed up at Cameron while I tucked a strand of my hair in behind my ear. "So, you have boats, planes and automobiles ... do you own a train to add to the list?"

"No, but we do have a helicopter. And I haven't really mentioned the houses in various locations around the world."

My voice lodged in my throat, rendering me speechless. I shook my head realizing I had so much to learn about him and his family. How was my heart going to survive all of this?

The crew — a boat captain, a deckhand and a waiter, greeted all of us before setting sail over the water and anchoring in a spot with an uninterrupted view of the Harbour Bridge. Looking up at the towering arch before me, I could see the tons of pyrotechnics strapped to her arches, ready to fire and show off to the world. The vibe in the air was electric and contagious. Thousands of people lined the edge of the harbor ready to watch the bridge light up the night's sky and welcome in the New Year. We could hear their cheers, their music and see their festive behavior even from out here on the water. My stomach wouldn't stop fluttering as the countdown toward midnight grew closer.

Robert, Peter and Cameron cooked up a storm on the barbecue while the waiter attended to our drinks and set out the meal accompaniments on the table. When it was time to eat, I could have sworn I was at the buffet of a five-star restaurant.

With overfull bellies from eating too much, everyone was standing around chatting in the lounge area when Cameron took my hand and led me outside to the deck. The cool harbor breeze was welcoming as we stood leaning against the back railing. The harbor was now covered with hundreds of smaller boats, full of people eager to watch the fireworks. All of the craft on the water were keeping a respectable distance from the monstrosity we were on.

"You want to know something funny," Cameron said, leaning over and looking over the side of the boat. "This boat even impresses me."

"I'm glad you agree it's ostentatious."

"It certainly is, but boats aside," Cameron lowered his voice and turned to face me, "now we have jobs, does it change your timeframe for moving to Sydney, or do I still have to wait until the end of January? We only have six weeks until we start work and I was hoping you could come down earlier."

I entwined my fingers with his and smiled. "All I need to do is go home, pack up my room and drive my car down here. There's not a lot to sort out. What I lived with at university is all I own. I should spend a few days with my parents before I leave, but otherwise that's it." The thought of moving now was even more exciting than before and my parents were ecstatic when I told them about the job. "When can we get in to the apartment? We'll have to go shopping for everything. I don't have any bedding, pots, pans, cutlery, furniture … absolutely nothing. Are you up for it?" I was rattling on with gibberish to hide the fact I was so excited and couldn't wait to move in with him.

Swooping toward me, he kissed me. Was it because he wanted me to stop talking? He picked me up in his warm embrace and swung me around in circles before he placed my feet back on the ground. He kept his hold on me to ensure I was steady on my boat legs. As I regained my balance, I was captured by his gaze. His blue-metallic eyes were mesmerizing in the sparkling night lights. He brushed his fingertips softly down the side of my face and sent tingles racing to every nerve ending in my body. Even after all this time, I was bewildered the chemistry between was as electrifying and as intense as the very first day I touched him in the lecture hall all those months ago.

"I am looking forward to it. Domestic bliss awaits us. I love you and I'm so excited we're going to be living together. I know it's a big step for you leaving home and moving down here to be with me. I'll be forever grateful." He caressed my cheek with the palm of his hand, leaned in and touched his lips to mine.

His kiss lingered, but something wasn't right. His heartbeat raced beneath my touch. His lips were tense and there was a tremble in his touch.

Maybe he was feeling seasick? The boat was rocking and rolling around a bit.

I touched his face, "Are you okay?"

Cameron nodded and took hold of my hand. His hand was definitely clammy. Oh God, I hope he wasn't getting sick again.

"The last few days and weeks have been crazy." He said, "No, make that the past few months. But what happened to your dad the other week reminded me of how short life can be. You've helped me through so much and I've changed for the better over the past year. You've shown me the person I want to be and have believed in me every step of the way. You're the light at the end of the tunnel." His hands squeezed mine tightly while he took a long deep breath. "There is just one more thing ... I never want you to doubt how I feel about you or for your trust in me to waiver. I know you think this is all like a fairy tale some days but I want to make it your reality. I've mulled it over and over in my head on how I can alleviate your concerns, and I've only been able to come up with one clear solution." His Adam's apple lurched in his throat when he swallowed. His eyes had never looked at me with such intensity before and the sound of his voice engrossed me. "I want to live every moment and share everything with you. I look forward to spending every day learning more about you and building our life together. You're my dream come true. I want to bind myself to you forever. I'm truly, madly and deeply in love with you. So Wilhelmina Cayton...will you marry me?"

What ...?

My mouth gapped open and I stared at him. The sea breeze disappeared. The boat stopped rocking beneath my feet. The city lights faded to black. The universe melted from existence. All that remained was Cameron and me.

He wants to what?

A smile touched the corner of his lips. He let go of my hands and fumbled in his shorts pocket. He pulled out a pale blue velvet pouch and slid out a beautiful silver ring. I gasped and covered my mouth with my fingertips when he held out the ring. The princess cut diamond sparkled and dazzled before me. With shaking hands, he took mine in his and bent down on one knee. "Sorry," he said, his eyes full of emotion. "I should've knelt down before." He asked me again. "I love you so much. Will you please marry me, Wiley?"

My hand quivered. I struggled to draw in a breath. I couldn't swallow and my ears still rang with the sound of his words. Cameron was what I wanted more than anything else in my life. Jobs didn't matter. The sun rising and setting didn't matter. The air I breathed in didn't matter. Cameron was all I needed. "This is definitely a fairy tale. You make me feel like I'm in heaven every day. There's nothing in the universe I want more than to be with you. We've endured so much already, more than anyone ever should within their entire lifetime. We've always come out on the other side so much stronger than before. I love you and will always be yours. So, yes. Yes, I'll marry you," My knees buckled when he slid the ring onto my finger, stood up and smothered me with a kiss.

Struggling to catch my breath and control my racing heartbeat, I took a closer look at the diamond swimming around my finger and twisted the sparkling gem between my fingers. It was way too big. I'd have to get it resized. "Cam, it's gorgeous!"

"Just like you, beautiful."

For so long all I wanted was to do well in my studies, get a good job and have a successful career. When I lost my internship I gave up hope. When I lost Cameron, I thought I had nothing left. But somehow, after losing everything, even nearly my life, I had made it through and gained so much more. Cameron was the best thing that ever happened to me.

"Hey lovebirds, what's going on out here?" Lisa interrupted us when she stepped out on to the deck.

Cameron took my hand and turned it toward her.

She stopped, stared and calmly called out. "Mum? Dad? I think you better get out here. You have to come and see this."

My legs were jelly and I could hardly stand up; Cameron literally had to hold me for support. His heart still pounded rapidly in his chest as I leaned against him.

Robert and Margaret walked outside. "What's going on? See what?" Margaret asked while looking all about.

"Look?" Lisa said pointing at my hand.

Cameron's breath hitched in his chest. "I asked Wiley to marry me and she said yes."

"Aaaagghhh!" Margaret shrieked, skipped across the deck toward us and gave us a massive hug. "That's fantastic! Oh, did you get a ring? Show me quick!"

I held my hand up for her to see.

"Oh Cam, it's beautiful. A platinum Tiffany engagement ring. I've taught you to have good taste, if nothing else." She hugged him again and gave me a kiss on the cheek.

Tiffany? Again? Not wanting to think of the dollar value hanging around my finger, I changed the ring onto my middle finger so it wouldn't fall off.

Robert came over and shook Cameron's hand and drew him into a huge hug before smothering me as well. I couldn't have found a nicer family to become part of; they made me feel so welcome.

"I'll go get the Verve and some glasses," Lisa called out, heading back into the boat. "We need to celebrate!"

***

The fireworks were magnificent. We stood out on the deck, watching them explode and pop loudly off the bridge. My heart pounded in my chest as each one boomed and lit up the sky.

I glanced up at Cameron beside me, his arm draped lazily across my shoulders. With him in my life, a new job, a new home, and becoming a part of an incredible family was beyond my wildest dreams. It was crazy, I know, but I was in love and everything felt right.

The fireworks continued to burst above welcoming in the New Year. The future was looking bright with exciting new adventures. A new life was about to begin with no more distractions.

Thank you

Thank you for reading Distractions
It would be appreciated if you could take a moment and leave
a quick review on Amazon.
http://amazon.com/author/taniajoyce

Quarterly Newsletter

For staying in touch with new releases, news and events, sign
up to
Tania Joyce's quarterly newsletter.

Subscribe to Quarterly Newsletter:
http://taniajoyce.com/newsletter/subscribe

Follow Tania Joyce

You can follow and find Tania Joyce on the following social
media platforms.

Web: http://taniajoyce.com
Facebook: https://www.facebook.com/taniajoycebooks
Twitter: https://twitter.com/TaniaJoyceBooks
Pinterest: https://www.pinterest.com/taniajoycebooks/
Goodreads: https://www.goodreads.com/taniajoyce
Instagram: https://www.instagram.com/taniajoycebooks/
Book Discussion Group:
https://www.facebook.com/groups/949340895151718/

Other Books by Tania Joyce

Propositions - Strictly Business Book 1

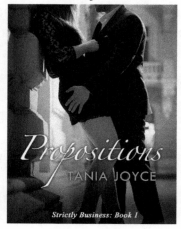

No strings attached ... or so she thought.

Following years of sacrifice and struggle, Jessica Mason now co-owns a successful marketing agency in Sydney. All Jessica wants to do is focus on growing her business and maintain the lifestyle she's worked so hard to achieve. But everything changes when her agency wins a major contract for the opening of the new Somers Hotel and she has to take on the account.

Nate Somers is a workaholic trying to please his retiring father. When he meets captivating, go-getting Jessica, the prospect of a short-term love affair sounds like a proposition he'd be crazy to decline.

But when Jessica spends a weekend away at her favorite vineyard retreat, she runs into Troy Smith, the ex-boyfriend who left her broken and vulnerable years ago. Things don't go to plan when the well-kept secrets from her past are revealed and Troy starts weaving his way back into her life.

With her business at stake and hearts at risk, Jessica's future is destined to change. Who will end up making Jessica a proposition she simply cannot refuse?

Available in eBook and print at:
Amazon | iTunes | Kobo | ... and more.

Acquisitions – Strictly Business Book 2

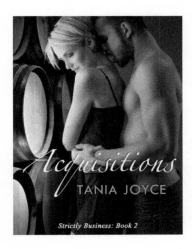

A new start. A short term project. That's all it was meant to be.

Losing his wife in a car accident has left Troy Smith doubtful of ever finding love again. He's tried, but failed. Now he thinks he's found solace as a hard-working business partner at Gumtrees Winery.

Kelleigh Johnstone needs a break from dealing with the mess and debt her fraudulent ex-boyfriend left behind. The opportunity to manage a project in the Hunter Valley seems like the perfect escape.

When these two strangers meet, a one-night stand delivers unexpected surprises. Troy is shocked when he finds out Kelleigh represents the company trying to purchase his vineyard for a new golf resort. In order to protect his home and community, Troy must do whatever it takes to stop the project from proceeding.

Kelleigh and Troy may be on opposite sides of the boardroom table, but when they are together the attraction is hard to deny. With livelihoods at stake and broken hearts vulnerable, who will risk everything for another chance at love?

Available in eBook and print at:
Amazon | iTunes | Kobo | ... and more.

CPSIA information can be obtained
at www.ICGtesting.com
Printed in the USA
BVHW07s0952101018
529783BV00003B/450/P

9 780994 577450